Holly Ever After

Laura Ashley Gallagher

First published in 2023

Copyright © 2023 Laura Ashley Gallagher

All rights reserved. No part of this publication
may be reproduced, stored in a retrieval system,
or transmitted, in any form, or by any means
without the prior permission of the publisher.

ISBN: 9798864992524

DEDICATION

To all the good girls,
Happy Holiday

ONE

Oh, sweet baby Santa Claus, what have I done?

My car groans to a halt in front of a dilapidated cottage that, to put it mildly, has seen better days. Maybe even better decades. I shove the car's door open and practically fall onto the frozen earth, my heels digging into what I hope is just mud and not a part of the town's sewage system. If I needed a sign that I've officially hit rock bottom, this might be it.

But at least everything at rock bottom is mine.

I frown at the peeling paint, and the windows that look like they're screaming, "Help me, for the love of God!" At least the walls are sturdy, and the roof is still

1

intact. I can work with that.

My father and brother unloaded my furniture when it arrived yesterday, so at least I can set my ass down somewhere. I'll somehow have to ignore everything else until I get started on cleaning tomorrow. This crumbling monument to bad life choices is my new home, and I'm going to make it work if it kills me.

It might actually kill me.

I drag my luggage out of the car, each wheel on my suitcase wailing like a cat in distress as it rolls over the uneven ground. "Come on, you. No complaining," I mutter to it as if it can hear me. Maybe I've gone mad. Conversations with luggage tends to be a red flag.

I fumble for the cottage keys in my purse, dropping my phone in the process. It lands face down. Of course it does.

"Please don't be cracked, please don't be cracked."

Thankfully, it's still in one piece. Unlike me.

Finally, the door creaks open, and I'm hit by an odor that's a mix between aged cheese and grandma's attic. But at least my things are here. Silver linings and all that.

I cough, realizing that my extensive collection of scented candles is about to serve a greater purpose in life.

At least I'm home. Home is Pine Falls, the town with more trees than people and more gossip than the Internet. I unpack a couple of essentials—laptop, some clothes, and an emergency stash of chocolate. As I set up my little writing nook, I catch my reflection in the window.

And what a reflection it is—twenty-seven years old, a recently un-engaged romance novelist with a bad case of writer's block.

I feel like a fraud writing books about happily ever afters with mind-blowing sex that only ever happen in a fictional world. How am I supposed to write another novel when any relationship I've ever been in has ended in heartbreak, and I haven't had sex in so long I've practically regrown my virginity?

I grin at my reflection, deciding to find humor in the absurdity of it all. Fuck it. Why not? If I don't smile, then I'll cry.

Even if my life feels like a draft that needs major revisions, it's still my story to write.

I should get cleaning first, but this writer is on a deadline. It's my third to be exact because I missed two while my life was falling apart. I'm sure my agent and publisher are fit to kill me and drop me all at once. My last book, much to my surprise, hit number one, which means the pressure is piling on for the next.

I sink into my makeshift writing nook, cracking my knuckles like a pianist about to perform a concerto.

I can do this.

But when I open a new document on my laptop, my eyes dance between the blinking cursor and the clock ticking away, two relentless reminders that time waits for no writer.

Hell, who needs a deadline to feel the pressure? Life is doing an excellent job on its own.

I decide to take a break, telling myself it's for inspiration and not because I've just typed and deleted the same sentence five times. I lean back and close my eyes as I try to massage the headache beginning to bloom.

My phone lights up with a message from my ex-fiancé, Adam.

Adam: Can we talk?

I hit delete, my finger pressing down a little too hard on the screen as if trying to erase him from my life. If only it were that easy.

I take a steadying breath when a pounding at the door startles me. This isn't a soft, neighborly knock; it's a drumroll, a forewarning of the storm about to engulf my new sanctuary.

With a sigh, I close my laptop and brace myself for impact. Swinging the door open, I'm instantly smothered in a floral-scented cloud of chaos. Mom barrels through the doorway like a Tasmanian devil in designer heels.

"Oh, Holly! This place is so…rustic!" She casts a judgmental eye around, her voice a pitch higher than usual.

"And by rustic, you mean…?"

"I mean, you'll need a Christmas miracle to have this place ready for a tree." She's already fussing over the throw pillows as if their arrangement will transform the room.

I'm slightly offended on behalf of my old cottage. "It just needs a good clean and a lick of paint."

She nods, unconvinced. "Sure, honey."

Dad lumbers in after her, his presence instantly calming like a weighted blanket. He gives me a bear hug so tight it nearly cracks my spine.

Ah, relief.

"It's good to see you, sweetheart," he says, smiling.

"And you, Daddy."

Just when I think we've reached maximum occupancy, my brother, Mark arrives, balancing his three-year-old, Mia, on one arm and holding the hand of his very pregnant wife, Rachel, with the other.

"Hey, sis." He grins, navigating the toddler minefield that is my living room with surprising grace.

"Hey yourself." I lift Mia into my arms. "Missed me?"

Mia giggles, her eyes twinkling with mischief. "Cookie? Play?"

Ah, yes, the universal language of nieces everywhere—sugar and playtime.

Before I can offer her some chocolate, Mom chimes in: "Speaking of play, you have to participate in the Christmas games this year. You haven't been home for Christmas in years. We need you for the treasure hunt, and you know how competitive the Johnsons get."

Christmas games? Treasure hunts? Competitive neighbors? What parallel Christmas universe have I moved into?

I glance at Dad for support, but he simply shrugs, his eyes saying, "You're on your own for this one."

"I'll think about it," I say, wiggling out of commitment like a seasoned politician.

Mark smirks, clearly amused. "You might as well say yes. She'll badger you until you do."

Traitor.

But before I can open my mouth, my phone buzzes on the coffee table. The screen lights up with yet another text from Adam.

Adam: You moved? What the actual fuck, Holly?

More texts come streaming through.

Here we go again.

He obviously doesn't know the meaning of "I never

want to see you again."

It's been three months and he's been relentless.

I don't have the mental compacity to deal with any of this today, so I silence it and turn it face down before my mother gets a chance to peek. The last thing I need is her grilling me about it.

I've been dodging the truth, tangoing around the reasons behind the sudden end of my engagement. My family has always been there for me, a tight-knit circle of trust and support. So why haven't I told them the real reason I ended my engagement?

Embarrassment. That's the root of it. I've built a career around penning romance novels, crafting tales of perfect couples and grand love stories. Admitting my own has crumbled, that it wasn't the fairy tale I'd hoped for, makes me feel like an intruder. Like I'm failing not just at love, but at understanding it.

And I don't want their pity or the *I told you so* looks. I don't want them to dissect every memory, trying to pinpoint where things went wrong. It's easier to keep them at arm's length, to deal with the heartbreak in solitude.

I'll tell them, eventually. When the words find their way and the sting fades a little more. But for now, I keep my silence, choosing to protect the delicate remnants of my pride.

"So, do we have a deal?" Mom raises an eyebrow. "Will you join our team?"

"Fine," I sigh, defeated. "I'm in. Just let me find a decent pair of running shoes, and maybe a crash helmet."

"Excellent. We'll crush the Johnsons this year!"

Jesus.

Dad chuckles, giving me a sympathetic look. "Your

mother takes no prisoners when it comes to Christmas games."

I remember.

"Or anything else," I mutter under my breath.

Mia tugs on my shirt, her tiny face a mix of confusion and curiosity. "Games? Play?"

I hoist her up in my arms. "You bet, kiddo, but these games involve more strategy and less tickling."

Dad finally manages to detach Mom from the décor planning long enough to suggest they leave and let me settle in. "Come on, Karen. Let's give Holly some space. She's got unpacking to do, and we've got a Christmas strategy meeting to plan."

Mom gives me a quick hug, slipping a not-so-discreet sachet of lavender into my hand as she does. "For the smell, darling."

"We can stay?" Rachel offers, resting a hand on her swollen belly. "Help with the place?"

I give her a sideways hug. "Your only job is to rest. You've already got your hands full." I crouch, tickling Mia and kissing her cheek. "And I promise," I tell her, "When this place is all done, we're having a sleepover."

She giggles and claps her hands.

God, I missed them.

Mark sighs. "Ah, sleep would be nice." He pulls me into a hug that feels just like home before whispering, "You sure you can do all of this on your own? I've got to work but I can help in the evenings, or I could call Sean—"

"No!" I back away. "I want my return to be peaceful and quiet. I'm going to lock myself away for a few days, clean, and see if I can write some sentences that are coherent enough to read. Then I'll get stuck into all of the big jobs around here. I would prefer my return not to result in a murder."

He rolls his eyes and shakes his head. "You realize you're an adult now? You and Sean could try to get along."

My poor, innocent big brother. "He's your best friend and that's your burden to bear, but it doesn't mean I have to suffer too."

"You know he could have this place fixed up in no time."

"Great, maybe while he's here he can dig a hole big enough for me to bury him in."

Mark dips his chin. "Point taken. No Sean. With the business taking off and everything going on with Brenda, I'm not sure he'll even have the time."

I rear back but remain steady on my feet. "What's wrong with Brenda?"

I know Sean and his mother have had their troubles throughout the years. I always thought the woman had the patience of a saint when we went a little crazy in her house, but now that I'm older I realize she was probably drunk. A mixture of emotions churns inside me—shock, confusion, and a touch of sadness. Brenda Colson was always kind to me, even when her own life seemed to be unraveling at the seams. But it wasn't easy for Sean growing up either. Most times, he played the parent rather than the other way around.

Mark blows out a breath. "Sean says he's handling it, but I think he's in denial. Her memory isn't what it used to be, and she's confused a lot. She's just... different. She walked into the bar last week and demanded a drink. Sean had to practically carry her out of there."

My mouth falls open. "Brenda?" The woman has been sober for years and worked hard at it.

He nods, the worry causing the corners of his eyes to crinkle. I know Mark has always seen her as a second mother.

"I should go see her."

"Let me run it by Sean first. I'm sure she'd love to see you, Holl, but she can be… well… erratic."

Something akin to guilt burns in the pit of my stomach. "Why didn't you say anything?"

"You were in the city living the dream. You know Sean will look out for her."

I nod. He might be an asshole, but he's an asshole who loves his mother.

As if on cue, Rachel's eyes widen. "Baby's kicking! Mark, do you want to feel?"

While Mark rushes over, awed by the sensation of his unborn child moving, I realize just how much I've missed this—my overwhelming but loving family. For all their quirks and invasions of personal space, they're mine. And right now, that means more to me than any well-decorated, sweet-smelling home ever could.

The door closes behind them, leaving me in a mess of luggage, scented candles, and leftover familial warmth. With a sigh, I pick up my phone and delete another text from Adam. His digital footprint is fading, but the emotional one? That's going to take some time.

I contemplate going back to my laptop to write but know it's going to be a wasted effort. I haven't written a creative sentence since my breakup. Instead, I grab the cleaning supplies I bought on the drive here, light some candles, and get stuck in, all the while hoping I don't hit off something that will cause the entire house to crumble down around me.

TWO

Three paint cans, two nervous breakdowns, and one impulse scarf purchase later, I finally emerge from the labyrinthine aisles of the home goods store.

It's Pine Falls in December, a magical little snow globe where Christmas spirit blasts through outdoor speakers like some North Pole version of Big Brother. It's cold enough to freeze a snowman's butt off, yet I'm sweating like a turkey on Thanksgiving Eve. Must be all that stress-induced cardio from dodging small-town gossip and inquiries about my love life. Or lack thereof.

I stagger towards the Falls Cafe, my arms weighed down by home improvement supplies, my mind weighed down by the creeping realization that my humble abode might require the skills of someone more qualified than a romance novelist with commitment issues.

I push open the café door, immediately greeted by a gust of warm air that smells like fresh coffee and cinnamon. "You made it out alive!" Molly, the owner, calls out from behind the counter.

"Do I look that bad?" I ask, easing my armload onto a table and collapsing into a chair.

She winks and slides a creamy concoction across the counter. "On the house. You look like you could use it."

"Is it laced with something stronger than espresso?" I sip the frothy beverage. It's like a Christmas hug for my insides. "Maybe you could ask your husband to slip me something?"

Molly's husband Archer owns the bar next door, aptly named Molly's, which is nauseatingly cute considering he named it after her.

"Don't tempt me. I have a stash of Irish cream for emergencies," Molly replies. "What's the deal? You look…"

"Like shit?"

"A little tired."

I take a deep breath. "The cottage. It's going to need some work."

She tilts her head thoughtfully. "Why don't you just ask Sean?"

"Why is he everyone's answer?"

"Because he's got his own business doing exactly what you need. I assumed he would be the obvious choice."

Sean freaking Colson. The only human being capable of making me consider bodily harm as a viable communication tool. "I'd rather remove my own spleen with a spork."

Molly laughs. "That bad, huh?"

"Let's just say, the less I see of Sean, the better it is for public safety."

Sean has been a part of my family since… well, forever. My parents treat him like the other son they never had. I get it. He didn't have the best family life growing up, but it doesn't mean I have to like him. I swear, he goes out of his way just to piss me off.

She pushes a plate toward me. "Well, this won't fix your house problem, but it will fix your hunger problem. Welcome home."

On the plate is one of Molly's famous Christmas pastries—flakey, buttery, and shaped like a Christmas tree. It's nostalgia and home in every bite.

Maybe I could do this. Fresh paint, a few repairs, and I'd have a writer's haven, a sanctuary. All without any interference from irritatingly talented carpenters who have known me since I was in braces.

"Thanks. You're a lifesaver."

"Anytime. And think about calling Sean. There's not many in the way of good tradesmen around here, especially this time of year. A woman can only do so much with a paintbrush and denial."

"Denial's my middle name," I joke, but my laughter dies as I catch sight of the time. It's late afternoon, and if I don't start on the painting now, I'll be doing it by the light of my phone.

I chug down the last of my coffee, grab the pastry for the road, and sling my scarf around my neck, bracing myself for the icy air outside. As I step out into the snowy streets, the holiday jingles echoing from shop to shop, I remind myself that this is home. It's where I belong.

Even if home requires paint, repairs, and a potential confrontation with Sean.

But for now, it's just me and the open road—or rather, the icy, treacherous path back to my cottage.

Oh, the things we do for the promise of a fresh start.

THREE

I'm halfway through painting my living room—a soft, inviting shade of teal that I'm hoping will magically transform this space into something habitable—when there's a knock on the door. I glance at the clock. It's too late for a postal delivery and too early for the apocalypse.

I contemplate not answering, but the knocking intensifies.

"For the love of God," I mutter, throwing down my paintbrush and jogging to the door. My hair is pulled into a haphazard bun, and I've got more paint on me than the walls at this point, but I really couldn't care less.

When I swing the door open, I need to tip my head back to meet a face that belongs on the cover of GQ magazine rather than at my doorstep.

I know under that beanie there's hair dark as rich soil, his eyes a shade even deeper. A jawline that could cut glass and a smile that, if rumors are to be believed, has a 100% success rate in melting the panties off women from here to Timbuktu. God, he's infuriatingly good-looking. His red flannel shirt is open, revealing a simple white T-shirt underneath that does nothing to hide his trim waist. His shoulders are broader than I remember.

When was the last time I saw him? It's been ages. Probably shortly after Mia was born. When I said I avoided him at all costs, I wasn't kidding.

Then he flashes that megawatt smile, and my brain finally catches up with the program.

"Sean, what the hell are you doing here?"

"Nice to see you too, Squirt."

"Oh, for fuck's sake, don't call me that," I snap.

I hate that nickname. A nickname he created for me after I snuck into one of his parties when I was only sixteen. In my naivety, I had gone a bit too hard on the beer and was feeling woozy, lightheaded and almost embarrassed about how drunk I was. One second my head was in a toilet bowl, the next, I was in the passenger seat of Sean's car while he cursed me out, mumbling something about how he was going to kill me for going to the party when he warned me not to. I vaguely remember telling him to stick his lecture up his ass. At some stage during the party, I had stuffed a beer can in my bag. I have no idea why. But I later sat on it in the car. It resulted in an explosion of beer. Sean's car smelled like a brewery for over a week, and I waddled in home looking like I pissed my pants. He snuck me into my house with his hand over my mouth to stop me from giggling, then put me to bed like the gentleman he isn't.

And that damned name? It stuck. For Sean at least.

"And wow," he adds, ignoring my protest as he steps inside and looks around, "this place has got...

charm. Yeah, let's go with charm."

I squint at him. "Are you calling my house ugly?"

"I'm calling it a work in progress."

"Such a diplomat." I cross my arms.

"I wear many hats, but today, the carpenter's hat is on. At least I'm going to try to put it on. Not sure what exactly it'll take to save this place. It might be easier to just knock the damn thing down."

I gasp, horrified. "You will do no such thing!"

He laughs. "Relax, Holls. I'm here to help."

"You're here to give me grey hairs." I narrow my eyes at him, still not fully convinced that tearing down my new sanctuary isn't part of his agenda. "What are you really doing here?"

He looks slightly uncomfortable for a moment, which brings me immense satisfaction. "Mark asked me to come take a look at the place. Help out if I could."

Damn it, Mark.

I should have known he wouldn't listen to me.

"I've got it handled, thank you very much," I insist.

He looks unconvinced but shrugs. "Suit yourself."

Then, with an air of nonchalance that riles me up, he strides into the kitchen like he owns the place. I follow, feeling a little like a territorial cat chasing off an unwelcome guest. He reaches up and opens a cupboard to inspect it. The door promptly falls off its hinges and clatters onto the countertop.

"Seriously?" I mutter, staring at the fallen cupboard door. Even the furnishings are conspiring against me.

"I guess this doesn't fall under the charming category."

"I can fix it myself." I reach for a screwdriver from the utility drawer that I had already filled with tools.

The only problem? It sticks and refuses to open.

Sean leans against the counter, arms folded. "I suppose you'll be fixing the cantilevered joists in the ceiling and the subfloor that's buckling too?"

"The what in the where now?"

As if on cue, something from the living room makes a loud, distressing cracking noise. We both turn to look just in time to see a section of the ceiling trim fall off and land in the middle of my half-painted room.

I let out a groan that morphs into a hysterical laugh. "Oh my God, I'm living in the Money Pit. I'm Tom Hanks laughing manically into a hole in the ground."

Sean stares down at me. "Now you see why I'm here?"

I sigh, my shoulders slumping in defeat. For the first time, I consider that maybe—just maybe—I can't do this all on my own.

"Fine, you win," I concede, looking at the fallen cupboard door and then back to Sean's infuriatingly smug expression. "But if you're helping, you're doing it my way."

He raises his hands in mock surrender. "Your kingdom, your rules, Squirt."

"For the love of—please don't call me that."

He laughs, that deep, throaty sound that I hate to admit is somewhat infectious. "Alright, alright. What's first on the agenda, boss?"

I glance around my crumbling cottage, considering where to start. "Well, I was painting, as you can see," I say, gesturing to the half-painted wall. "But I'm thinking structural integrity is more important at this point."

"Smart choice," he says, walking over to the section of trim that had fallen. "Don't worry, structurally, the place is sound. It just needs some TLC. But this wood is rotting. You'll need to replace it, not just paint over it."

"You can do that?"

"With my eyes closed, but I'll keep them open for your sake."

I roll my eyes but feel a small twinge of relief. "Okay, what do we need?"

"We?"

"Yes, we. If you think I'm letting you tear apart my house unsupervised, you're wrong."

He grins, apparently pleased by my concession to let him help. "Do you own any power tools?"

"Do kitchen appliances count?"

He bursts out laughing. "No, they don't."

"Then no."

"Alright, I'll bring some from my shop tomorrow. We'll get started bright and early."

I pause, finally letting it sink in that Sean is going to be here, in my space, fixing things.

"Tomorrow it is," I say, but I can't keep the sigh out of my voice.

"That's settled then," he says, turning abruptly to leave. "Have my coffee ready, won't you?"

"Excuse me?"

"I work better when I'm caffeinated."

"Well, so do I. But I don't see you offering to make coffee for me."

A grin tugs at the corner of his mouth. "You'd trust me with your coffee? Color me flattered."

"You're insufferable."

"And yet, you're the one who needs my help."

With that, he steps out of my crumbling cottage, leaving me standing amidst the chaos.

Well done, Holly. You've managed to ensnare the one carpenter in Pine Falls guaranteed to make your life a living hell.

This is going to be a very long renovation.

FOUR

"Why the hell did I agree to this?" I mutter, rubbing a hand over my face as I look at my cluttered workshop. It's organized chaos. Nails here, screws there, sawdust everywhere. Only I understand the intricate layout of this madness.

I pick up my tool belt, strapping it around my waist. Tools find their respective homes in various pockets. Can't show up to a job site unprepared, especially not one that's... well, Holly's.

Mark, that son of a bitch. He knows Holly and I fight like cats and dogs. Always have.

But she's also his little sister, which by some

unwritten rule makes her my responsibility too.

"Headed out, boss?" My apprentice, Caleb, smirks as he watches me load the truck. "Who's the lucky client today? You look so excited."

"Your sense of humor's gonna get you fired one day," I shoot back, not bothering to answer his question.

"Aw, you wouldn't do that. Who else would put up with your grumpy ass?"

"Get back to work, kid," I grumble, though there's no heat in my words.

Truck loaded, I take a final look at my list. Got everything? Check. A sinking feeling in my gut because I know exactly where I'm headed? Double check.

As I drive, memories flood back. Holly, covered in paint from head to toe yesterday, looking as frazzled as I'd ever seen her. Why does that image bring back a rush of nostalgia? The Holly from yesterday oddly reminded me of the Holly from our childhood—always in some sort of mess, and always somehow dragging me into it.

That old pounding resurfaces in my chest as if it was waking from a deep sleep. I take a long inhale, ignoring it. It'll go away. It did before.

I pull up to her cottage and park my truck. A glance at the house has me muttering curses under my breath. It really is a shithole.

But as much as I hate to admit it, if anyone can turn a shithole into a home, it's Holly. She has this way of breathing life into things, people too. Even when those people want to strangle her sometimes.

I grab my toolbox and head for the front door, taking a moment to brace myself. I'm about to step into the lioness's den. And this lioness? She bites.

Deep breath. Here goes nothing.

"Morning, Squirt," I say as she opens the door.

Her eyes widen then narrow almost immediately.

She throws her head back with a groan and walks away, muttering, "Oh, for fuck's sake."

There's that pounding again, reminding me it never really left. Each beat is more bruising than the last.

Thump.

Thump.

Thump.

I try to suffocate it, swallow it down, take a fire extinguisher to it and smother it but nothing works. Especially when she looks over her shoulder at me, that same scowl still on her face.

"You coming in? Or are you going let us both freeze to death?"

Thump.

Thump.

Thump.

Fuck.

Why did she have to move back? Why did she have to move back looking like that?

I was doing fine.

Now? Well now I'm stuck renovating this cottage for the only woman I've ever loved.

FIVE

I'm measuring and cutting pieces of crown molding for the living room. The miter saw roars to life, drowning out whatever Christmas carol is emanating from Holly's phone. *Deck the Halls* maybe? Or *Jingle Bell Rock*? Doesn't matter; they all blend together after a while.

As I align the saw with my pencil mark, I can feel her gaze drilling into me from across the room. It's distracting as hell. You'd think she was watching a bomb technician at work.

Finally, I set down the saw and remove my safety goggles. "You know, you're supposed to look away when people are working with power tools. Ever heard of safety first?"

She shrugs, paintbrush in hand, obviously trying her best to refurbish an old bookshelf that's seen better days. "I am being safe. It's you who's wielding that thing like it's Excalibur."

"Listen, Squirt. I've got this under control. Why don't you focus on making that bookshelf less of an eyesore and let me work my magic here?"

Her eyes narrow dangerously. "Quit calling me Squirt, and maybe, just maybe, I'll consider it."

"Quit staring. I'm good at my job. You don't have to supervise."

"Who says I was supervising? Maybe I was just admiring your... technique."

"My technique, huh?"

"Yeah, like, how *not* to do things."

"Ouch. You really know how to wound a man's pride."

She grins, pleased with herself. "It's a gift."

Her phone changes tune, shifting to another holiday song.

"Enough chit-chat. I have molding to cut, and you have a bookshelf to... whatever you're doing to it."

"Improving it," she says defiantly.

"Sure, let's call it that."

With a huff, she stands before tippy-toeing awkwardly. She's trying to reach another paint brush on the top shelf, and it's not going well. Christ, she's like a kitten trying to reach a high branch. Didn't she grow at all since we were kids? I could swear she stopped at twelve and hasn't gotten an inch over five-foot-four.

Her jet-black hair is swept up in a messy bun, a few rebellious strands framing her face. That face—those light blue eyes that could pierce through steel, lips I've seen her bite when she's concentrating—they're features I've had to remind myself more than once not to stare at too long. And yet, I find myself looking anyway. My eyes trace down her figure to where her jeans hug her ass, and it's like my hands have a mind of their own, itching to—

Fuck.

Mark would drive my head through a wall if he knew the thoughts I'm having about his little sister.

"Here, I can get it," I say, stepping in behind her. She tenses as I get closer, a stiffness creeping into her shoulders.

Ignoring her reaction—or maybe because of it—I press my front to her back, my height advantage obvious. She smells like paint fumes and cinnamon, a weird combination that I find oddly intoxicating.

Careful not to get paint on my shirt, I reach up effortlessly and grab the paint brush. "This what you were after?"

She lets out a shaky breath as she takes it from me. "Yes, thank you."

"Ah, she has manners. Who knew?" I rear back, quick on my feet as she makes a genuine attempt to bite me. "So vicious."

She groans, and I grin. She may drive me up the wall, but damn if it isn't a fun ride getting there.

We spend the next hour in silence, but I can't help noticing that her phone buzzes every few minutes. It's sitting on a nearby table, and each time it vibrates, she casts a side-eye glance at it like it's an object of dread. She never answers.

"You sure you don't want to get that?"

"It's nothing," she says, but there's a crack in her voice that tells me it's anything but nothing.

I put my tools down and wipe my hands on a rag, my mind racing with questions I have no right to ask. "Holl, everything okay?"

She's visibly annoyed, her brows knitting together in that way they do when she's frustrated. "I don't remember inviting you into my personal life."

And there it is. A brick wall. Not that I blame her,

it's really none of my business. I've never been great with emotional stuff, especially not with women. Mark has always been the sensitive one, not me. My forte is physical labor and tangible results—emotions are just too messy.

She exhales, almost like she's trying to release whatever's bothering her. "Sorry. I'm just stressed, that's all."

"Stressed is starting to sound like your middle name."

"Yeah, well, Holly 'Stressed' Winters has a ring to it, don't you think?" She offers a smile, but it's too tight to be real.

I decide to let it go. If she wants to talk about whatever's bothering her, she will. Until then, I've got work to do.

Picking up my tools again, I turn back to my work, but my mind keeps wandering back to her. If anyone is going to stress her out, it's me, no one else.

But what can I do? Even if I tried to help, she wouldn't let me.

After a while, her intense supervision shifts from me and her bookshelf to her laptop screen. She's staring at it like it holds the secrets of the universe, but her fingers are hovering above the keys, frozen in place.

"Having a problem writing your sex books?"

"Shut up, Sean," she snaps without looking away from the screen. Her cheeks are flushed, but it's hard to tell if it's from irritation or embarrassment. With Holly, it could be either—or both.

"If you need inspiration, you know where to find me." I wink at her even though she's not looking.

She makes a gagging sound. "Gross."

"I'm just offering my services. Very generous of me, don't you think?"

"Your ego is the only thing generous about you."

I bark a laugh, pleased that I can still get a rise out of her. "Touched a nerve, did I?"

She rolls her eyes and mutters something under her breath, but she doesn't respond. Instead, she huffs and turns her attention back to her laptop, her fingers now flying across the keys.

Inspired or not, she's writing, and that means she's too busy to supervise me. Perfect.

SIX

I can't believe I'm waiting for Sean Colson. And he's late. According to my mom, he's inundated with work. So why, pray tell, is he gracing me with his ever-irritating presence?

When he finally walks in—tools in tow and flannel shirt screaming "I'm a lumberjack and I'm okay"—he doesn't even greet me.

"I don't suppose you're ever on time." I can't help myself.

"Time is a social construct," he retorts, avoiding eye contact.

"Really? And here I thought it was a unit to measure

27

the passing of life, something we all have a limited amount of."

As he turns to me, I'm reminded of how much he towers over me, a little imposing in a way that's strangely familiar. It's no wonder I could never keep a boyfriend in high school. Between Mark, my over-protective brother, and Sean, his intimidating best friend, potential boyfriends didn't stand a chance.

"What? Why are you looking at me like that? You're the one that's late. Walking in here like—"

He looks at me, eyes narrowing, before striding over, placing his thumb and index finger on my lips, and pressing them together.

"You hear that, Squirt? Silence. It's bliss."

I swat his hand away. "Did you just silence me? Like, physically silence me?"

His action brings back memories of a thousand little arguments—of him hiding my favorite books just to get a rise out of me, of the shared Sunday dinners when we couldn't look at each other without squabbling over the mashed potatoes. In those moments, I hated him the most.

I'm reminded of when I hit puberty, and I might have had a mild, teeny tiny little crush on him.

Okay, it was huge. I swear it consumed my life for an entire year. I lost so much oxygen in that year from holding my breath when he looked at me that it's obviously affected my adult life.

I got over my crush… eventually. I mean, I'm a grown woman. I can admit that Sean is hot, but it would give me so much more satisfaction to just kick him in the balls.

He shrugs, a smirk playing on his lips. "I'm giving you a sample of what I enjoy—silence."

I feel my face redden. "I don't recall inviting you here to enjoy yourself."

"I don't need to be here, Holly. Got plenty of other things to occupy my time."

"Then why are you here?" I'm seething but also genuinely curious. "Please, go do those other things."

He sighs, his demeanor changing for just a moment as he scrubs a hand over his face. It's then that I notice his work attire—a faded navy flannel shirt over a white tee, dark work pants, and steel-toed boots. There's something unexpectedly appealing about a man in work clothes. It's annoying how attractive it is, and that realization makes me even more infuriated.

Ignoring my directive, he turns his back to me and gets on with his work.

"Fine." I grab my coat and keys and head for the door. "I'm going into town. Enjoy your precious silence."

He grunts, which I interpret as a goodbye in 'Seanese'.

I step out, welcoming the fresh air as a temporary escape from the intensity inside. In town, Pine Falls is in its full festive glory—a stark contrast to the atmosphere I left behind.

I find myself inside a quaint little bookstore. The owner has me sign some of my books he has in store and take a picture for social media which makes me smile. The familiar smell of paper and ink brings a sense of comfort. I've done countless press tours, but there's something about being home, in this little bookstore and seeing my books on the shelves that always brings me the most pride.

Perhaps a new book will be a suitable distraction. Yet even as I leaf through the pages of a promising mystery novel, my mind can't help but drift back to Sean. The sight of him in his work clothes, his unshaved jaw, even the arrogant way he smirked at me—everything floods back, and I'm annoyed with myself for even letting him invade my thoughts.

My phone vibrates in my pocket, jarring me from my reverie. It's Adam again. My stomach knots. I've lost count of how many times he's tried to contact me since I walked out of our shared life. And each ignored call, each deleted text, they all feel like tiny victories. But also like a door I haven't completely shut. I silence my phone and tuck it back into my pocket, feeling the weight of it like never before.

I make a hasty purchase—anything to busy my thoughts—and step out into the chilled air.

As I step out of the bookstore, my boots crunch against the freshly fallen snow that blankets the cobblestone pathways of the town square.

"Well if it isn't Holly Winters finally coming to see her best friend."

Turning, I see Jackie, my childhood friend, who's currently trying to manage a gaggle of hyperactive kids. They're huddled around a table filled with half-finished Christmas ornaments, construction paper, and—good Lord—is that glitter?

"I told you after our last weekend together that I never want to see you again," I say but smile at the memories. Jackie came to visit me in the city after my breakup from Adam. I'm sure we had fun, but I can only remember the hangover from hell that lasted a week. "This is your idea of fun, huh?"

She rolls her eyes. "Oh, please. This shitshow is what they call teaching. But don't let the arts and crafts fool you. It's a goddamn war zone. You try telling

Timmy over there not to eat the fucking glitter."

I bite my lips together, suppressing a laugh. "You always did have a way with children."

"Screw that," she says, taking a break to stand beside me. "So, what brings you to town? I thought you'd be buried in your little cottage, avoiding humanity."

I sigh. "Sean's helping me with some house repairs."

She raises her eyebrows. "Sean? Jesus, that's like putting a bull in a China shop and expecting no breakages."

"He's driving me up the freaking wall."

She shoots me a sympathetic smile, probably picturing the many public arguments me and Sean have gotten into over the years.

"Well, if you're looking for a distraction, I'm setting you up. He's perfect for you—"

"No, no, no," I cut her off, shaking my head. "I'm not in the dating game right now."

"Holly, you need to get out, have some fun. Remember fun? That thing adults do when they're not busy adulting? The last time I spoke to you, you were three days in the same sweatpants while drowning in Ben & Jerry's over a guy who didn't deserve you anyway."

Caramel Chew Chew really had my back.

Before I can argue, she continues, "Look, even if you don't want a date, you're coming to Christmas dress up at Molly's bar. No excuses. I need a wing woman. Don't worry, you have two weeks to prepare."

A wing woman for a night out at Molly's? God help me. "Okay," I relent, more for her sake than mine. "But I'm not being set up."

"Deal," Jackie says, sealing my fate. She tilts her

head toward the kids at the stall. I shoot them a quick wave. "Want to help with this lot?"

I back away slowly before she physically makes me stay. "Sean is more child than I can handle right now."

She pouts while simultaneously getting wrapped in tinsel. "You're the worst friend."

"But I love you."

"Yeah." She blows a hair from her forehead. "I love you too."

Strolling around the bustling square, I can't help but get caught up in the excitement as everyone prepares for the upcoming Pine Falls Games. It's still weeks away, but this town takes their games seriously. Vendors set up their stalls, kids dart around with the electric energy that only comes with the holiday season, and families snap photos in front of a grand, awe-inspiring wooden arch. The arch is a masterpiece, the wood dark and rich, adorned with intricate carvings of snowflakes, reindeer, and pine trees. A delicate lacework of vines and holly wraps around the columns, converging at the top in a beautiful Christmas star that seems to glow in the setting sun.

As I admire the craftsmanship, my old high school teacher Mrs. Thompson and her husband Doug sidle up next to me. "Isn't it gorgeous?" she says, nodding at the arch. "Sean did that, you know."

I resist the urge to roll my eyes. Of course, he did. "It's beautiful," I admit.

She leans in, her voice a conspiratorial whisper. "I have to ask, when is your next book coming out? They're my secret pleasure, you know."

A bubble of laughter threatens to escape, but I manage to hold it back. "Hopefully soon," I say, cheeks flushing a shade of pink I'd rather not analyze. Ever since Sean's inappropriate yet oddly stimulating offer for "inspiration," my writer's block has mysteriously vanished. My mind keeps projecting his image onto the cowboy in my story.

God help me.

Feeling the need for some liquid courage—though settling for caffeine—I make my way to the coffee cart in the square. I order two large coffees. My eyes land on the display of festive cookies. On a whim, I grab two: a cute Christmas tree one for myself and a Grinch cookie for Sean. Because if anyone embodies the spirit of the Grinch right now, it's him.

Armed with my caffeine and cookies, I head back to the house. I step in, closing the door softly behind me, and immediately the tension in the air hits me like a ton of bricks. Sean is where I left him, engrossed in his work, tools and wood shavings scattered around him like the aftermath of some carpentry war zone. His flannel shirt stretches across his broad shoulders, sawdust clinging to the fabric and his work boots. He doesn't even look up, and it's infuriating how a man can look so damn attractive while being so damn annoying.

"Thought you might need this." I place the Grinch cookie and coffee next to him and set my own on the kitchen counter. He finally glances up, eyes meeting mine for a split second before falling on the cookie.

"What's this? A peace offering?" he grumbles, not pausing his work.

"If it is, would you accept it?"

He chuckles darkly, grabbing the cookie and taking a bite before meeting my eyes from across the room.

The muscles in his jaw tick. "If there's one thing I'm sure of it's that I will never know peace around you."

"You sure you don't want to leave?"

He stops, power drill in hand, and sighs. "Look, I said I'd help you, so I'm here, alright? Don't make me regret it more than I already do."

I feel a pang of something—guilt, maybe, or sympathy. But my pride won't let me show it. "Fine, stay," I say, my voice softer. "Just don't expect me to sing *Kumbaya* with you."

He grins, a real grin this time, and for a moment, the tension eases. "Wouldn't dream of it."

The moment I sit back down at my writing desk, I can't help but take in the changes around the cottage. Despite the temptation to label Sean as a mere thorn in my side, the reality is more complicated. The man is skilled, damn it, and my place is already looking more charming.

The old, worn shelves are replaced by sleek, sturdy oak that seamlessly fits with the rustic decor. There's a finesse to his handiwork—clean lines, smooth surfaces, and joins so precise they're almost invisible. It's not just competent work. It's art. Each new addition transforms the room, making it feel both fresh and familiar, like a beloved book you've read a dozen times but can't help diving into again.

The way he's arranged the wooden panels in a geometric pattern reveals an attention to detail that's both impressive and infuriating, mainly because it reminds me how he's not just the brawny builder with calloused hands; there's a thoughtful brain behind those dark eyes, too.

And then there's the fireplace. My old, underused fireplace now looks like something straight out of a home design magazine. He's retiled the hearth with intricately patterned tiles that capture every hue of the room, turning what was once merely functional into a focal point. It's an undeniable improvement, a stark contrast to the chipped, dated tiles that were there before.

I hate that I love it all so much. The improvements are exactly to my taste, even though we never discussed it in detail.

I refocus on my laptop screen, painfully aware that if Sean's handiwork can inspire anything, it's the drive to make my own work just as good. And just like that, my fingers start to dance across the keyboard.

SEVEN

The man is insufferable. It's been a week. A week is all it takes for Sean to drive me insane.

Most of the time we don't even speak, and he still manages to find my last nerve just to stomp all over it.

He's a barbarian. Yesterday, he drank water straight from the tap. Who does that? He didn't use a glass, just suctioned his mouth around the streaming water. His tools are flung around with a carelessness that's borderline artistic, and he breathes. That's it. He just breathes.

I've been pounding on my keyboard all morning, sitting at my kitchen table wearing every layer I own. Sean is wearing his work clothes, no jacket, hat, scarf, gloves, or thermals. How is he not freezing his balls off?

I can't feel my fingers.

"Can you please close the door?" My teeth are clacking so much I'm surprised they don't crack.

He wipes a bead of sweat from his forehead before looking up at me. "I'm using strong adhesive. Do you want to choke on the fumes? I already told you that you should get out of here for the day."

I roll my eyes, or at least I think I do. My eyeballs are probably frozen too. "I've got things to do here. Like die from hypothermia. Besides, I don't want to leave. I'm finally writing again, and I don't want to jynx anything."

"When your fingers fall off from frost bite you won't be worrying about what you write."

I flip him the middle finger and smile. "They look like they're still working just fine to me."

He runs a frustrated hand over his face. "Can you just go inside your bedroom? I'm cold looking at you. Get under a blanket or something."

I open my mouth to reply, but how can I tell him that my room is a Sean-free zone? My desperate-for-creativity brain has detached Sean's unbearable personality from the Adonis-like body it inhabits. Oh, and it's a masterpiece. My fingers are burning up the keyboard, but my eyes are feasting—on the straining muscles, on the jeans hugging his thighs as he climbs, and on the flash of abs when he stretches. As of yesterday, the cowboy in my story is now a part-time carpenter.

I can't tell him any of that so instead I shake my head, ignore the heat crawling up my neck, and get back to work.

It's another hour of solid writing before a question comes up in my story, so I dive straight to the source. I steeple my gloved fingers, eyeing Sean before I ask, "Why did you become a carpenter?"

I think he grunts at me.

"Seriously, Sean."

He keeps going with his work. "I like it."

I wait for him to continue, but he doesn't.

"That's it?" He is useless for this backstory in my book. "There has to be more."

"Jesus was a carpenter. I felt inspired. Merry Christmas."

I don't even think he's religious.

"Sean?" I smile sweetly and try to bat my lashes.

When he finally looks at me, he cocks a brow. "You sick?"

I throw my head back with a groan. "There has to be a genuine reason. I know you've always been good with this sort of thing but—"

Sean cuts me off, finally directing his full attention toward me. "Is that a compliment, Holly Winters?"

"Maybe," I reply, my voice laced with a mix of annoyance and coaxing. "You gonna answer my question if it is?"

His eyes narrow to slits, studying me intently, causing an uncomfortable stirring in my stomach. "Seriously, have you got a fever?"

"Sean!" I cry out, my patience threadbare.

He's standing there, his stance solid and unmoving, arms crossed over his chest, hammer hanging loosely from his hand, and his eyes—those piercing eyes—analyzing every inch of my face.

"Why do you want to know?" he asks, his voice gruff but laced with a hint of curiosity.

I throw my hands out, still shivering, "Because we're probably going to die here, and I just want to know before I freeze to death!"

He looks lost in thought for a minute, returning to his work, his movements meticulous and calculated. I don't think he'll answer, the silence stretches thin, but then his voice breaks through, softer, more intimate.

"After my father left, Mom and I... we didn't have much." He looks at me then, eyes a medley of old wounds and reluctant vulnerability. "But you already know that part."

He proceeds, every word heavy with memories. "One Christmas, she... she couldn't get out of bed for weeks. She was just... lost in this dark place." His voice tightens. "So, I started making decorations, thinking maybe they'd cheer her up. I carved nearly every decoration on the tree from pieces of wood."

A smile pulls at the corners of my lips, involuntary but genuine. I remember that. Sean gave everyone their own decorations that he made himself as presents that year. I was eleven; Sean couldn't have been more than fourteen.

His words drip with sarcasm, a smirk playing at his lips. "Now, I think you, of all people, know just about everything there is to know about me. Anything missing you'd like me to enlighten you about?"

Maybe it's the remnants of the romance I'm weaving on my laptop, or maybe it's a sudden lapse in judgment, possibly a brain injury, but before I can censor myself, the words tumble out, unbidden. "Have you ever been in love?"

Even he seems taken aback by the question, his eyes widening a fraction before he schools his features into a semblance of impassivity, and he just stares and stares.

Oh, I want to retract the words and suck them right back into my big mouth.

"Sure," he finally mutters, severing the eye contact to immerse himself back in his work.

"With who?"

Shut up, Holly.

Shut. Up.

"Oh," I finally blurt. "Ashley. Of course it was Ashley."

Why do I always forget about Ashley?

He's almost glaring at me before he says, "Yeah, Ashley."

"Anyone else?" It's definitely a brain injury. I can't stop talking.

"What is it with you and obsessing about my love life. You've been in love enough for all of us."

If my mouth wasn't hanging open and I could feel my feet, I might notice how he works his jaw back and forth as if trying to relieve the tension. "Excuse me? What's that supposed to mean?"

"It means you're in love with falling in love. How has that worked out for you?"

The air abandons my lungs and forgets to come back, the pounding under my breasts making it hard to breathe.

"First there was Brad, then there was Leo, then, oh what was the accountant guy?"

"Danny."

"Right, him. And now Adam. Although he almost got you down the aisle, so he deserves some credit."

He's joking, right?

Something in my questioning has hit a nerve, but what the hell was it? Was it asking him if he was ever in love, or bringing Ashely into it?

I study him, really study him, but his eyes are laser-focused, his features carved from granite.

I try to inhale a steady breath, but it does nothing to alleviate the ache in my chest.

It's true, I've always been a relationship kind of girl, but who the hell does Sean think he is?

For once, I was trying to be nice, and look where that got me. The air around us seems to crystallize with tension, a sharp contrast to the slow burn spreading through my veins. Every bit of warmth seems to have congregated around my heart, simmering and bubbling, threatening to overflow, and all because of a few, well-aimed words from Sean.

Swallowing hard, I force myself to move.

He obviously sees the hurt in my eyes because his face drops. "I was kidding, Squirt."

"Sean, I swear if you call me that one more time, I'll stick that hammer so far up your ass, you'll substitute for a candy apple. And next time, maybe refrain from commenting on things you know nothing about." The burden of carrying what Adam did to me weighs on my chest, causing tears to sting my eyes.

Panicked, he takes a step forward but stalls, running a hand through his hair. "Fuck, Holl, I didn't mean... I'm sorry."

I almost topple over. An apology from Sean? Unheard of.

Instead of letting it go, the words spill out. "You seem to be keeping pretty meticulous tabs on my love life. Bet that's what you do hiding away in the mountains."

He laughs, and I almost lunge for him. "What?"

"I'm just saying, it could be worse. I could build myself a cabin in the mountains and hide away."

"Like me?" he guesses... correctly. I nod. "Fair assessment."

But I'm seething now, and I can't stop myself. "Well, maybe if you weren't so busy messing around with other women behind Ashley's back, you wouldn't need to hide away."

His laughter dies in his throat.

Our chests are heaving, eyes locked in a duel, each breath etching frost in the air between us. This is what it always comes down to with us. Pure animosity. It's a slow buildup of little squabbles until one of us can't contain it anymore, and it boils over, resulting in this. A vacuum of hate.

"Where the fuck did you hear that?" he finally snaps, his voice rough, eyes blazing with suppressed anger.

I search my mind, but I can't come up with an answer, probably because I don't have one. Jesus, did I just assume that's what happened and ran with it until I believed it to be the truth? Sean's a womanizer. I know it. He knows it. But now, guilt and embarrassment are crawling into my chest, making me want to curl up in a ball somewhere, far away from the heat of Sean's stare as he waits for a more intelligent answer than silence.

But I don't have one.

He scoffs, his gaze unwavering. "You always did have an active imagination. How about you leave it for your books this time?"

The sting of shame paints my cheeks a fierce red, and it's a struggle not to avert my gaze, not to admit defeat. But the words of apology are lodged in my throat, imprisoned by a mixture of pride, pain, and a whirlwind of unresolved emotions. So I stand there, my silence a loud echo in the space around us, wishing the earth would open up and consume me, freeing me from his penetrating eyes and the undeniable truth in his words.

He disappears into another room before a word of apology can escape my lips, and the next two hours blend into nothing but clattering keys and the buzz of power tools.

I should apologize, I know I should.

I stand to go to him, but there's a scratching sound that tears me away from my internal battle, forcing my eyes to roam around.

Empty.

Sean reappears, stalling at the doorway as his gaze locks onto something on the floor.

"You've got mice," he announces, his tone detached.

Never in my life have I moved so fast. I climb onto the table. I'd cling to the ceiling beams if I was sure they wouldn't fall down.

"Sean, you better not be messing with me. You know I hate mice," I nearly wail, my hands trembling as my eyes dart to the floor.

But Sean, he's the epitome of calm, the embodiment of ice cold. He approaches, every muscle in his body a tense line, veins in his forearms prominent. Then, with a suddenness that leaves me breathless, he clasps my chin between his fingers, forcing our gazes to lock.

"There's no mice," he states, his voice a sharp whisper. "In future, don't believe everything you hear."

A wave of realization crashes over me.

Well played, Sean. Well played.

EIGHT

"Holly?" The door swings open, Rachel's exhausted face peeking out from inside. Her eyes are wide, her cheeks flushed. "I... I wasn't expecting visitors."

I smile, noticing how even her lips are swollen. Poor Rachel. "It's only me."

Her mouth tilts, but her cheeks are still burning red. "It's just..." She looks around, trying to find her words. "To hell with it. The place looks like a dump. I can't bend over to pick anything up from the floor, and I'm pretty sure Mia is already jealous of the new baby. She's been glued to my hip all week." Her shoulders sag forward as if getting it off her chest was a weight released.

"Looks like I'm right on time. I'm here to kidnap Mia."

I've never seen a face light up so bright. "Really?"

"Yeah, I thought we'd go ice skating."

"You are my angel." She steps aside to let me in. "It might give me a chance to tidy this place."

I press my hand to her shoulder. "Relax. Go to bed

and sleep. I can give the place a tidy when I get back with Mia."

She blows out a long breath. "I think I married the wrong sibling."

"Of course you did. Now where is our little girl?"

She must have heard me because Mia comes barreling my way, a dangerously large Lego tower ready to topple in her chubby hands. "Lolly!"

My heart aches. I love that she can't pronounce my name yet.

"Hey, girlie. Want to come to the ice rink?"

I kneel to her level, watching her eyes light up, her grip tightening around her colorful Lego tower. "Uncle Sean?"

Damn, this girl loves Sean.

I'm still smarting from the whole mouse fiasco. Sean and I, well, we're not on speaking terms unless absolutely necessary. It's a silent, awkward dance, avoiding each other's gaze, quick "morning" and "night" being our only exchange.

"He's super busy, honey." I keep my voice light, not wanting to dampen her excitement. "But we can see if he wants to come, just for a little while, what do you think?"

Her little head nods vigorously, her curls bouncing. "Uncle Sean! Uncle Sean!" she chants, her little legs carrying her out the door before I can even blink.

I exchange a helpless glance with Rachel, who just shakes her head. "You've opened Pandora's box now," she teases.

I shrug. "I'm about to face him anyway, might as well have a cute kid as my shield." I wink, heading out the door after Mia, my heart thumping in my chest.

The workshop's noises grow louder as we

approach, and there he is, immersed in his work, unaware of the storm heading his way.

"Uncle Sean!" Mia's voice pierces the air, her arms flailing around.

His head snaps up, his eyes widening as they lock onto the tiny human running towards him. A smile plays on his lips as he scoops her up into his arms. "Hey, munchkin, what's up?"

Her arms wrap around his neck, her voice a whisper, "We go ice?"

His brows furrow, his gaze flickering to me. Our eyes meet, the air between us crackling. "Ice skating?"

I force a smile, my nerves dancing in my stomach. "Yeah, thought it'd be fun for Mia, break the routine a bit."

"Uncle Sean come?" Mia's hopeful voice breaks the tension, her eyes shimmering with excitement.

His gaze lingers on me for a moment longer before he looks down at Mia, his voice soft. "I'd love to, munchkin, but I have a lot of work…"

Mia's face falls, and damn, it's a punch to the gut. He seems to feel it too, his face softening. "Maybe I can join you guys later?"

"Promise?"

He smiles, pressing a kiss to her forehead. "Promise."

We still haven't spoken a word to each other. We're somehow still trapped in this strange air of silence.

Swallowing my pride, I step closer, but he doesn't meet my eyes. "It's not the only reason I came."

"No?" he asks, his eyes on Mia as he smiles at her.

"No. I wanted to apologize for the other day. I shouldn't have assumed—"

"No, you shouldn't," he clips.

We've fought before but I've never heard his voice so cold. I hit a raw nerve I never expected to encounter.

"I'm sorry," I finally say, for once pleading with him to look at me.

He dips his chin and lifts his head. "I'm almost finished up here. I'll meet you both at the rink."

Oh.

"Okay, good," I mumble, scooping Mia into my arms.

He returns to work which I guess is my cue to leave. Before I exit the workshop, he calls my name. I spin around to see that stupid half-smile on his face before his gaze finds mine.

"Me too."

He doesn't have to say it. I know he means he's sorry too.

Mia's little hands play with the strands of my hair, her voice soft as she hums a tune.

I strap her into her car seat, glancing back at the workshop. I can see his silhouette through the window, moving, working.

"Lolly, we go vroom vroom on ice!" Mia kicks her feet as we pull into town.

"Yes, baby girl. We go vroom vroom on ice."

"Sean coming?"

Jesus, this kids obsession with Sean is becoming concerning.

"He's coming."

Her tiny hand slips out of mine the moment we approach the town square where the outdoor ice rink is already set up. Her excitement pulls her towards another little girl. They rush into each other's arms, hugging.

"Izzy!"

"Mia!"

Well, damn, that's about the cutest thing I've ever seen.

"This your friend?" I ask.

She nods.

"Isabel, you can't just run off like that!" A woman with a warm smile and a camera hanging around her neck appears, her eyes scanning between the kids. When she sees Mia, her face lights up, "Hey, sweetie, you going on the ice today?"

Mia's head bobs up and down, her eyes glittering with anticipation.

"I'm Beth." She extends her hand towards me. "These two have play dates together every week."

"I'm Holly, Mia's aunt. It's nice to meet you," I respond, shaking her hand. For some reason I feel like I should know her. "Seems like the girls are quite the pair."

She laughs softly. "They're troublemakers."

I believe it.

Suddenly, a familiar voice rings out, "Little Holly Winters!" My heart leaps, recognizing the voice instantly.

I spin around to see a pair of very familiar eyes, one of his hands steadying himself on the barrier of the ice rink, the other holding the hand of another little girl. This one is older, ten maybe.

Mom had told me he settled down since returning to town.

"Logan!" A squeal escapes me as I rush to hug him. "I heard you moved back." I pull away to look at him, his tattoos, and those same kind eyes.

"It looks like I'm not the only one. How are you doing, kid?"

48

"I'm good. Who's this beautiful little girl?" She blushes a bright pink at his side.

"I'm Hannah," her voice is quiet, and she almost shrinks behind Logan's back.

"Nice to meet you, Hannah." I turn to look at Logan. "Look at you, all domesticated now."

He flashes me a megawatt smile. I think it's the first time I've ever seen him smile that way. I always thought Logan only smiled with a twitch of his lips.

Beth observes the reunion, her gaze flicking between Logan and me, the light catching her camera lens.

Then I realize… I look between them. "Oh, this is your Beth?"

He looks over at her, a flicker in his gaze. "The one and only. Holly worked the reception at the tattoo studio when she first moved to the city," he explains to her as she stands at my side. "She was younger then and a pain in my ass."

I nudge him playfully. "The old man looked out for me."

Beth laughs, her eyes glittering with something unspoken between them. It's intense, and I suddenly feel like I'm intruding.

"Wait." Beth turns to me. "You're Holly Winters. *The* Holly Winters."

"Am… I…" Why do I always stutter over this part? I'm still not used to it when people recognize me. "Yep."

"Oh my God, Logan bought me your books last year. I loved them."

I feel the heat creep up my neck. "Thank you. That's really kind."

"Logan!" She pushes him and he wobbles on the

ice. "You never told me you knew her."

"Because I knew you'd react like this," he deadpans.

She rolls her eyes. "Well, it's lovely to meet you, Holly. I'm going to get the little one and join Twinkle Toes on the ice." She winks at him, but he merely grunts back at her.

"And you?" Logan's gaze probes, "How's life treating you?"

"It's good, settling in, learning to live the small-town life again."

His gaze rolls over my head as Mia lets out a giddy, "Uncle Sean!"

A part of me was hoping he wouldn't come, but a bigger part of me knew he would because he loves Mia.

I feel the warmth of his presence behind me while he's standing there, Mia clasped in his arms.

"Hey," I whisper, not meeting his eyes.

He dips his chin.

Sean and Logan fall easily into conversation about something over the barrier of the rink. It would be interesting, I'm sure, if I was actually listening, but all I can think about is how close Sean is.

It's annoying how attractive he is, especially with a kid in his arms.

Relax, ovaries, we've got time.

Sean takes a step back, heading off to grab some skates. I open my mouth to call out my shoe size, but he cuts me off. "I know what size you are."

I turn back to Logan, his eyes drilling into me. "What?" I snap, crossing my arms and leaning into my hip.

"Do I sense something between you—"

"No."

"I think I do." His eyes are all narrow, studying my

face like it's a freaking map.

"I think you're getting old, and your senses are off. Go play with your family." I tilt my head, signaling towards Beth and the little ones.

He chuckles, that easy laugh that I remember so well, before pushing off the barrier, "See you around, kid."

Watching him skate away, I shake my head. It's going to be a long, long day.

NINE

"You coming or what?" Holly calls, skating onto the ice with Mia by her side.

"I'm coming, just give me a minute," I mumble, glancing down at the ice.

The hesitancy must be written all over my face because Holly skates back, a mix of amusement and disbelief in her eyes. Mia, clinging to her skating aid, seems more steady on her feet than I feel. A smirk crosses Holly's face, and I can almost hear the gears in her head turning.

"Just lean on me," she says, stretching out her hand.

She's not fooling anyone. I can see how she's almost

choking on the suppressed laughter.

I glare at her. "I don't need your help."

"You still can't skate, can you?"

I ignore her.

"When was the last time you came to the rink?"

I pretend to think about it. "When I was sixteen."

Her eyes swirl like she's searching through her memories before her eyes widen. She leans in so Mia can't hear. "Oh, for fuck's sake. You haven't been here since you broke your leg?"

"I can do some damn ice skating." I look down at Mia's skating aid. "Do they have those for adults?"

Holly rolls her eyes before bursting out laughing. "Why the hell did you agree to come?"

Isn't it obvious? "Mia asked."

"That's sweet and all, but I'm not spending the night in the emergency department."

I place one foot on the ice, the skate instantly slipping from under my feet. "How about you give a man some silence, Squirt. I'm trying to concentrate, and your voice is scratching at my brain."

She skates circles around me, making it look so damn easy, her laughter echoing in my ears. It's infuriating and intoxicating at the same time.

"Come on. Even Mia is doing better than you," she taunts, pointing at the three-year-old who's happily gliding around with her skating aid.

"Mia's got more practice."

"It's her first time."

"I've seen that kid climb a tree. She's not human."

"She's a toddler!"

I shoot her a disgruntled look, my fingers gripping the barrier tighter. "Can you just shut up for one damn minute? I'm trying not to die here."

"Oh, dying is the least of your problems. I'm more concerned about you breaking a hip, old man."

I grit my teeth, and my eyes narrow. "I'm two years older than you. I'm not going to break anything."

"Yeah, yeah, keep telling yourself that. Maybe it'll numb the pain when you fall on your ass." She laughs as she effortlessly spins around me, her hair flying out behind her.

I take another step, focusing on my balance, ignoring Holly's relentless teasing. But then she stops in front of me, blocking my view, and offers her hand again. "Come on, hold my hand. It'll be less embarrassing than holding onto a penguin skating aid."

Mia tugs on my coat. "Hold Lolly's hand. It's fun."

Holly leans down to Mia, whispering loud enough for me to hear, "I don't think Sean knows how to have fun, sweetie."

I finally lock eyes with her, a challenge sparking between us.

"Look, you can either hold my hand, or I can call an ambulance in advance. Your choice."

"I choose option three: you skating away and leaving me the hell alone," I snap, but I want her to stay, to keep challenging me, pushing me.

She pretends to ponder, tapping her finger against her lips. "Hmm, tempting, but I think I'll stick around, watch the show. It's not every day you get to see a grown man wobble like a newborn deer."

"Mia?" I smile down at her. "Tell your auntie to zip it."

She giggles. "Zip it, Lolly."

"Hey!" Holly scowls.

She leans in closer, her breath warm against my cheek. "Let's go, Bambi. I don't have all day."

I roll my eyes, pushing away from the barrier, slipping and sliding, trying to find my footing, all while Holly's laughter rings in my ears, light and beautiful, and damn her, despite everything, I'm starting to enjoy her company a little too much.

It's easier to be this way with her. It's easier to pretend because if I acknowledge anything more, I'm screwed.

Holly hates me because I'm her brother's best friend who drives her crazy.

I hate her because when she was nineteen something changed, and she made me fall in love with her without even knowing what she was doing.

"I prefer Thumper," I mutter, finally moving away from the barrier, my legs shaky but determined.

"Thumper it is then. Come on. Let's go." She beckons me like a dog and for a full minute I stare at her and list all the ways I could shut her up. Every one of them includes my mouth on hers.

Back to trying not to die.

I exhale deeply, struggling to focus on the ice beneath my feet rather than the infuriatingly attractive woman taunting me.

"You're doing great," Holly says, spinning around me with the ease of a professional, her laughter mingling with Mia's giggles.

"I'm going to thumper you in a minute," I grumble, attempting a glide and nearly toppling over, my arms flailing.

"Aw, you think you can catch me?" She chuckles, her eyes gleaming with mischief, skating backward, her movements smooth and controlled.

"When I catch you, you'll wish I hadn't," I threaten, but there's no real heat behind my words. I'm too focused on not breaking anything vital and too distracted by the way Holly's eyes light up every time she laughs.

She twirls around me like a damn fairy on ice. Her movements are graceful, her laughter enchanting, and I'm so caught up watching her that I almost forget about the ice beneath me. "Like this, look." Holly puts one foot in front of the other like a pro.

My jaw clenches, but before I can retaliate, my foot slips, and I find myself crashing down, my pride cushioning my fall. "Fuck!" I groan.

"Oh, down goes Thumper!" Holly laughs, but she's immediately by my side, offering her hand. "Need some help there?"

I glare at her extended hand.

"Come on, don't be stubborn."

Reluctantly, I take it, feeling a spark of warmth, an unexpected jolt of electricity.

Her hand is soft, warm, and engulfed in mine.

My eyes are drawn to her, to the way the cold air reddens her cheeks and how her breath creates little puffs of fog in the air, to the way her eyes seem to be shining brighter than the lights above us.

"You're still a pain in the ass. Don't let this let you think otherwise."

"Oh, I wouldn't dream of it." She presses her lips together, the corners of her mouth twitching into a smile that does strange things to my heartbeat. "It's clear you're utterly enamored with me."

My brows raise sarcastically. "Enamored? Someone's been writing too many romance novels."

"Maybe you should try it sometime. Might loosen you up a bit," she quips back, her smile blossoming into a full grin that's contagious, and despite my reluctance, I find myself smiling back.

"I am loose!" I nearly slip again, my arms windmilling as I try to regain balance.

"Sure, as loose as a rusty bolt."

Mia's laughter joins ours. "You're funny, Uncle Sean."

"Funny looking maybe," Holly mutters under her breath.

Thirty minutes later, I feel like I finally have the hang of it. Sure, one hand is still clutching the railing as Holly and Mia effortlessly skate around me, but all in all, I'm practically a pro. At least, that's what I tell myself.

Now, Holly is skating with Mia in her arms, a maneuver that seems impossibly difficult. How the hell does she do it?

Feeling a surge of confidence, or perhaps it's foolhardiness, I push off the railing and glide into the open space of the ice rink. The smooth slide of the skates on the ice, the absence of immediate disaster—it's not so bad.

And then it hits me: how the fuck do I stop?

I see Holly's eyes widen, her body tensing, bracing for impact. She's in my direct path, and with Mia in her arms, there's no way she can dodge in time.

Mia's voice rings out, sharp and clear, "Stop, Uncle Sean!"

The warning comes too late. I collide with Holly, the impact sending us sprawling to the ground. Instinctively, I grab her waist, trying to brace our fall. I groan as they come down on top of me. A flurry of limbs and cold ice, my back absorbing the brunt of the fall.

Everything goes silent for a second. I stare up at the

clear, night sky, holding my breath, waiting for a sign that anyone is injured. Holly is still flat against me, with Mia safely enclosed in her arms. The cold seeps through my clothes, but the warmth from Holly and Mia blunts the chill.

Then, the silence breaks. They both look down at me and burst into laughter, and despite the pain shooting up my spine, a laugh bubbles up from my chest.

"Are you guys okay?"

Holly's eyes meet mine as she glances over her shoulder. "Yeah, we're okay. You, on the other hand…" she trails off.

"I'm… I'm good," I insist, trying to sit up. Every muscle in my back screams in protest. "A few bruises, maybe, but I'll live."

"You sure?"

I nod, gritting my teeth against the discomfort. "Yeah, yeah. I'm sure."

Eventually, we manage to untangle ourselves. Holly stands, still holding Mia, her arms protective around her.

She looks down at me. "You really need to work on your stopping."

"Or you need to work on your dodging."

"Next time, I'll be prepared for the human missile."

"Okay," I breathe, reaching up for Mia and pulling her into my arms from where I still sit on the ice. She wraps her arms around my neck while I double check she's not hurt. "How about we get out of here and get some hot chocolate?"

"Marshmallows?" Mia asks.

"Lots of marshmallows," I promise then groan. "Just once I'm sure this human missile hasn't broken anything."

TEN

"Who left the lights on in the car? Holly, did you forget again?" Dad yells from the window as I make my way to the door. A minute later, he pops his head out again. "Never mind, it was me."

Welcome to family dinner night at the Winter's residence, a circus wrapped in chaos, dressed up as a gathering.

A knock on the door interrupts my thoughts.

"Holly, would you get that?" Mom shouts from the kitchen, her voice competing with Dad's power tools running in the background. He decided tonight was the perfect time to fix a loose cabinet handle.

I open the door, smile already on my face. When I see it's Sean, my shoulders slump, but not as much as they used to. He holds a bottle of wine in his hands and his infuriating smirk on his face.

"What are you doing here?"

"Your mom invited me. As she always does. You'd know that if you had come home more."

Ugh. He's right. "Well, I'm home now. Come in."

As we head into the living room, the family chaos fully unfolds. Mark is chasing Mia around the coffee table. Rachel is flipping through a pregnancy book while simultaneously devouring a plate of cheese puffs. Mom is still in the kitchen, the clattering of pans and bowls a background symphony to this madness. And Dad's now debating whether to continue his one-man DIY show or to actually join us for dinner.

"Sean! How are ya, buddy?" Dad hollers, ditching the screwdriver on the table and enveloping him in a bear hug.

"You know I can fix whatever you need," Sean offers.

"Ah, it keeps me young."

Mark and Sean share a hug, while Mia climbs into his arms. It's effortless for him. I can feel the scowl on my face soften as I watch. Rachel waves a cheesy hand at him.

Mom pops her head out of the kitchen, an apron covered in something that looks like a failed science experiment. "Sean, darling! Where's your mother?"

He tries to hide the flinch, but I see it. "She was tired."

"Oh, that's a shame," Mom breathes. "Well, you know what to do. Make yourself at home."

And just like that, he's swallowed into the family

circus, fitting right in, as if he belongs here. The familiarity of it all hits me like a ton of bricks. It's both comforting and irksome.

My phone buzzes on the table. Another message from Adam. I resist the urge to throw it out the window, settling for flipping it face-down instead. I glance up to find Sean watching me, a knowing look in his eyes. I divert my gaze, annoyed at myself for caring what he thinks.

"So, Dad, you fixed that cabinet yet?" Mark asks, trying to wrangle Mia into her highchair.

"Nah, but I think I've successfully stripped the screw," Dad replies proudly.

Mom rolls her eyes as she walks in, holding a tray of steaming garlic bread. "Oh, Holly, could you help me set the table?"

"Sure."

I snatch a piece of bread as I pass by and follow her into the kitchen. The chatter and clatter of the household dim to a hum as we lay out plates and forks, working in sync in a way only a mother and daughter can. The shared silence is a small sanctuary.

"So, you and Sean seem to be getting along well," Mom ventures carefully, a gleam in her eye.

I stiffen. "We are not getting along. We are... coexisting. For your sake."

She hums, arranging the cutlery meticulously before fixing what I've already laid out. "Coexisting is a start. But I heard you went ice skating together."

"We brought Mia to the ice rink together."

"Well, whatever is going on, it's nice not to see you both bickering all of the time. I always said—"

"Stop right there. I swear, if you start on with any of your matchmaking—"

"I wouldn't dream of it," she interrupts, but there's a playful mischief in her eyes that says otherwise. "Besides, I still have hope for you and Adam."

My heart sinks into my stomach. I should tell her. Get it over and done with. "Mom—"

"We all have our rough patches, honey. God knows me and your father have seen our fair share, but you power through. You were about to marry the man. You must have loved him."

"I did," I whisper feeling that familiar burn in my chest. "I did love him."

"I can't even count how many times I stayed awake at night imagining my little girl in my wedding dress."

Tears form in my eyes as a boulder size lump of guilt settles in my stomach. It was always my dream to take my mom's dress and redesign it for my wedding. We had so many plans.

And Adam ruined all of them.

I try to smile but it falters. "Don't count me out yet. Just because I'm not marrying Adam doesn't mean I will never get married."

She exhales, leaning against the counter. "I know, sweetie. But sometimes…" She pinches her lips together as if pondering if she should say what she's about to say. My mom has never been one to hold back and she's not going to start now so I brace myself for impact. "You just… you tend to run from things when you're scared."

Grant me patience.

"That's called instinct, mother. It's not a flaw."

My fight or flight has always leaned towards flight.

"You never told me what happened between you two."

I hum and haw like I'm about to break into song.

She's also holding a large knife that makes me reluctant to breathe a word of what Adam did. My mother might be a little overbearing but she's protective to a fault.

"He… um—"

Dad appears in the kitchen doorway, his expression half apologetic, half exasperated. "Can't find the bigger screws," he announces, like it's a national tragedy. Mom merely hands him a bowl of salad and shoos him back to the dining area before turning her expectant gaze back to me.

"It just didn't work out," I say because I'm a coward, and that knife is razor sharp.

A part of me wonders if she already knows. My mother has this weird superpower of being able to read me better than I can myself. I'm convinced of it when her lips quirk, her shoulders drooping like she was holding her breath for my answer.

"Well," she says, a smirk tilting on her red painted lips as she returns to cooking. "Like I said, you and Sean are getting along better."

"Oh God." I roll my eyes. "Don't read too much into it. He's fixing my house. I need to be nice to him. We'll be back to contemplating murder soon."

"Well, at least you didn't pour the wine over his head this time."

"The night is still young."

Now it's her turn to roll her eyes. "I knew when I went into labor with you on Christmas Eve that you were always going to be dramatic."

She continues with a story I've heard a thousand times. How her waters broke on my Grandpa's shoes as they were about to have family dinner. How my father ran every red light and sprinted into the hospital screaming that his wife was having a baby but forgot that wife and left her in the car in the middle of all the chaos. She tells me how she stayed up all night and into Christmas day while in complete agony. And how I didn't arrive until one minute before the clock struck twelve. I just made it on time to have my birthday on Christmas Day.

Even when she's finished, I can sense her unasked questions, her unsaid worries dancing in the silence between us. I know she cares, maybe too much sometimes, and the knowledge that she is restraining herself from delving deeper makes me love her even more. But right now, I'm thankful for the temporary reprieve, for the breath of air before diving back into the swirling emotions waiting for me in the silence.

∞∞∞∞

In the middle of dinner, little Mia is attempting acrobatics from her chair before my father sweeps her into his arms. "Careful or you'll end up like your aunt here with your little arm in a cast for six weeks." He chuckles, winking over at me.

The room erupts into laughter, and I can feel my face turn scarlet. "Dad, seriously? You had to bring that up?"

Mark joins in, "Oh man, how could we forget? You tried to impress us by jumping off the treehouse and ended up with a broken arm."

Sean's eyes are on me. "Not just a broken arm. She screamed like a banshee and blamed me for daring her, remember?"

"Oh, I remember." I glare at him. "You told me I was too chicken to do it. 'Just a quick jump, Squirt,' you said. 'What could go wrong?'"

Sean grins wider, clearly relishing the trip down memory lane at my expense. "Well, you were never one to back down from a challenge."

"No, and you were always one to push my buttons," I shoot back.

"Okay, you two," Dad interrupts like when we were children. "No bickering at the dinner table.

Mom chimes in, not letting the opportunity go to waste. "Well, Holly, Sean, speaking of challenges, the Christmas games are coming up. You two would make a fantastic team for the couples' events!"

Seriously?

Where did she get that notion?

I stare at her as if to say, "What the hell are you doing?"

She tips her head back and pretends not to see me.

Everyone freezes.

Sean raises an eyebrow and our eyes meet. My face is already red, but now it feels like it's on fire.

"Um, yeah, I'll think about it," Sean finally says, breaking the silence, but the undercurrent in his voice suggests he's considering anything but.

The daggers I throw his way confirm it.

I will tie your balls around your neck if you agree.

He arches a brow as if he can read my mind, so I scratch my nose with my middle finger.

I know, so mature.

I don't care.

The bastard only smirks and winks at me, but I can read his mind just as well as he can read mine.

Challenge accepted.

∞∞∞∞

After dinner, Mom asks me to fetch a box of decorations from the shed. As I make my way back to the house, clutching the dusty box in my arms, I notice Sean. He's standing a few feet away, phone pressed to his ear.

I know eavesdropping is terrible, but I can't help myself. I slow my pace, lowering the box onto the snowy ground as quietly as I can. His voice is tense, frustrated even, as he argues with someone on the other end of the line.

"Nobody took your money, Ma... Don't get worked up... Look, I'll be there soon, okay?"

He ends the call abruptly and slips the phone back into his pocket. He runs a hand through his hair, a gesture that I remember from our childhood, one that he resorts to when he's stressed. It's then that he notices me standing there, awkwardly holding the box of decorations.

"You hear everything you needed to?" he snaps, visibly annoyed. "Going to add to the town gossip?"

His words sting. It's on the tip of my tongue to fire back, but I swallow it down. "Come on, Sean. I know we're not exactly best friends, but you know me better than that."

He looks at me, really looks at me, for the first time tonight, and his shoulders slump. "Sorry, Holl."

I pick up the box and start walking again, but the awkward tension between us has shifted, become something more fragile. "Is there anything I can do?" I finally ask, breaking the silence.

He rubs the back of his neck, hesitating for a moment. "Honestly, I don't know. She's... she's not doing great. She hates doctors. I'm trying to get her help, but she's so damn stubborn."

There's a vulnerability in his eyes that I haven't seen in years, and it tugs at something deep inside. Whatever our past issues, this is a man struggling with a crisis that no one should have to face alone.

"I'm sorry," I say softly.

"Yeah, well," he shrugs, looking away. "It is what it is. I better get going."

"Sean," I call as he walks away. "If you need anything…"

"Don't worry your pretty little head about a thing. See you tomorrow, Squirt."

ELEVEN

SEAN

I wake up in my childhood bedroom, a room wallpapered in the distant echoes of adolescence— vintage band posters, a deflated football, dusty trophies from a time when life was simpler. The bed's a little too small for my adult frame, and the mattress feels like a slab of granite under my back. I haven't slept in this room since I was eighteen, hell-bent on escaping to the freedom of adulthood. But these days, I find myself back here more and more, and not because I'm nostalgic.

A dull throb pulses behind my eyes, evidence of a late-night filled with restless sleep. Rolling out of bed,

I drag myself to the window and peer through the worn curtains. It's a dreary morning, the sky clouded over with a thick blanket of gray. Somehow, it feels fitting.

When I arrived last night, the house was an even bigger mess than usual. The disarray had a desperate quality to it, as if someone had been searching for something—something important, something urgent. I found my mom in the middle of it, her eyes clouded with confusion and frustration.

"Where's my money, Sean? I know I had it right here," she had said, rummaging through a pile of mail and old receipts. She looked up at me, her eyes lacking the clarity they once had.

It took me all of two minutes to find her purse sitting on the kitchen table, her wallet buried under some crumpled tissues and old grocery lists. Her money was right where it should be.

"I need to take my medication," she insisted afterward, her fingers trembling as she tried to open a childproof cap.

"But you've already taken it, Ma," I reminded her gently.

Her eyes narrowed, mistrust clouding her gaze. "Are you sure?"

I sighed. "Yes, I'm sure. I gave it to you this morning."

As I stand here now, staring at the four walls that once defined my world, I can't escape the sinking feeling that I'm in over my head. I should hire someone to help clean the house, but the thought makes me uneasy. The last two housekeepers I hired didn't last a week. My mom's unpredictable moods and increasing paranoia scared them off, leaving me back at square one.

I run my fingers through my hair, pulling at the roots as if I could yank out the stress and uncertainty tangled there. What am I going to do? How do you care for someone who's slipping away right in front of you, their mind unraveling thread by fragile thread?

I need a solution, and I need it fast. But for now, the weight of the unknown pins me down, heavy and unyielding, as I brace myself for another day of challenges I'm not sure I'm equipped to handle.

As I sit on the edge of the bed, my gaze drifts to an old family photo perched on the worn-out dresser. It's a snapshot from a rare moment of happiness—Mom smiling with a youthful sparkle in her eyes, and a much younger me, grinning ear to ear, totally unaware of the storms that would soon cloud our lives.

Times were never easy for us. Mom did her best, but when life threw its punches—and it often did—she sought solace at the bottom of a bottle. And Dad? Well, let's just say he lacked the courage to be the man he should have been, vanishing from our lives and leaving a hole too large for either of us to fill. The burden, by default, fell on my shoulders. Bill payments, groceries, even comforting my mother after one of her drinking binges—all responsibilities that should have never been mine to begin with.

Maybe that's why the Winters were such a haven for me. They took me in when I needed an escape, showed me what family could really be about—warm dinners, laughter, unconditional support. It was like stepping into a different world whenever I crossed their threshold. They did what they could to help, but it wasn't their place to fix a home that was so fundamentally broken. Still, their kindness provided a contrast, a model for what I wanted in my own life someday.

I got out as soon as I could, eager to break free from the suffocating atmosphere of my home. I worked my ass off for every success, for every ounce of stability and peace I now have. There were years when resentment for my mother built up like plaque, a bitterness that was hard to shake. I blamed her for the hardships, for the chaos, for all the nights I spent lying awake wondering what kind of mess I'd have to clean up the next morning.

But as the years roll on and I see her deteriorating before my eyes, resentment gives way to something softer, more tender—pity. It's hard to hold a grudge against someone who's becoming a stranger even to herself. She tried. I know that now. She fought her battles the only way she knew how, armed with inadequate weapons and outdated armor.

Taking a deep breath, I push off from the bed and head downstairs to the kitchen. Ma is already there, seated at the worn-out table that has seen better days, just like us. I can tell she's a bit disoriented, so I put on a reassuring smile. "Morning, Ma. How about some eggs and toast?"

Her eyes meet mine, clouded but appreciative. "That sounds lovely."

I get to work, cracking eggs into a skillet and placing slices of bread in the toaster. The familiar routine brings a sense of normalcy, a small reprieve from the worries that have become a constant backdrop. As I plate the eggs and toast, I make her a cup of herbal tea, something to calm her nerves.

"There you go," I say, setting the plate and cup down in front of her. I linger for a moment, watching her take small bites, then announce, "I've got to head out."

"Working again?"

I nod.

"You work too hard. You need a break."

I kiss the top of her head. "It's almost Christmas. I'll take a break then."

A nod from her is all I get, and I exit the house, locking the door behind me.

∞∞∞∞

I pull up to Holly's cottage, gravel crunching under my truck tires. I told her I wouldn't be by until later, but the guys have the workshop and other jobs covered, and I find myself with some free time. Her car is in the driveway, so I know she's home.

I knock, listen, but no answer. I turn the doorknob and push the door open. As it swings ajar, the strident sounds of *Last Christmas* by *Wham!* blare from a Bluetooth speaker somewhere inside.

"Holly?" I call out.

Nothing.

Then she appears, shimmying out of her room, completely engrossed in her own world, belting out the lyrics. She's dressed in just her underwear, her hair up in a towel.

I freeze.

My mind stumbles for a second, unsure of where to look or what to do. She's... energetic, uninhibited, and completely unaware of my presence.

It's only a split second. It should be too little for me to notice, but I do. I notice when her eyes open, they lock with mine. Her chest rises and falls which is doing very little to distract me from the swell of her breasts inside the lace of her bra. Her skin is like ivory, except for the peek of her nipples through the material.

I should stop staring. I'm practically devouring her from where I stand, but I can't. I can't stop my eyes from drinking her in. The curve of her hips. The legs that are fucking criminal to hide under all the winter clothes she's been wearing since she's been back.

She's all exposed skin and vulnerability, and something tightens in my chest. Holly was always pretty, beautiful even. That type of beauty you look twice at because you can't believe you've seen it the first time. But seeing her like this—unfiltered, unprepared, radiant in her own space—flips a switch in me.

My gaze darts back to hers, and I watch the hot flush creeping to her cheeks.

It takes three seconds for all color to drain from her body.

Her eyes go wide, her mouth opens in a soundless *O*, and she lets out a scream that has birds flying out of the trees surrounding this cottage. In a scramble, she grabs the towel from her head and clutches it to her chest.

"Sean, what are you doing here?"

Instead of apologizing, I can't help but let a smirk cross my face. Maybe it's the ludicrousness of the situation, or maybe it's the unexpected tension filling the room. Either way, I lean against the wall and cross my arms over my chest, eyes unabashedly sweeping over her.

"Look at you, Squirt," I drawl. "Do you always parade around in lingerie when you have guests?"

"This… this isn't lingerie, and this is my home." Her eyes flash with fire. "I don't expect people to just walk in."

"And yet, you're still standing here half-naked," I point out.

That seems to hit just the right button. She's more angry now than embarrassed, I can tell. It's reckless, but I admire the hell out of her when she drops the towel entirely and mirrors my stance, leaning against her bedroom door in nothing but her underwear. It's a standoff, laced with a heat that neither of us can completely ignore.

I clench my jaw, feeling my spine go ramrod straight because the only thought entering my mind is how I want to fuck that attitude right out of her.

"What's your excuse, then? You're still staring."

"More like checking if you've grown up," I shoot back. "Clearly, you have, at least physically."

She arches an eyebrow. "Nervous, Colson?"

"Me? Never."

I take a step toward her.

She doesn't back away.

If anything, her brow arches higher, a silent dare. Another step, and another, until I'm towering over her, close enough to hear her uneven breaths. Something has shifted. I feel it. We're not playing anymore.

My hand reaches out almost of its own accord, curling fingers under her chin to tip her head back. Her eyes lock onto mine, wide and challenging. I use my other hand to move the wet strands of her black hair away from her shoulders.

God, I should leave, I should get out of here before—

Before what? Before I kiss her full lips, which are slightly parted now? Before I forget that she's Holly and I'm Sean, the guy she hates, and who's supposed to be renovating her house, not contemplating the totally inappropriate thoughts running through my head?

It's my last chance to pull back, and I take it just before I lean in so close our mouths are almost touching.

"Better get dressed, Squirt. Walking around like this is a safety hazard." I run my thumb over her bottom lip, feeling her shiver against me. "I'm a man that possesses plenty of self-control, but those panties might just push me to the limit. Don't test me."

TWELVE

I stare at my reflection in the mirror, my towel now securely wrapped around me.

Did that just happen?

I huff and turn away from the mirror, reaching for my clothes. My wardrobe suddenly feels too casual, too mundane for this mess of emotions.

My heart is still racing, and I can't help but wonder if Sean is as unsettled as I am.

I shake my head. "You've got to be kidding me, Holly," I whisper, pulling on a pair of jeans and a simple t-shirt.

I take a deep breath and march out of my room,

determined to act like an adult who absolutely did not have a flirtatious spat in her underwear. As I step into the living room, the noise stops abruptly.

Sean sets down his drill and wipes his hands on a rag. "All dressed now, I see."

I roll my eyes, refusing to let him rile me up again. "Thanks to you, I now know that my locks need fixing."

"You're welcome."

An awkward silence fills the room, both of us keenly aware of the lingering tension. To break it, I clear my throat and veer the topic to safer grounds.

"So, what are you working on?"

He glances at me, amused. "The list you gave me."

I pretend to ponder. "Ah, yes. The list that magically omitted any mention of door locks."

I take a closer look at the wooden paneling he's been working on. The wood has intricate carvings etched into it—tiny, delicate leaves and swirls that give the whole wall a more rustic and elegant vibe.

"This wasn't in my list," I say, genuinely impressed. "This is amazing."

Sean puts down his drill and steps back to admire his work. "I thought some detail would give the place more character."

I nod, completely captivated, not just by the work but also by how his eyes light up and his entire demeanor changes when he talks about it. "How did you do this?"

He picks up a smaller, more intricate tool from his toolbox and waves it in the air as he talks. "It's a technique called relief carving. You take a chisel and hammer, and you basically sculpt the wood. Takes a bit more time, but the results are worth it."

The look on his face is almost gooey, like he's a kid talking about his favorite toy.

"You really love what you do, huh?"

He looks at me and his eyes soften. "I do. There's something about taking raw materials and turning them into something functional. It's rewarding."

For a minute, I see Sean in a new light. Not as the annoying, smug guy who walked into my home uninvited, but as a craftsman passionate about his work, someone who finds joy in creating something beautiful. And for a fleeting second, that makes him incredibly appealing.

"Hmmm," is all I manage to say. Then, not wanting to give him too much credit, I add, "So how much is all this really going to cost me?"

He arches a brow, looking offended. "Just keep the coffee coming."

I take a step back. "Sean, you're going to charge me for all of this. And I am going to pay you. I'm not expecting you to do this for free."

He moves closer and presses his fingers to my chin, lifting my face just as he did earlier. I try to ignore the flip in my stomach.

"Oh, but your sparkling personality is all the payment I need," he says, mocking me.

I open my mouth to argue, but he cuts me off, his voice turning serious. "Your family has done so much for me over the years. Let me do this."

"I don't need your charity."

"It's not fucking charity. Can't I help out a friend?"

I almost choke on the word. "Friend? Since when are we—"

"You know what, Holly? You can pay me after all." Relief washes over me until he continues, "Pay me with some damn silence."

"You're impossible," I mutter, picking up a paintbrush and dipping it into a can of paint. Walls that are now, thanks to Sean, ready for some color. I hate that. "Impossible to deal with, impossible to understand, and impossible to get rid of."

"Ah, but you wouldn't want to get rid of me. Who else would put up with you?" He winks at me, grabbing his own paintbrush.

Fuck it.

The walls can wait.

He looks like he could use a little color in his life.

With a flick of my wrist, I swipe the paintbrush down the front of his shirt. "Suits you."

The bastard doesn't even flinch. "You know I get dirty for a living?"

God, why did I just clench my thighs?

He smirks with that smug *I-want-to-slap-it-off-his-face* look before sticking the paintbrush to my forehead and running it down my face.

"You asshole. I just showered."

"That was a tactical error on your part, wasn't it?"

I fire back, but I can't help the laugh that escapes my lips. "Seriously, what are you, twelve?"

Before either of us can take the paint war further, my phone buzzes loudly on a nearby table.

Sean's eyes flick from my face to the phone and back again. "Someone's been blowing up that phone for weeks. Are you finally going to answer it?" he asks. There's a piercing intensity in his gaze, as if he can see right through me.

I hesitate. My heart pounds in my chest for reasons I don't want to examine right now. If I don't answer, I know he's going to have questions—questions I'm not ready to answer.

"Yes," I say, but my voice cracks midway, betraying my unease.

Reluctantly, I put down the paintbrush and pick up my phone.

It's Adam.

A tiny, involuntary shudder runs through me.

"Excuse me," I mumble, avoiding Sean's probing eyes as I step out into the crisp, frosty air that nips at my face. The paint is already beginning to dry on my skin.

I hate myself when I smile.

I slide the screen to answer. "Hello?"

"Holly, it's Adam," he says, as if his name on the display wasn't clue enough.

There used to be a time when his voice would evoke something other than anger in me—a time when he was my anchor. Now, I'm taken aback by the utter indifference that washes over me.

"I know."

He starts speaking, but I'm hardly listening. All I can think of is how desperately I want this call to end so I can go back inside, back to the warmth of the cottage, back to Sean. And that realization hits me harder than any words Adam is saying.

"Why didn't you tell me you moved?" he demands, a hint of betrayal lacing his voice. "I had to hear it from Sue when I called last week. That's really low."

"You called my agent?"

"What else what I supposed to do? You're not returning any of my texts or calls."

Or emails, I want to finish for him but don't.

"You lost the privilege to know anything about my life when you slept with half of Manhattan."

"We could work things out, you know. I could even come to see you," he suggests, as if doing me a favor. "I'd love to see your new place."

Is he serious?

A laugh, bitter and cold, escapes. "You're not stepping one foot in my new life. I don't want to see you, ever."

My voice gets louder, frustration fueling each word. I'm vaguely aware that Sean might hear this, but right now, I can't find it in me to care.

Adam tries to cut in, but I've reached my boiling point. "Adam, can't you just let it go? It's been three months. Move on. I'm done. There's no more to be said. I played second best in your life for long enough."

"But Holly—"

"I'm busy. Have a good life." With that, I end the call with a satisfying finality.

I push the door open and step back inside. The moment I do, my eyes lock onto Sean, who's standing ramrod straight. The muscles in his biceps strain against the fabric of his shirt, his eyes stormier than I've ever seen them.

I start to walk past him, dropping my gaze to the floor, but it's his words that keep me rooted in place.

"What the fuck did he do to you?" His voice is low, tinged with a protective anger that I've heard from him before. But this seems more punishing, deadly.

My mouth opens, but no words come out. I'm wrestling with my own mix of emotions—shock, gratitude, and a surprising vulnerability I didn't know I was capable of feeling around him.

"He didn't do anything," I finally manage to say, my voice softer than I'd like. "I did it. I walked away. That was my choice."

"Was it also your choice for him to sleep with other women?"

I feel every barrier come up, anything to block it out. To block him out and the way he's looking at me. Murderous.

"That's none of your business."

His hands ball to fists at his sides. "I'm making it my business."

"Well, don't. You weren't even supposed to hear that." I try to keep my voice steady, but I can hear it tremble. "What happened between Adam and me is my business, not yours."

"Your business?" His voice rises in incredulity. "You're here, in the middle of nowhere, isolating yourself from everyone who gives a damn about you, and you say it's none of my business?"

"I didn't tell anyone because it's humiliating, okay? Is that what you want to hear? I didn't want their pity, and I sure as hell don't want yours."

As if betraying me, a single tear escapes, trickling down my cheek. I bat it away furiously. He doesn't get to see me cry.

I can see the way he looks at me change. It's a look I've never seen from him before and never wanted to—something between confusion and pity.

"Fuck you, Sean," I spit out, venom in my voice. "You should leave."

Surprisingly, he doesn't fight me on it, but then again, Sean has never been great with emotions. Seeing a woman cry renders him mute and incapable of knowing what to do with his limbs.

There's no insistence, no pressing me to talk things out. Just a taut line of his jaw that tells me he's boiling with an anger I can't fathom. He grabs his coat from the hook near the door, forcefully pushing his arms through the sleeves.

"If you want my opinion—"

"I don't." My own walls are up, high and unyielding, and I don't want his insight or judgments breaking through them.

"Well, I'm giving it anyway." His eyes meet mine, stormy and intense. "Look at me, Holly."

Reluctantly, I lift my eyes to meet his.

"He's a fucking idiot," Sean says, his voice so low it's almost a whisper. "When you get a chance from someone like you, you don't risk it. Not for anyone, not for anything."

And just like that, he turns, walks out the door, and leaves.

THIRTEEN

SEAN

She probably didn't expect me to return, especially after her outburst a few days ago. But here I am. I've invested too much time and energy into this place; I want to see it through to the end. The quicker we finish, the sooner we can stop this awkward dance around each other.

To move things along, I've brought two of my crew members, even though they're needed elsewhere. We have to wrap this up today—for both our sakes, but perhaps more for Holly's than my own.

As I lay the final piece of her dark wooden floor, I grind my jaw, attempting to alleviate the tension that's been coursing through me since overhearing that phone call last week.

That son-of-a-bitch cheated on her.

I never liked the guy; he was a conceited jerk who looked down his nose at everyone. And all the while, Holly was too smitten to see his true colors. But to cheat on her? That's a new low, even for him.

Now I understand why she got so heated about me and Ashley. Even if she was wrong, it obviously pinched a raw nerve somewhere.

It's her expression that's seared into my mind: the distant look in her eyes framed by snow-laden trees outside her living room window, her bottom lip chewed raw, and the single tear that broke free. No one has the right to mess with her like that, especially not with her heart. No exceptions.

Mark has been concerned about her. He keeps asking if I know what's up since I've been around, working on her house. I've had to lie to him. Holly's story isn't mine to tell.

His concern isn't misplaced, though. She's been uncharacteristically silent since that call—no snarky comments, no jokes. She's even stopped retaliating when I try to provoke her. I'd rather she hurl insults at me than see her this muted.

She's been hammering away at her laptop lately. I remember how she used to fill notebook after notebook with her stories before the family got a computer. Then, she began printing her tales and handing them out for everyone to read. It's surreal to think that little Holly has turned into a best-selling author.

Whatever she's working on, it doesn't seem to be lifting her spirits. Eventually, she took refuge in her bedroom, possibly to avoid my presence or sidestep my questions. When even that didn't work, she donned her boots, snatched her laptop, and muttered, "I'm going to the café. If you burn down my house, I swear I'll kill you."

She's been gone for hours now.

The final floorboard slots into place with a satisfying click, and I straighten, taking a moment to survey the work we've done. The room has transformed from a shell of its former self into something livable. Something that should be a source of joy. But Holly's absence fills the room like a dark cloud, casting a shadow over everything.

My phone buzzes in my pocket, pulling me out of my thoughts. I pull it out, half-expecting, maybe even hoping, it's a message from her. But it's not. It's a client, asking about another job, another house to repair and remodel. Business as usual.

Except it's not. Nothing feels usual anymore, not since I heard that call, not since I saw that tear fall from her eye.

The question nags at the edges of my mind: Why is this affecting me so much? Holly is an adult. She's been away from this town for years, living her own life, building her own world. She's clearly capable of handling herself—even if she still needs a step stool to reach the top shelf of her kitchen cupboards.

So why can't I shake this feeling? Why does the thought of her, of what she's going through, sit so heavily in my chest?

Because I'm a fucking idiot who thought her return wouldn't affect me, but I'm suddenly twenty-two again wondering why my stomach knots when she's close or why none of the women I'm with challenge me like she does.

I shake my head, as if physically dismissing my concerns could also shake them from my mind. "It's not my problem," I mutter to myself, picking up the last of my tools.

"Hey, Sean," Mike calls out, one of my crew. "We're heading to Molly's for a drink. You in? You look like you could use one."

"Or two," adds Dave, flashing a grin. "It's Friday, man. Work here is done. Time to celebrate a little, eh? It's Christmas."

I hesitate for a moment. Holly's face, her words, that unshed tear—they all flash before my eyes. But then I push it all aside. She's not my responsibility. And they're right; it's been a long week, and God knows I could use a drink.

I grab my jacket. "Let's go."

As we walk out, locking up behind us, I take one last look at the house. It's finished, but as I climb into my truck and we head toward the bar, I can't shake the feeling that some things are still very much unfinished. And for the life of me, I can't decide whether that's a good thing or not.

∞∞∞∞

The moment we step into Molly's Bar, I'm hit with the warm, familiar scent of aged wood and spilled beer.

We grab stools at the bar, and I give a nod to the owner, Archer, who is busy slinging drinks.

I don't even have to tell him what we want. He's already reaching for the glasses.

Mike takes a long gulp of his beer when Archer sets it down on the counter. "So, you're all quiet tonight, man. What's up? Woman trouble?"

I snort, shifting in my seat. "What makes you think it's about a woman?"

"Come on, it's always about a woman," Dave chimes in, grinning over his own pint. "Either you've got one that's driving you crazy, or you're coming up with a plan on how to get rid of one."

Mike nods in agreement. "Exactly."

I roll my eyes, taking another sip of beer to buy myself a minute. "You two sound like a pair of fucking agony aunts."

Dave laughs, loud enough to catch the attention of a few others at the bar. "Hey, sometimes, a man's gotta vent. You've been wound up tighter than a drum lately." They both share a conspiratorial look and smirk. "You know, the last time you got this tense, Holly was back in town."

"Bullshit," I sputter.

"She winding you up, big man?" Mike chimes in, nudging me.

"Fuck off, Mike, unless you want to get acquainted with my fist."

He sucks in a breath, holding back his laugh. "Defensive."

"Fired," I shoot back.

"Someone's a little touchy."

"Again, fuck—"

"I don't write porn... or maybe I do. So what? You know what, sir…"

My eyes dart toward another voice getting louder with every word.

And there she is.

Holly, perched on a stool, beer in hand, schooling two men I recognize as Jeff and Ace—local mechanics and members of The Kingsmen motorcycle club. That doesn't seem to faze her in the slightest. They're sitting awkwardly on their stools, not sure whether to laugh or listen intently. Her laptop is open in front of her; obviously, she didn't go to the café like she told me.

She digs into her bag and slides a copy of her own book across the counter to Jeff. "Read this. Your wife will thank you."

Jeff and Ace puff out their chests, smug expressions painting their faces. "We know how to please a woman just fine, thank you very much."

Holly tilts her head, looking at them like they're two lost puppies. She pats each of them on the chest and says, "Oh, of course you do. But do me a favor? Read it anyway. You might be able to put away the GPS in order to find a woman's clitoris."

A wave of laughter sweeps through the bar, leaving Jeff and Ace fumbling for a retort.

"She told you, boys," someone roars.

Holly grins, taking a satisfied sip of her beer.

Jesus Christ, I need to get her home.

I scrub a hand over my face, down the rest of my beer, and make my way through the crowd. She doesn't notice me until I'm right behind her.

Leaning close, I whisper, "Easy there, champ. You haven't even been back an entire month yet and you're already inciting a riot."

I feel her shiver, her back briefly pressing against me. When she turns around, her eyes are a little glossy. Not drunk, but well on her way.

"What?" she says, batting those long lashes at me. "You think you could use some lessons too?"

I ignore that comment. "You said you were going to the café."

"Yeah, well, sometimes coffee just doesn't cut it."

Someone at the bar shouts, "Hey Holly, why don't you read us some of the stuff you're working on?"

She's got bigger balls than most of the men in this place. I have no doubt she's about to open that laptop and do it. My gut tightens at the thought. I'm not about to let her read a steamy scene to a room full of booze-fueled guys—and some very interested women.

Before she can even lift the screen, I reach over and snap her laptop shut. A chorus of boos erupts around us, and she gives me a look so icy I almost expect frost to form on my shirt.

"Scrooge," she mutters, glaring at me.

I stand my ground. Let them boo all they want. Some lines shouldn't be crossed, even in the name of entertainment.

Annoyed, she slaps my hand away and fumbles to open the laptop again. "I'm reading it, Sean."

"Like hell you are. I'm taking you home."

"I'm not going anywhere with you."

Suit yourself.

So I do the only thing I can think of to stop her. I grab the laptop from the counter, tuck it under my arm, and stride out of the bar. I hear her loud objections as she slides off the stool and stomps after me.

I'm fuming now, too, but this is the most animated I've seen her all week.

Give me all you've got, Squirt. Let me see that fight.

Once outside, I open the back of my truck and lock her laptop securely inside. She's right behind me, cursing me out, calling me a *fucking barbarian* and everything else under the sun.

She reaches me just as I turn, her body pressed against mine in her haste. I wrap an arm around her waist to steady her, spin her around and pin her to the side of the truck. Her breath escapes in a startled whoosh, and the falling snow catches in her ebony hair and sticks to her lashes.

"Listen to me. I'll be damned if I let you read a fucking sex scene to a bar full of horny men."

"Excuse me?" Her eyes flash, her chest rising and falling rapidly. "Who the hell do you think you are, dictating what I can or can't do?"

"I think I'm the guy who's been busting his ass fixing your house while you've been sulking."

"Sulking? Are you kidding me?"

"Then what would you call it?"

She huffs, indignant. "None of your business."

"For some reason, it feels like it should be."

"Why? Because you've appointed yourself my guardian angel?"

"Someone has to look out for you."

"I can look out for myself."

"Could've fooled me."

She glares at me, her eyes flickering like flames. But then something shifts. I notice a heat in those eyes that isn't entirely anger. My own blood runs hot in response. God, why does she have to get under my skin like this? Why does she have to find that last nerve and grate against it so damn much?

"Maybe I want to get under your skin," she says, her voice a notch softer now. "Ever think of that?"

"You're doing a hell of a good job, then." The heat in my voice has turned from frustration to something else entirely. "But that doesn't mean you should go back in there and—"

"And what? Be myself? Live my life? You don't get to control that."

"I'm not trying to control you," I snap, more harshly than I intend. "I'm trying to protect you."

"From what?" she challenges, her eyes searching mine. "The big bad world?"

"From getting hurt again."

The words hang in the air, heavy with a meaning neither of us wants to dissect here and now.

For a long moment, we simply look at each other, the snow falling gently around us. The world, for this brief moment, feels impossibly still.

Then she breaks the silence. "I don't need protecting. Not from you, not from anyone."

"Maybe I need it," I find myself saying, the words slipping out before I can stop them.

Her eyes widen, and her quick pants send little clouds of cold air swirling around that maddeningly tempting mouth. A mouth that, right now, I want nothing more than to silence with my own.

Jesus Christ, what is she doing to me?

"I don't need a babysitter. I'm not *your* sister, remember?"

"I've never been more aware of that in my life."

I let my arm drop from her waist, taking a step back to put some much-needed space between us. She shivers slightly, whether from cold or the absence of my touch, I don't know.

She crosses her arms over her chest. "I'm not going home. I came to the bar to blow off some steam. I'm still feeling pretty steamy, so I'm staying."

"You're really a writer?"

She almost stomps her foot.

And did she just growl at me?

This fucking woman.

"Fine, stay."

She brushes snow off her sweater, looking anywhere but at me. Taking a deep breath to muster whatever control I have left, I make a split-second decision. In one quick movement, I swoop down and hoist her over my shoulder in a fireman's hold.

"What the hell are you doing? Put. Me. Down!" She screams, kicking her legs and pounding my back with her fists.

I tighten my grip, making sure she can't squirm her way free. "I've been working on your house all day. The least you can do is buy me a damn drink."

"So you kidnap me?" she shouts, still kicking and twisting.

"Not kidnapping. Consider this forcible persuasion. You're going to sit down, far away from the crowd of horny men you've stirred up with your writing, and you're going to have a drink with me."

I feel her go momentarily still, and it's enough to tell me I've made my point. Now we'll see if it holds.

I take her back inside the bar, my grip still firm around her. As we re-enter, I lower her down slowly, finally releasing her back onto her feet. A mix of cheers and boos greets us. Clearly, our little spat has become the evening's entertainment.

She immediately folds her arms across her chest, giving me an icy glare. "Forcible persuasion, huh? What's next? Are you going to club me over the head and drag me back to my newly remodeled cave?"

"Tempting, but no. Though I think you'd be pretty impressed with how the cave's turned out."

She rolls her eyes but can't hide the smile tugging at the corner of her lips. "Alright, Neanderthal, what's it going to be? Beer? Whiskey? A Cosmopolitan to match your delicate sensibilities?"

I laugh. "Whiskey. Neat. And you?"

"I'll have the same. If I'm going to endure a drink with you, I'm going to need it strong."

I signal the bartender, ordering two whiskeys. As the drinks are poured, the atmosphere between us shifts. The tension's still there, crackling in the air like static, but it's different now—more electric, less hostile.

We clink our glasses together, a mock toast to our continued aggravation of each other. As the liquid fire trickles down, warming me from the inside, I find my eyes locking onto hers.

She breaks the gaze first, a slight flush coloring her cheeks. "So, you finished my house." She changes the subject, trying to steer us away from the dangerous territory we're skirting. "Thanks, by the way." That one sentence almost killed her to say, I know it. "It's beautiful. But if you installed a beer pong table while I was gone, I'm going to kick your ass."

"Damn," I say, feigning disappointment. "There goes my housewarming gift. And you're not kicking anyone's ass. I saw you get in a fight with a cardboard box last week and lose."

"It was huge!"

We both laugh, the tension momentarily diffused but not forgotten. It lingers, like a ghost we both acknowledge but neither of us is willing to exorcise just yet.

"Alright, let's cut the crap," she says suddenly, setting her glass down with a determined clack. "Why did you really drag me back here? Just for a drink?"

I consider playing it off, but something in her eyes tells me she's not in the mood for games anymore. "Honestly? I didn't like the idea of you becoming the evening's entertainment. Call me old-fashioned."

She pulls back, her eyes searching mine as if looking for something—approval, challenge, I don't know.

"Alright, carpenter boy, you've got yourself a deal. Let's finish these drinks and you can show me all your hard work on my house. But I warn you," she says, picking up her whiskey glass again, "I have very high standards."

"And I aim to meet every single one." I clink my glass against hers one more time.

Christ, we're flirting.

I'm playing with fire.

We finish our drinks, but we don't leave, neither one of us quite ready to be alone for too long in fear we'll strangle each other or... Or what? Why do I suddenly fear being alone with her?

Because I want to rip off that oversized sweater and see what I saw when she came out of her room in just her underwear? Because I want to see more? Because I want to hear the sounds she makes when she screams my name?

Yep, time for another drink.

She keeps chewing that fucking lip, so I reach across the table and pull it away from the hold of her bite.

"Stop that?"

"What are you going to do about it?"

I inhale a steadying breath, ignoring the swell in my jeans.

"Just stop it," I warn.

She raises an eyebrow, intrigued but cautious. "Fine, but only if you promise to stop looking at me like you're about to either kill me or kiss me."

I don't even think she realizes that she's called me out, but when I don't reply, her eyes widen and her throat bobs on a swallow.

I look at her, really look at her. The whiskey is blurring the lines. "Okay, let's cut the bullshit. We're going to talk. Honestly. No dodging, no deflecting."

She takes a deep breath, the first sign of vulnerability I've seen from her. "Alright, shoot."

So I do. We talk about life, the past, our dreams, our fears. Every topic is a loaded gun, but for the first time, it seems like neither of us is aiming to shoot to kill.

"Alright, different question then. I've known you've wanted to be a writer since we were kids, scribbling stories in your notebooks. But why romance? Why not sci-fi or mystery?"

She leans back. "Because love is the one mystery that everyone wants to solve. You can have aliens and murders in a book, but if there's no love, something's missing. Besides, who doesn't like a happy ending?"

"Fair point."

She pauses to think. "Why'd you stay in this town? You could've taken your skills anywhere."

"This is home. Simple as that."

She nods, as if she gets it. And maybe, for the first time, she really does.

"Do you ever write based on real-life experience? Like, are any of those hot, bookish carpenters inspired by anyone we know?"

She laughs, a full, hearty sound that sends a shiver down my spine. "I'll never tell. A writer has to have her secrets. But I will say, life informs art, not the other way around."

I find myself leaning closer, captivated. "So, if I read one of your novels, will I find traces of you in them?"

She bites her lip, and I have to restrain myself from reaching across the table again. "Maybe," she finally says, looking me straight in the eye. "Or maybe I'm just that good at making it all up."

For the first time in so long, I see her guards are slipping. It might be my only opportunity to ask, so I do. "You doing okay?"

She laughs, but it's awkward, and not her. "Oh, come on. Don't go soft on me now?"

"For once, can you answer a serious question? I won't ask again if you don't want me to. No judgement. Pretend for a minute we don't want to insult each other as a hobby. Just two people that have known each other forever."

She swallows hard, clearly wrestling with whether to let her guard down completely. After a long pause, she exhales and speaks softly, "Okay, fine. You really want to know? Adam was cheating on me with so many women I lost count."

"Jesus, Holly," I say, the words escaping before I can rein them in. "That's—"

"Yeah, it's messed up. The real kicker is I went through his phone one day because I had this gut feeling, you know? And there they were—pictures that no fiancée should ever have to see."

She takes a moment, as if gathering her thoughts or maybe her strength. "But the scariest part is, I thought I loved him, yet it was so easy to leave, like flipping off a switch. You were right about what you said with me and my relationships."

Guilt lodges in my stomach. "Holly, I didn't mean—"

"No, you were right and that's probably the only time you'll ever hear me say that so record it if you'd like." She smiles at me. It's one of those crooked smiles she flashes when she's pretending and trying to hide the sadness. It's as if her mouth can't betray her and doesn't tilt fully. "That's what terrifies me the most, you know? That maybe I'm incapable of the real thing."

The vulnerability in her eyes hits me like a freight train, and I'm momentarily stunned into silence. Here's this strong, independent, fiery woman laid bare, and I find myself feeling protective of her, angry for her, and, if I'm being honest, relieved that she's no longer with that bastard.

"Maybe it's not that you're incapable. Maybe it's that you never really had it with him to begin with."

She looks up, locking eyes with me, and I see a glimmer of something that might be hope—or maybe it's just the alcohol.

She lets out a soft laugh before draining her glass. "Maybe you should write a romance novel. You seem to have it all figured out."

Draping an arm over the back of my chair, I lean back. "If I wrote a romance novel, I'd ruin women everywhere. They'd all be hunting for a guy who can build a house with one hand and make a five-course dinner with the other."

"A Renaissance man, huh? You can build and cook?"

"I can microwave like a champ," I shoot back.

"And here I thought you were just good for heavy lifting and scowling."

"See? I'm a man of many talents. But in all seriousness, you deserve someone who values you, who gets you. Adam clearly didn't, or he wouldn't have done what he did."

She's quiet for a moment, staring into her empty glass as if it holds the answers to life's most complex questions.

"You're unexpectedly wise for a man who thinks a five-course dinner involves different flavors of chips," she teases, but the smile she gives me is genuine, and in that moment, I feel like we've crossed some invisible line.

Yeah, we're definitely playing with fire here. But damn, what a good burn it is.

FOURTEEN

"Hate...whiskey," Holly groans, her voice echoing off the porcelain.

"No more whiskey for you," I affirm, securing her hair back as she heaves again into the toilet bowl.

She glares at me weakly, her eyes bloodshot and desperate. "Stop...lookin'."

Can't do that, darling.

Keeping her hair out of the danger zone, I gently rub circles on her back. Her breaths come out in ragged bursts between her low groans and occasional dry heaves. Honestly, I've never seen someone so small produce so much...well, you get the picture.

"I think I'm done," she mumbles, her head drooping dangerously close to the toilet seat.

I scoop her up, placing her gently on the vanity. I make sure to keep a stabilizing hand on her as I reach for a washcloth and soak it in warm water.

She doesn't fight me, probably too exhausted to even keep her eyes open, let alone object. As I gently dab the cloth against her forehead, I can't help but chuckle at the ridiculousness of the situation.

"Stop laughing at me," she mumbles, her words slightly slurred, eyelids fluttering as she fights against sleep.

"Not laughing at you. Laughing with you."

She cracks an eye open, regarding me with an unimpressed stare. "M'not laughing."

"I beg to differ. I saw a smirk." I continue to wipe her face gently with the cloth. Her cheeks are flushed from the alcohol, but beneath that, I catch a glimpse of the embarrassment coloring her skin.

"Asshole," she murmurs, her eye slipping closed again, but there's no real heat behind it.

I put toothpaste on her toothbrush and hand it to her.

I knew she was tipsy at the bar, but I didn't realize until the ride home when she started singing—no butchering—her version of *Bohemian Rapsody*, just how drunk she had got.

I feel her eyes on me as I run the cloth over her forehead and down her neck before handing her a glass of water to rinse her mouth.

She waves her hand. "Look away."

"You puked like you were possessed by Satan, but you won't let me see you spit out your toothpaste."

"Look. Away. Sean."

I do and turn back just in time to catch her before she tumbles off the vanity.

"You've got—" She hiccups. "You've got amazing bone structure." I hold back another laugh as she reaches out and runs her fingers across my jaw. With her touch, the smile drops from my face. Instead, all I can focus on is how her fingers are creating a trail of fire across my skin. "I hate how handsome you are."

"Yeah, well, I hate how beautiful you are too," I tell her, rinsing the cloth.

"Why do you always look out for me?"

I run my thumb over the blush returning to her cheeks. "You're my best friend's sister. I've known you since we were both kids."

She rolls her eyes. At least I think she does. "That's a boring answer, especially after you just watched me vomit."

"You've made a habit of that over the years." I wink at her. "I remember a similar situation when you were nineteen."

"Oh my God. The New Years Eve party." She gags again.

I don't know what I'm searching for in her returning gaze. Maybe it's recognition. Does she know that's the night I started falling for her?

"I mean," she says slowly, her eyes slightly glazed from the alcohol, "I was a disaster that night. What with the neon green Jell-O shots and the dare to do the worm dance in the living room." Her face scrunches up. "Why you guys let me do that is beyond me."

"To be fair, we were all pretty sloshed. But you... you were a sight."

She grins weakly, eyes still heavy with exhaustion. "Did you have to carry me to the bathroom then too?"

"No, but you threw up on my shoes."

"Ugh." She throws her head on my chest with a loud groan. When she doesn't get back up after a minute, and there's nothing but the sound of her even breathing, I know she's asleep.

Careful not to wake her, I bring her to her bedroom and put her down under the sheets. She barely moves as I pull off her boots and cover her.

God, she's so fucking beautiful. Her hair is fanned out across the pillows, her cheeks flushed from alcohol, a hint of a smirk quirking on her full lips.

I wonder what she's dreaming about?

Just looking at her brings the memories swimming back.

That New Year's Eve night is burned into my brain like it happened yesterday. I'd walked into the party with the usual excitement and anticipation that came with ringing in a new year. The house was already buzzing with energy, the bass thumping from the speakers. But all the noise faded to the background the moment Holly entered.

I had never seen her quite like that before. She was no longer the little girl with scraped knees and hair constantly in a messy bun. That night, she wore a glittering dress that hugged her figure, showing off her long legs. My eyes were instantly drawn to her, and a feeling I couldn't quite understand took root deep inside.

Throughout the night, I found myself subconsciously tracking her every move. I laughed when she laughed, tensed when another guy approached her, and felt a pang of jealousy I'd never felt before. It was all so new, this intensity, and I didn't know what to do with it.

When I'd walked upstairs, it was to catch a break from the suffocating realization that something had changed. But the universe seemed to have other plans for me when I found Holly in the bathroom, struggling with the aftermath of one drink too many. As I held her hair back and made sure she was okay, there was a weird sense of déjà vu.

Once she'd cleaned up, we descended back to the

main floor. The party had died down, most people gone or passed out in different parts of the house. But in the middle of the wreckage, it was just me and her. I sat her on the kitchen counter, handing her water to sip on, and when she was coherent enough, made her some coffee. It felt oddly intimate, feeding her, the silence only broken by her sleepy murmurs.

She sobered up and didn't leave. Either did I.

I was already hyper-aware of every touch, every glance, every little smile she gave me. She was right there, and yet, it felt like there was a universe of unspoken words between us.

We laughed, and Christ, but she has a laugh that would make any man weak at the knees. I thought about leaning into kiss her more than once and then thought better of it.

It was the early hours of the morning when we settled on the couch, our tired bodies sinking into the soft cushions. As the hours ticked on, I felt her snuggle closer to me, her head resting on my chest. She was already asleep, but somehow that affected me more. That even in her sleep, she crept closer.

And I knew, from the moment I felt her pressed against me, I knew I was fucked.

FIFTEEN

HOLLY

I feel the press of kisses dancing up my inner thigh as my heart is ready to explode in my chest. Every touch of his lips has me grinding my hips into the mattress. My back arches, heat coiling low in my belly.

Calloused hands grip my thighs, pulling me closer as my knees fall to the side, inviting him in.

One flick of his tongue and I feel like I'm going to come undone, my body wound so tight I'm sure I'm ready to combust.

"Oh, God," I cry out, as his tongue flicks back and forth before soothing the burn and creating circles with his tongue on my clit.

"So fucking good," I hear him growl.

My head feels heavy when I look down at him. Our eyes meet and that dark stare burns me where I lie, pinning me to the bed.

I couldn't move if I wanted to, and I don't fucking want to.

He shoots me his signature smirk before he devours me like a man starved.

"Sean, don't stop."

The pressure builds and my head tosses from side to side as I try to keep my eyes locked on him. I can't. My head falls back as the intensity of his mouth on me swells. I'm so close to exploding. I need him to give me release.

"Sean," I cry out.

His head rises, making my body go cold, my eyes fly open, and I realize why he stopped.

"No." I try to wiggle away, but he holds me tight, pushing me back to the mattress, his face right there when I look at him. He's so close, I can feel his hot breath on my face. "Please."

Great, now I'm begging, and I don't even care.

"How do you want to come?"

"I want your cock inside me," I sob. "I need you."

"No. You're not coming until I give you permission. Understand?"

Do I understand? How the hell can I understand when I can't even think straight, when my body is throbbing with such need, tears fall on my cheeks.

"Say it," he leans in, his mouth a hair away from my neck. "Say you understand."

"I understand," I cry out. "I understand."

"Good girl." He crawls up my body to kiss my neck.

My head flies back as his words sink in. He smiles

wickedly down at me. I can't believe the things he says to me, the things he makes me feel.

And good girl?

Holy shit.

Gasping when his mouth covers my nipple, I arch into the feeling. His tongue swirls around until I'm panting and whimpering. It's so intense I'm going insane as he moves on to my other breast.

"Sean."

"Not yet," he whispers, flicking my nipple with his tongue.

"I need to—"

"No," he says, smirking down at me.

"Please," I cry, as his teeth nip at the tip of my nipple. "Please," I plead again, as he bites down hard.

"Please what?"

I'm fisting the bedsheets so hard my hands are beginning to spasm, but I don't care. I need this. I need him.

The heat builds and builds, but there's a distant buzzing distracting me.

You've got to be kidding me.

Somehow, I know I'm asleep and this is only a dream, but I don't want to leave.

Not yet.

But that damn buzzing won't stop.

My eyes snap open, my chest rising and falling frantically as my gaze darts around the room.

Oh.

My.

God.

I just had a sex dream...about Sean.

I grab the pillow next to me, press it to my face, and scream.

What is happening to me?

Am I ill?

With the heaviness still knotted in my belly, I grab my phone with a loud sigh. My head is pounding like it's a drum in a rock band. Squinting, I see a text from Jackie reminding me of the Christmas dress-up night at Molly's Bar later.

The idea of going out again makes me want to be sick.

I need a shower. I need to get dressed. I need food. But most of all, I need an orgasm, and I need to do it while imagining anybody but Sean Colson.

Reaching into my drawer for my trusty vibrator, I leave out a breath when it buzzes to life, and stare at it. "You can't call me a good girl, but you'll have to do."

∞∞∞∞

Ten minutes later, I force myself out of bed and into the shower. It helps, a little. The steamy water loosens the knots in my muscles and the minty freshness of toothpaste cleanses the bad decisions of last night away. A bit.

Feeling marginally human again, I walk into my newly refurbished living room, still unable to believe how beautiful it turned out. Cozy, inviting—the place screams for a Christmas tree and some garland, maybe even a wreath. It's a testament to Sean's skills, the guy knows how to bring a house to life. Christmas decorations are going on my to-do list today.

Deciding a cup of coffee is my next step toward salvation, I head into the kitchen. That's when my heart almost stops.

Sean is there. Shirtless. Brewing coffee like he owns

the place. He looks like a model in a Calvin Klein ad, if Calvin Klein models built houses and fixed things for a living. Thighs like tree trunks, a chiseled chest, and biceps that tell the tale of a man who knows hard labor. His chocolate brown hair is a tousled mess, making him look irresistibly sleepy and rugged.

"What are you doing here...in my kitchen...exposing yourself?" I finally manage to stutter out.

His laugh is a low rumble, both intimate and disarming. He pours coffee into a mug and hands it over. "Thought you might need this."

I eye him skeptically as I take the cup. "Did you spit in this?"

He rolls his eyes, but there's a smile tugging at his lips. "No, only cream. The way you like it."

"Um...thanks," I say, still in mild shock. "But coffee doesn't answer my question. What are you doing here? And why aren't you wearing clothes?"

The smug bastard winks at me. "For the inspiration."

I groan.

"You got drunk. I slept on the couch," he explains.

"Were you listening when I told you I could take care of myself?"

He pinches my chin between his fingers and tips my head back, locking eyes with me. "Of course I was, Squirt. But you were also attempting to give a rendition of *Bohemian Rhapsody* with incorrect lyrics. So, I thought it was safer to stay."

I can't help but laugh, even though I'm slightly horrified at the thought of drunkenly singing anything, let alone a Queen classic.

"Fair point," I concede.

"Besides, if I had left, I never would have heard that

performance this morning."

I squint at him, confused, until my hungover brain catches up.

No.

He. Heard. Me.

I'm going to die.

Pass away.

Deceased.

R.I.P.

"This is not happening," I mumble, putting the coffee down on the counter in fear I'll drop it. My limbs have forgotten how to function. So has my mouth as it flaps open and shut with no words coming out.

To make matters worse, he's not teasing anymore. His eyes are hooded, a slight tilt to his lips, as my sex drive comes speeding back to life.

The vibrator wasn't enough.

"Stop looking at me like that."

He tilts his head. "Like what? Like I didn't just hear you make yourself come."

I throw my head in my hands. "OH. MY. GOD. Never say that sentence again." Because my thighs are hurting from clenching them so hard. "Why the hell were you listening?"

Did I hit my head last night?

"It was hard not to. You're surprisingly loud for such a little thing."

"Shut up, Sean. Shut up."

I try to turn away from him, but he grabs my chin again, tilting my head back. "Interesting."

"What's interesting?" I try to snap at him, I really do, but there's too much heat in my voice.

He runs his thumb over what I'm sure is the furious

blush staining my cheeks. "You're embarrassed."

"Obviously."

"You're a grown fucking woman. In your own home. Don't apologize, don't be embarrassed.

I take a ragged breath, knowing he's right. This isn't the 1950s. I don't need to be afraid of my sexuality. I don't need to apologize for exploring it. And I don't need to put up with his shit.

But he's a master at getting to me. Always has been. So when his thumb rubs circles over my throat, all I can do is swallow and smell his goddamn delicious scent. If you've never smelled a man brewing coffee, try it. There's something about it that makes me want to rub against him. Rub, and rub, and rub some more.

"Did you hear me?" His voice is low, husky.

I'm so horny.

I hear you. I hear you loud and clear and every cell in my body is screaming for you. But I don't dare say it. Instead, I shake my head.

His hands move to my face, his thumb sliding under my jaw, and his lips are hovering millimeters from mine.

I can do this.

I can ignore him.

I can do this.

Before I can do anything, he pulls away, his gaze never leaving mine as he lifts a brow.

He knows I want him.

He knows I'm practically crawling up his body.

That grin he loves to flash when he's about to get what he wants spreads across his face.

I'm screwed.

He schools his features into that same smug impression. "As much as I'd love to stay for round two,

I've got to go."

What?

I swear I almost cry.

It's an aneurysm. It's the only explanation.

Or a life-threatening surge in hormones that make me so horny I'm ready to drop to my knees in front of him.

It doesn't matter. When he leaves, I'm going to hit my head so hard against the wall I'll knock some sense into myself.

"Okay," I whisper.

Okay?

Get a grip, Holly.

Grabbing my coffee mug, I follow him into the living room where he's sticking his feet into a pair of jeans that I didn't notice before. The jeans are at the end of the couch, neatly folded, and I wonder how long he's been awake.

"Damn," I mutter, "those were some good abs."

"Did you say something?" he asks, pulling his shirt over his head.

"Nothing," I say quickly. "Just noting that you actually fold your jeans. Who knew you were so domestic?"

He chuckles, grabbing his boots. "I'll have you know, I'm a man of many talents."

Oh, God, I'm painfully turned on. "Is that right?"

He winks at me.

Bastard.

"Where are you off to so early in the morning?"

Why do I sound so needy? Why don't I care?

"I'm meeting your brother later to help him assemble a cot for the baby. You know, brotherly bonding with drills and screws."

"Ah, yes, masculinity at its finest," I quip. "Making furniture while discussing the game last night."

"Exactly, you're catching on."

I shake my head, my heart doing that weird little fluttery thing that I absolutely refuse to analyze right now.

"See you around," he says, heading for the door.

"See you," I reply, feeling oddly disappointed as he closes the door behind him.

I beat the heel of my palm against my forehead and instantly regret it. I'm turned on and hungover and I'm still hungry.

My eyes flicker to my phone, reminding me of the text from Jackie about the Christmas dress-up night at Molly's. Ugh. I quickly tap out a reply.

Me: Jackie, for the love of God, I have nothing to wear tonight. Also need a tree. And I'm hungover. Send help!

I don't mention how I want to climb Sean like a tree because I don't have the energy to explain.

Her response comes through almost instantly, with the characteristic Jackie flair.

Jackie: Get your hungover ass ready. One hour. We'll grease you up with breakfast, find the bushiest tree in the lot, and buy something that makes you look like a ho-ho-ho, but classy.

I snort, thankful my mouth is empty of coffee.

Me: Classy ho-ho-ho, got it. What's for breakfast? My liver has demands.

Jackie: Your liver can write me a thank-you letter. I'm introducing you to the breakfast burrito that should be illegal. Heart attack wrapped in a tortilla.

Me: Ah, you truly are the Santa of shitty mornings.

Jackie: Merry fucking Christmas, bitch. Let's deck your halls.

SIXTEEN

I've just spent half an hour laughing, cringing, and debating with Jackie over a rack of the most offensive holiday clothing I've ever seen. Who knew Santa could be turned into such a sex symbol?

"Look at this," Jackie exclaims, holding up a sweater that reads "Jingle My Bells." She giggles uncontrollably, the kind of laughter that happens after one too many mimosas. "You should totally get it!"

"Ha, very funny. Unless you want me to pick out your outfit too? How about these leggings? They say, 'Santa's Favorite Ho'."

Jackie snorts. "Please, I've got some class."

We both erupt into laughter, drawing the attention of nearby shoppers who probably think we've lost our minds. And maybe we have.

I'm still torn between two ridiculous options: an elf costume that's more lingerie than clothing, and a naughty Mrs. Claus ensemble that's just screaming for trouble.

My phone buzzes, startling me out of my holiday-induced moral dilemma. It's a picture from Sean. He's shirtless, flexing next to a half-assembled baby crib. The caption reads, "Some daily inspiration for your porn books."

I burst into laughter, so much so that Jackie gives me a worried look. "What? What's so funny?"

"It's Sean."

"Aww, is lumberjack daddy checking up on you?"

I roll my eyes. "Don't call him that."

"But he is, though. With all those muscles and flannels, he's just an axe away from a lumberjack calendar. December, specifically."

I turn my phone to her. "He sent me this."

Her eyes go wide. "Holy mistletoe. I mean, if I didn't know any better, I'd say he's auditioning for a spot in *Magic Mike: Christmas Edition*."

I roll my eyes but can't suppress a smile. "Knowing my brother took this picture somehow makes it less sexy and more...bizarre."

She winks at me. "Speak for yourself."

Feeling oddly bold—maybe it's the mimosas or maybe it's the laughably sexy Mrs. Claus outfit in my hands—I snap a quick picture of it and send it back to Sean with the caption, "I make my own inspiration."

The bouncing dots appear almost instantly, then disappear, and reappear again. Ah, the suspense. Did I manage to make Sean speechless?

His reply pops up on my screen.

Sean: You're going out in public like that? You trying to give the entire town some daily inspiration too?

The subtext is clear—somehow, the thought of me

being the center of attention in that outfit doesn't sit well with him. It's protective, slightly possessive, and it sends a little thrill through me.

Jackie glimpses at the screen and winks at me. "Wow, looks like Mr. Handyman wants to be the only one nailing something tonight."

∞∞∞∞

"Ah, The Heartstopper," Jackie coos, practically salivating as the waitress sets down a gargantuan platter in front of her. It's piled high with fried eggs, bacon, sausage, and a thick layer of hash browns swimming in gravy. "Isn't she beautiful?"

"She's stunning."

She snorts and digs in. "Don't be jealous."

I raise an eyebrow at her as my breakfast burrito arrives. It's the size of a newborn, stuffed to the brim with scrambled eggs, sausage, and cheese. It's a heart attack wrapped in a tortilla, but I'm not one to judge. After the mimosa-fueled morning and yesterday's drama, I deserve this.

"So, what's the game plan for tonight?" she asks, her mouth full of hash browns.

"First, we eat, then we decorate my sad, undecorated tree. And after that, we go to Molly's and unleash our holiday havoc upon the world."

She laughs, clinking her coffee mug against my juice glass. "Here's to holiday havoc and bad decisions."

"May they haunt us for years to come."

SEVENTEEN

I'm standing in my living room, fingers lightly brushing the frilly hem of my "Sexy Mrs. Claus" outfit. What on earth possessed me to choose this? Sure, it's warm and cozy inside my cottage, but outside, the snow is falling in thick blankets, and this outfit is not built for a winter wonderland.

My eyes roam the room, settling on my newly decorated Christmas tree in the corner. Its twinkling lights cast a soft glow on the pine-scented room.

A faux fur rug sprawls in front of a fireplace, where a fire crackles and pops, its flickering light dancing across the room. Vanilla and cinnamon-scented candles are scattered on end tables, filling the room with the sweet, comforting aroma. A stack of well-loved holiday books sits on the coffee table next to a bowl of pinecones and a few sprigs of holly. A cozy knitted blanket is folded over the arm of my favorite reading chair, practically inviting me to curl up with a cup of hot cocoa.

Everything about this room screams Christmas and warmth. It's like a holiday hug that I never want to end.

Just as I'm about to reconsider my outfit choice, I hear a car horn honk loudly outside. It's Jackie, no doubt, and she's probably just as ridiculously dressed as I am. With a sigh and a quick glance at myself in the mirror—Red lips? Check. Santa hat? Check—I grab my coat and head for the door.

∞∞∞∞

We pull up to Molly's, and even from the outside, it's clear the place is buzzing with an electric energy that only a live band can generate. As we walk in, I immediately understand the reason for the crowd. On stage, Jaxson King, the lead singer of the Savage Saints, is belting out a rock rendition of *Jingle Bell Rock* that has the entire place on its feet.

The Savage Saints have won multiple Grammys, toured the world, and reached a level of fame that most bands only dream of. Yet, every year, they come back to Pine Falls to play a Christmas gig at Molly's. It's their homage to their roots. The bar practically vibrates with the bass and the crowd's excitement.

Looking around, it seems that everyone got the memo about dressing up. It's like a Christmas carnival of ridiculous attire.

Jackie, who's dressed as a sexy gingerbread woman complete with gumdrop buttons and frosting swirls, sidles up to me with a grin.

"Hey Mrs. Claus, ready to find your Santa?" she shouts over the music, winking at me.

I laugh. "I don't know, there's a lot to choose from. How about you? Ready to get baked?" I gesture at her outfit.

"Honey, I'm always baked. But don't let me crumble alone. Let's get some drinks."

"Alright, but only if we can avoid the Santa shots. I heard they're made with peppermint schnapps and regret."

She guffaws, clutching her gumdrop-buttoned belly. "Peppermint schnapps and regret are my middle names, darling."

We push our way through the sea of ridiculous outfits, toward the bar, feeling both utterly absurd and perfectly at home.

Standing at the bar, Jackie and I are approached by a couple of guys wearing what can only be described as haphazardly-assembled elf costumes. Both are attractive, but in that vanilla way—great for a Christmas party hookup but not necessarily life-changing.

"Hey, Mrs. Claus, can we be your elves for the night?" One of them winks, oozing confidence.

Before I can even muster a polite rejection, a deep voice cuts through the din of the crowded bar. "Hands off my wife. That's my Mrs. Claus."

I turn around and lock eyes with—Santa? No, wait, it's Sean. I'd recognize those piercing eyes anywhere. He's in a full Santa outfit, complete with the bushy white beard hanging around his neck, looking both ridiculous and strangely sexy at the same time.

Mark then appears next to him, wearing what appears to be a Christmas tree costume? He's got tinsel wrapped around his torso and an actual star headband. I can't decide if it's stupid or endearing, so I settle for stupidly endearing.

"Hey," Mark says to the would-be elf suitors, "how about you find another sleigh to hitch to, eh? This one's family-only."

The two guys size up Mark and Sean for a moment before nodding and slipping away into the crowd, looking deflated.

I roll my eyes so hard they nearly get stuck. "Really? What are you guys, my Christmas chaperones? I'm not sixteen."

Jackie, never one to miss an entrance, just grins at them. "Hey, boys."

I shoot my brother a quizzical look. "What are you even doing here? Don't you have a pregnant wife at home?"

"She kicked me out. Said she wanted a night off from my overbearing holiday cheer. Can you believe that?"

Overbearing is an understatement when it comes to my brother during Christmas, so yes, I can absolutely believe it.

Even in this crowd, I can't shake the sensation of Sean's eyes on me. Burning into me, more like. I risk a sideways glance and find him grinding his jaw so tightly I'm surprised it doesn't snap.

I glare at him as if to say, *What's your problem?*

The laser-focused sweep he gives me, from my red boots to my fur-trimmed hat, answers the question without a single word. It's the outfit.

Frustrated, I extend my middle finger discreetly toward him—just enough to let him know what I think of his silent criticism. "Mark doesn't seem to have a problem with my outfit, and last time I checked, I'm twenty-seven, not seventeen. So, you can stuff your judgment in a stocking."

Sean's eyes glint mischievously at the challenge, and there's a moment of electric tension that even Mark picks up on.

"Whoa, I'm not sure if I should leave you two alone or make sure you don't kill each other," Mark says, clearly enjoying the spectacle.

Sean takes a step closer to me. "No chance of the former happening, and as for the latter... well, 'tis the season for giving, not murdering, right?"

I seize the opportunity and grab at the fake white beard dangling around his neck. "Alright, if you're going to play Santa, then act like it. Why don't you be a good Santa and get these girls some drinks?"

The grin that creeps onto his lips is part devilish, part delighted. "Yes, Ma'am." He winks, pulling the beard back into place and heading toward the bar, giving me a lingering look that promises this battle of wills is far from over.

As Sean saunters off, the red velvet of his Santa suit clinging to him in all the right places, Jackie nudges me. "You're drooling, girl. That's my job."

"I'm not drooling, I'm evaluating," I retort, pulling my gaze away from Sean's retreating form.

"Evaluating what exactly? How well that Santa suit would look on your bedroom floor?"

"I was thinking more along the lines of how ridiculous we all look. It's like Christmas threw up in here."

"Speak for yourself. I look fabulous." She twirls, showing off her outfit.

"Only you could make green and red sequins work."

"Well, someone's got to do it."

I shake my head, still smiling. "You're crazy and I love you."

"And you're smitten with Santa," she says, still not letting me off the hook.

"I'm not—"

"Save it. Your secret is safe with me."

I roll my eyes but can't suppress a grin. "Fine, let's

just say, if that's Santa, I wouldn't mind being on the naughty list this year."

"That's the spirit! Now, let's see what kind of Christmas spirit Santa brings us from the bar."

Santa brings lots of spirit and keeps them coming. So much spirit that I'm not sure if I'm merry from the alcohol or from the intoxicating mix of Christmas music and eye candy.

Naughty Santa got us tipsy.

I wipe the sweat from my brow as Jackie and I dance.

Speaking of Santa, where is he?

I scan the crowd. It's a forest of Santa hats, ugly Christmas sweaters, and an elf or two. But there's only one Santa I'm looking for, and he's nowhere to be found. When I finally spot him, he's perched on a bar stool, having ditched the ridiculous beard and Santa hat. Now it's just the red suit. And damn it, how does he pull it off?

The outfit does nothing to hide those broad shoulders, the curve of his arms, or the toned shape of his body. I shouldn't be surprised. This is Sean, after all. Even in a Santa suit, the man would look like he stepped out of a magazine.

And those eyes. They find mine across the room, making me sweat for an entirely different reason. Perhaps it's the alcohol, or maybe it's the electrifying atmosphere, but I hold his gaze. Boldly, I sway my hips to the beat of the music, my skirt swishing around my thighs as if it's part of the performance.

I watch as he shifts in his seat, his eyes darkening a shade.

Mission accomplished.

The intensity of the moment stretches between us

like a wire pulled taut, humming with electricity. My heart pounds in my chest, each beat echoing in time with the music and his unwavering gaze. Thoughts I shouldn't be having flash through my mind, vivid and uninvited. Thoughts of his mouth on mine. Thoughts of what it would feel like to be pressed against him in that ridiculous Santa outfit.

New kink unlocked, I guess.

Just as I'm about to give in to whatever magnetic pull is drawing me toward him, my line of sight is blocked. A woman slides into the space next to Sean. I don't recognize her—likely a tourist—but what irks me is the ease with which they fall into conversation, both of them laughing like old friends.

A bubble of jealousy forms, unbidden but unmistakable. For all the times Sean has scared off any man that so much as looked my way, I decide it's high time for some payback.

I glance over at Jackie, but she's lost in her own world, headbanging to a punk-rock version of another Christmas tune. She won't notice if I slip away for a moment. Determined, I weave my way through the crowd, straight for the bar, straight for Sean.

Slipping myself between him and the woman he's chatting to, I make a show of hopping onto his lap. I drape my arm around his neck and pull myself close, as if I belong there.

"What the fuck are you doing, Squirt?" he hisses in my ear, the tension in his voice as tight as his grip on my waist.

Ignoring his apparent rage, I smile sweetly at him, then raise my voice for the benefit of our audience. "My goodness, Santa, did you forget you had a wife?"

The woman's eyes go wide, her mouth forming a

perfect O of surprise. "I'm sorry, he never said a thing. I'm not getting involved in this." She scrambles away, disappearing into the throng of Christmas revelers like a snowflake in a blizzard.

Sean glares at me, but I see the corners of his mouth twitch. "You enjoyed that, didn't you?"

I look up at him, all innocence. "What, you mean reminding Santa he's a married man? Always."

His jaw clenches, and for a second, I wonder if I've pushed him too far. But then he leans in, his lips almost touching my ear, and I'm too entranced to care.

"You just made the naughty list," he murmurs. "I hope you're happy."

The thrill that courses through me is immediate, electrifying. "Ecstatic," I reply, locking eyes with him. "Absolutely ecstatic."

EIGHTEEN

S<small>EAN</small>

It's confirmed. I want to fuck Mrs. Claus's brains out.

NINETEEN

HOLLY

I'm still sitting on his lap, my arm around his neck, and the tension is thick. I can't help but revel in the discomfort I've caused.

"Seriously, what was that about?" Sean mutters, his voice tinged with an irritation that's almost palpable.

"Just making sure no one else sits on Santa's lap." I push off him to stand. "You should be thanking me."

"Thanking you? For embarrassing me in front of a stranger?"

"You've never been embarrassed a day in your life," I shoot back, turning on my heel. "But if you can't handle the heat—"

"Don't even finish that sentence," he hisses, grabbing my arm as I try to walk away. "You're playing a dangerous game, Holly."

I yank my arm back. "Then maybe you shouldn't play."

The tension between us turns electric, a storm waiting to happen. I feel his eyes on me as I sashay back to the dance floor, but I refuse to give him the satisfaction of turning around.

Eventually, I've had enough. "I need some air," I tell Jackie, who nods, too wrapped up in the music to really hear me.

I push through the crowd and stumble out of Molly's, inhaling the icy air deeply. The cold feels good, cutting through the heat and frustration that's been simmering inside me all night.

I'm not alone for long. Footsteps approach, and I don't need to turn around to know who it is.

"What's your problem?" Sean asks, his voice icy as he steps in front of me.

"My problem?" I can't help but laugh. "You've been treating me like a misbehaving child all night. You're my problem!"

"You're acting like one!"

"Oh, fuck you, Sean. Go back inside to Malibu Barbie."

An incredulous laugh leaves his lips. I don't even feel the cold air on my skin because I am fuming.

He smirks. "You're jealous."

I swear I choke on air.

"Jealous? You think this is about jealousy?" I snap, rolling my eyes dramatically.

"I think it's about a lot of things, but sure, let's go with jealousy for now."

I cross my arms. "Not everything revolves around you. You've been so damn judgmental and overbearing tonight. Like you're some paragon of maturity. Look at you, dressed as Santa in a bar, and you have the audacity to judge me?"

He leans in closer, his breath fogging up the air between us. "God damn it. You know, for once, can you keep that pretty mouth closed?"

"Make me," I challenge, rolling my shoulders back.

He scrubs a hand over his face and growls, "You shouldn't have said that."

And then, in a beat, he's closing the distance, his hands cupping my face, and his lips are on mine. It's one of those moments when your soul leaves your body just to look back and check if this is really happening. And, oh sweet baby Santa Claus, I'm kissing him back.

The kiss isn't just a meeting of lips—it's a merging of years filled with tension, misunderstandings, and underlying emotions neither of us had the courage to confront. His mouth is demanding, but not overpowering, coaxing my lips open for a deeper connection. Our breaths mingle, hot and fast, as if we're both trying to catch up to the reality of this moment.

One of his hands slides down the side of my neck, his fingers tracing a burning path to my shoulder, before it comes to rest at the small of my back, pulling me impossibly closer. His other hand still cradles my face, his thumb brushing softly against my cheek, as if he's amazed that I'm real. It's gentle and sweet, a sharp contrast to the fervor of the kiss, and that duality shakes me to my core.

The world narrows down to the sensation of his lips

on mine, his tongue meeting mine in a dance as old as time yet new to us. I forget the cold, the people inside, the complicated mess our lives are. All that exists is this kiss, and for a brief, soul-shattering moment, it feels like coming home.

But then, reality crashes over me. I'm kissing Sean. I'm actually kissing him back. With that realization, I push him away, our chests heaving, eyes locked in a moment charged with...something. Three seconds pass. Three long, agonizing, life-changing seconds where I could walk away, but guess what?

I don't.

Then I pounce on him because I don't have energy to fight any more.

He grabs the back of my thighs, lifting me so I can wrap my legs around his waist, our lips meeting again in a kiss that's anything but calm. It's as if all the tension has all boiled over, and this, this right here, is the result. My back meets the wall, causing a shiver to crawl down my spine, and I'm thankful to the Christmas gods that there's no one out here to witness this lust-filled spectacle.

Because this is all it is, right?

It's lust?

Right.

I haven't had sex in over six months. Sure, it's been three months since my break-up from Adam, but we didn't touch each other for months before then, and my body is crying out for touch. The touch just so happens to be Sean's.

What the fuck, Universe?

His hands move to either side of my head, pinning me against the wall, not that I have any intention of escaping. His lips travel to the curve of my neck, planting hot, open-mouthed kisses that make my head spin.

"See what you've done," he growls against my skin, possessive and intense. "You drive me fucking insane, woman."

Then his mouth is back on mine, consuming me, devouring every thought, every doubt, until there's nothing left but the overwhelming sense of need that's rushing through my veins. The crisp night air does nothing to cool the heat radiating off us. If anything, it only serves to stoke the fire.

I'm so absorbed in the feeling of him, the heat of his body pressed against mine, the intoxicating scent that's uniquely him, that for a moment, I forget where we are, who we are, and how complicated everything has always been between us.

The universe be damned. Right now, all that matters is this moment, this kiss, this undeniable attraction that neither of us can ignore any longer.

"Holly?"

My eyes snap open at the sound of another voice, my pulse hammering in my ears. Sean's grip on my thighs tightens, and his eyes darken as they meet mine, filled with a mixture of confusion and caution.

It's then I hear my name again.

I look over Sean's shoulder and…what the hell?

"Adam?"

His expression is twisted into a scowl. "Is this what you've been doing since you got back home? Whoring yourself around?"

Sean steps away, lowering me to the ground before helping me to right myself.

Adam stands there, looking out of place yet strangely poised, a stark contrast to the casual festivity going on around him. He's tall but not as tall as Sean, with sandy brown hair, cut neatly in a conservative style. He's wearing a tailored coat over a crisp white shirt and dark slacks, the epitome of buttoned-up corporate good boy. His eyes are narrowed in judgment, lacking any of the warmth or depth I once thought I saw in them.

"I need to speak to my fiancée," Adam insists, his voice dripping with entitlement.

A humorless laugh escapes my lips. "Fiancée? Really?"

Sean's eyes flash. "I don't see a ring on her finger."

Adam scoffs. "That's a temporary situation."

"Sounds to me like it's pretty permanent."

I try to intervene, "Adam, I think you should—"

Adam looks at Sean as if sizing up an opponent. "I don't know what you think you're doing here, but Holly and I have a history."

"And it's just that, history," Sean fires back, cutting me off before I can speak.

"Who the hell are you to say that?" Adam snaps, his shoulders squaring.

"Sean," I interject.

His eyes soften when they look down at me, but I can see the anger he's holding by a thread swimming behind his last ounce of control.

He takes my chin, tipping my head back. "Yes, baby?"

He knows exactly what he's doing.

I close my eyes and leave out a steadying breath before pleading in a whisper, "Please don't."

Adam takes a step forward. "Holly, who the fuck does this guy think he is?"

"I'm the guy who was about to hear her scream my

name until you rudely interrupted."

Oh, no.

"Fucking whore." Adam's eyes go wild with rage just before he shoves at Sean's shoulders.

Sean might as well be a brick wall.

And then it happens.

"Sean, don't—"

His fist connects with Adam's nose. Blood instantly drips and stains the snow.

"Where's your manners?" Sean hisses, taking Adam by the collar to straighten him before dusting snow off his shoulders. "It's a pet peeve of mine when men don't have manners toward women."

Really?

Is he serious right now?

"Sean, stop it."

He looks at me, his eyes a turbulent mix of worry and unresolved anger. "I'm getting you out of here."

I shake my head, my voice quivering but resolute. "I need to talk to him."

His jaw sets, muscles tensing visibly. "The last thing you need to do is to talk to him."

Ignoring the biting cold that seeps through my ill-advised outfit, I stand my ground. "I have to put an end to this. Go back inside."

He hesitates, his eyes flicking between Adam, who's still nursing his bleeding nose, and me.

"Sean, please. Just go. I don't need a bodyguard. He won't hurt me."

His head shakes as if wrestling with himself. "Not a risk I'm willing to take."

Exasperated, I snap, "Will you stop playing the knight in shining armor? This is not about you."

A flicker of hurt crosses his eyes as he takes a step

back. "Fine," he mutters, but not before he tilts my head back with his knuckles. I've noticed it's a thing he does, always wanting to meet my eyes, and I'm starting to like it. "You need me, you know where I am. And for fuck's sake, call me, Holly, so I know you're alright."

"I will."

He glares at Adam one last time, a clear warning, before turning and walking away, disappearing back into the warmth of the bar.

I release a long-held breath and turn toward Adam, who looks pitiable with his bloodied face.

"Let me see," I say softly. He winces as I gently remove his hands from his nose, inspecting the damage. "This is your own fault."

He groans. "You're seeing someone?"

I shake my head. "No. It's Sean. You've met…lots of times."

I know Adam knows who he is. His ego just won't let him admit it.

"So this is what you were doing every time you came home?"

Three months ago, the accusation would have broken my heart. Tonight, it's a mild pinch.

"What? All three times I came home over the years?"

I wait for him to realize how ridiculous it sounds, but of course he doesn't admit to that either.

"We need to talk."

I nod, weary but resolved. "I know. Let's go."

TWENTY

Two hours, a tough but overdue conversation, and a headache later, Adam is finally gone. We talked, we argued, I made him shut up until he listened, and we cried. I did love him once. I loved the idea of the life we could create. But all of it is in my rearview. And it dawned on me as he sat across from me at the breakfast counter—the counter Sean installed—I didn't even hate him anymore. I felt...nothing. It was a strange sense of relief to lay it all out and salvage what we could... just separately.

I blow out a breath as I stare at myself in the mirror, Mrs. Claus outfit still intact, if not for some new wrinkles around the skirt from where Sean had bundled it in his fists.

I close my eyes, goosebumps erupting across my flesh as the memory of our kiss floods back. And then, his face when I told him to go. I hate how we left things.

We could just forget it, couldn't we? Pretend the momentary lapse in judgment never happened. Go back to the way things were. But we've crossed a line, and lines once crossed can't always be retraced. And it's not as if I'm only here in Pine Falls for the holidays; I'm here to stay.

Making my decision, I exhale deeply and snatch up my car keys. I open the door, gasping when I find Sean already standing there. His hands grip the sides of the doorway, and he's still wearing that ridiculous Santa suit. The scene is almost comical, and I'd laugh if it weren't for the intensity in his eyes. It's an electrifying silent moment between us.

Finally, summoning the courage, I manage to say in a voice far breathier than I would like, "He's gone."

A chill shimmies down my spine. I've willingly, hopelessly, stepped into his trap. There's heat in his eyes, but mixed with it is a layer of anger, a cocktail that thrills me more than it probably should.

He straightens, his jaw muscles flexing before he growls, "Fuck it. I don't care. He could have watched."

Taking that final, charged step toward me, he wraps his large hand gently but firmly around my throat, presses me against the wall, and kisses me, shattering all illusions of lines and boundaries.

I draw in a sharp breath as his lips meet mine.

The man doesn't just kiss me. He breathes me in, desperate as his kiss strips me bare, leaving me defenseless to everything Sean Colson.

I'm equally as hungry as I wrap my arms around his neck and pull him close, needing to stretch on my tiptoes even in my heels.

His tongue skims over my bottom lip before he draws it into his mouth and sucks.

The door slamming shut with his foot is all I'm aware of before he grabs my waist and hoists me up in his arms. His lips never leave mine as my back is slammed against the wall again before his tongue explores my neck. I throw my head back hardly recognizing the moan that leaves my mouth. The sound of ripping fabric is my only warning before I feel a graze of his teeth along my nipple.

"Oh God, Sean," I cry out.

He stills, his eyes locking on mine before he smirks and rasps, "Fuck, baby. Keep saying my name like that."

Then he sucks my nipple into his mouth, his hot tongue swirling around the flesh. I could come just like this, with his mouth on me.

His fingers dig into my ass under my skirt before he peels me off the wall, grabbing the back of my neck and walking with me to the counter in the kitchen. Sitting me down, he takes a step back like he's displayed a meal he's ready to devour.

I shudder, my breathing coming in heavy pants.

"If you want to back out, you better say it now because you've got about five seconds before I'm on my knees finally getting to taste you."

With those words, I lose my breath, my stomach clenching as I grab the edges of the counter to steady myself.

I shake my head, the need in his eyes making me nervous as I breathe, "On your knees then."

And. He. Drops.

His large hands knead my legs before resting at my knees. "Spread your legs and lean back."

Oh God.

Sean is on his knees… for me.

Let's not think about that too much. Especially when he licks his lips and bites down.

My legs are too weak to even contemplate holding together. With his hand under my thigh, he lifts my leg, letting my foot drop on the counter, spreading me completely before rubbing my clit through the lace of my thong. Instinctively, my head falls back with a moan.

"Eyes on me," he demands. "If I'm touching you, your eyes are on me. Do you understand?"

My lungs are burning, desperate for air.

"Holly," his voice is stronger now. "It's my one rule. Keep your eyes on me."

I can't help myself. "Rules? So bossy."

"I'd like for you to look at me when you're screaming my name."

I've died and gone to heaven. Or maybe it's hell. I don't care. I'll willingly burn. At least if I'm in flames, he's going to be right there with me.

"You seem quite sure of yourself."

He smirks, shaking his head with a husky laugh. "Oh, baby. Brace yourself."

He's still got that damn victorious smile on his face as he rips the lace fabric of my panties, his tongue immediately soothing away the burn. Shamelessly, I grind against his face, feeling the heat rush through my body.

He groans, lapping at my clit in long strokes. I'm ready to explode as he maneuvers his tongue between my folds, and I lose it, screaming his name and keeping my eyes on his just as he told me to.

I almost leap from the counter when he presses his finger inside, then another, fucking me until I'm nothing but putty in his hands.

Stroking me with a skilled tongue, I shudder with pleasure, my body tightening around his fingers as he continues to push me over the edge. His mouth moves from my clit to my inner thigh, his breath fanning over my skin.

He licks and sucks at my thighs until I'm a quivering mess beneath him, submitting to him in every way.

I can feel it, the raw waves of pleasure washing over me.

The vibrations of his voice hit my thigh as he demands, "Let go. Come for me."

He keeps licking, each stroke of his tongue more determined than the last. He knows exactly what I need, and how to drive me over the edge. My orgasm builds until I'm sure I'll go insane.

Sean notices too. "Come for me, baby. Let me feel it all."

"Oh fuck." I can't hold it back any longer, screaming out his name as I come undone in his arms. He doesn't let up, keeping up the same pace until every nerve in my body is alive and aching for more. Finally, when I'm spent and trembling, he slows down, pressing soft kisses on the inside of my thigh before standing to his full height.

Reaching out for me, he picks me up and spins me around, pressing on my shoulder and bending me over the counter.

"Do you remember the rule?" he asks, his voice gruff.

I do, and I can't help but giggle as he swats my ass gently. He does it again and I dig my nails into his arm, almost drawing blood. He pulls away and raises an eyebrow at me, a warning in his eyes.

"I'll tie you up if you don't behave."

I look over my shoulder at him, my heart beating so madly in my chest I'm sure he can hear it. My body is already begging for more.

He grabs both of my wrists in one hand and pulls them behind my back, pushing me further into the counter. His other hand slides around to cup my chin, tilting it back so that our eyes meet. The fire burning in his gaze makes me shiver; he knows what he's doing to me, and it turns him on even more.

"You need to keep your eyes on me at all times," he demands gruffly before pressing his lips against mine in a kiss that leaves me weak in the knees.

He pulls away, but I can feel his breath on my neck as he speaks. "Now, are you going to be a good girl, or do I need to tie you up?"

Holy shit.

Did he just call me a good girl?

I shiver.

Am I dreaming again?

Nope. That hot flesh pressed against my body is very real.

"Holly?"

"I'll be good," I promise, looking up at him through my lashes. "I'll be so good."

"Good girl."

I'm on fire. We both are.

His hands explore every inch of my body as he stands tall at my back. He runs his thumb over my lower lip, holding my gaze as he teases me and pulls away.

Groaning, he slides his hands around to cup my ass.

He's watching me. All of me. As if he's committing it all to memory, his eyes are dark and predatory.

His voice is low as he speaks, and I have to fight the urge to beg. "Do you want me inside you?"

"Yes," I say, my voice just above a whisper.

"Please."

He squeezes my hips and positions himself at my entrance. "You're so fucking wet, baby." Holding my dress up, he instructs, "Wider."

I part my legs wider, and he gives me another hard slap on my ass. I gasp out, the pleasure and pain of his palm against my sensitive skin driving me wild.

I know I'm dripping wet; I can feel it, and I can't take the anticipation anymore. I can't control myself. I'm desperate for him.

"Please," I whisper, "Please, Sean."

"I want to hear you say it," he says, rubbing the head of his cock against my throbbing clit. "I want you to tell me what you want."

I close my eyes and lose myself in the feeling. I don't want to think about the consequences of what we're doing. All I want to do is give myself over to him. I want him to take me, to make me his.

I need him to take me, just like this.

"I want you to fuck me," I whisper. "I want you to fuck me until I scream."

"Christ, you're perfect." He groans from deep in his chest, pulling my panties to the side, and slamming into me so hard, I scream.

Thank God I don't have neighbors.

His hand comes down, covering mine on the counter—it's an oddly comforting sensation, and I wonder if it was always there.

I'm still pulsing around him, my body humming with pleasure.

"You're so fucking tight," he groans, pushing my dress past my hips to pool around my waist.

He thrusts into me again, each stroke of his cock making my body scream for more. He wraps his arms around my waist and lifts me up, sliding me farther onto the counter. I spread my legs, the cool marble making me shudder. Grabbing my ass with both hands, he pushes inside of me again and again until I can hardly catch my breath.

I prop myself on my elbows, watching him. I can't tear my eyes away. His chest is heaving, a line of sweat trailing down his stomach and disappearing into his pants.

"I'm so close," I say, my voice breathy. He pulls out of me, and I swear I almost cry. "What are you doing?"

He grabs my hips to spin me around before sitting me on the counter and stepping between my spread legs. I'm smothered in everything that is him. His stature is too big, too intimidating, so masculine I'm drowning in it. He towers over me in a way he always has, but this is different. This is primal, possessive.

He presses himself against my entrance but stops when I let out a whimper.

"Like this?"

"Yes."

He pushes into me inch by inch, the sting quickly replaced with mind numbing pleasure.

Another orgasm is building, I can feel the heat unfurling between my legs until I can't support my own weight. It doesn't matter because he's there with his arm around my waist, holding me steady.

"That's right, baby," he rasps. "Come all over my cock."

When my head slumps, he wraps his hand around my throat forcing me to look at him.

It's too intense. It's too much when he looks at me like this. I can't pretend here.

And either can he. I see it in how his muscles strain,

in how his jaw clenches, and how he averts his gaze. He's close to slipping over the edge with me but he doesn't want to look at me when he does it. He doesn't want it burned into his memories like it will be mine.

Defiant I palm his face and force his gaze back to mine. We're both doing this…together. Whether he likes it or not.

"Eyes on me," I breathe out, repeating his earlier demands. "I want your eyes on me when you come."

I'm not sure if it's pain or anger in the molten heat of his stare, but it doesn't last long when he slams into me so hard my ass slides back on the counter.

Now he's angry, and there's a sick part of me that's happy about it.

"Fuck, Holly," he roars, his chest vibrating.

He wraps his arm around my back as I lock my legs around his waist, tightening my grip, refusing to ease up. I meet him thrust for thrust, my thighs quivering, breathing erratic.

My mind is a haze, but I still notice how the cords in his neck strain, the muscles in his biceps bulging as he holds me tights against his chest.

I want to close my eyes, but I can't. I need to see him.

I need to watch him as he falls. The expression on his face tells me he's desperate for control. It's there in the tremble of his fingertips, in the way he presses his lips together and loses himself in my body.

Sean's mouth falls open as he lets out a low grunt, and we both topple over the edge…together.

We remain still for long endless moments, neither of us knowing what to do now.

When I come back to my senses, he's looking at me with that twisted up face he always wears when he's worried.

A lump forms in my throat, but I quickly swallow it down.

"Don't say it," I say, leaning away from him. "Don't say anything."

What the hell am I doing?

My heart is pounding. My mind is racing. I can't believe we just did that.

I can't believe how right it felt, and I hate it.

I try to shimmy away, but he doesn't let me. Instead, he cups my face and presses his forehead against mine. "What's wrong?"

"Nothing," I say, closing my eyes.

He traces circles over my cheek with his thumb. He's so gentle with me. I keep my eyes closed, swallowing hard as I feel him move my dress back down, covering me.

"Holly?" he asks, pulling me off the counter. My legs are unsteady underneath me, and I stumble into him, but he catches me, wrapping his arms around my waist. "What is it?"

"I don't know," I say. "I just…"

"Did I hurt you?" he asks, stepping away and looking me in the eyes.

I shake my head. "No, no, it's not that. It's just…"

"Just what?"

"Sean, look what we just did. Me and you." My voice is getting louder, panic finally catching me after I ran from it earlier. "You're my brother's best friend. I hate you, remember? And you hate me."

He has the nerve to cock that stupid smirk at me. "You don't hate me, Winters."

"Oh, I do, Colson," I say, but my voice is a little husky from the heat still purring in my veins.

He takes a step toward me, the smell of us clinging to our skin. I tip my chin back, defiant, but then he stares down at me, pulling my lower lip with his teeth, and my legs lose function.

"It's okay." He smiles against my mouth. "I never hated you either."

He leans down and kisses me.

I don't fight. I hardly move because my brain is still adjusting to the fact that Sean is even this close to me. My mind might be struggling, but muscle memory works quick, as if his touch has branded me. Instinctively, I lean into him, deepening the kiss.

His lips are soft, his tongue tastes like me, and my body remembers exactly what to do. I'm so completely overwhelmed it's a wonder I can even remain standing.

My hands slide into his hair, holding him in place. I can't help it; the need to be even closer is too much. I feel like I should be angry at him. But I can't find it in myself to fight. I'm exhausted. I'm spent. It's been a long week.

He skims the pads of his fingers up my spine, and I shiver. "You sure you still hate me?" he asks against my mouth.

"Yes," I gasp. "I still hate you."

He kisses me again, deeper this time. I moan into his mouth and wrap my arms around him, pulling myself against his chest. My nipples pebble under my dress before I squeeze my legs together in an attempt to ease the ache between my thighs.

I'm still mad at him. I know I shouldn't be doing this. But, damn, it feels so good.

"Stop," I say, pulling away and holding him at arm's length. "I really do hate you."

"I know," he says, a grin spreading across his face.

"That's why I'm going to fuck you again."

My mouth falls open. "How? So soon?... Never mind. That's not the point. I'm being serious." This is wrong on so many levels.

He leans back but his hands don't leave my body as his eyes meet mine. "Do you want me to go?"

There's no bitterness. He's serious. He's giving me an out.

My eyes fall to the floor.

When I don't answer, he steps back.

It's too late for an out now. I know what he feels like, and my greedy body wants more. I want his scent to invade me, I want his hands on me, I want to feel him between my legs. I want him to envelope me until I'm blinded by it.

Once wasn't enough.

I might wake up tomorrow and hate myself, but I can't let him go.

I reach out, catching his fingers before he can step away completely. "Stay," I whisper.

He pushes his knuckles under my chin, his touch gentle now, soft.

"Look at me." I lift my gaze. "You want me to stay?"

I nod. "I want you to stay."

This time when he steps back, he takes me with him, lifting me into his arms, a shit eating grin on that gorgeous face.

"You don't have to look so smug," I tell him, hardly keeping my own smile at bay.

He throws his head back and laughs, making me want to slap it off his face. "Oh, baby," he says pressing a quick kiss to my swollen lips. "I love how you have no idea what to expect."

"And what's that then?"

He winks, walking us into the bathroom. I'm vaguely aware of his hand leaving my ass to turn on the shower.

"You'll see. First, let's get cleaned up." He kisses me as he walks under the sprays, Christmas costumes be damned.

TWENTY-ONE

The beam of light casting through my window stirs me from my sleep. A sleep I could easily fall back into because I'm cocooned in warmth, pulled tightly against a chest.

I peek over my shoulder.

Not just any chest.

Sean Colson is in my bed.

What have I done?

Still, I can't find it in myself to move. He's holding me so tight I don't think I could if I wanted to. I give myself a few minutes to stay this way because once he wakes and realizes what we've done, he's going to be out of here faster than a snowflake melting in July.

His even breaths sweep across the skin of my shoulder, reminding me of how naked I am.

Naughty Santa worked the nightshift.

I stretch, but it only reminds me of how sore I am… everywhere.

I definitely ho-ho-ho'd last night.

And Santa? Santa came more than once this year.

Bad Holly. So, so bad.

The silence is shattered as my phone buzzes, jolting me from my reverie. Then it buzzes again. And again. Each vibration stabs through the stillness, eroding the fragile peace of this illicit morning-after.

I fumble for my phone on the nightstand, squinting against the bright screen. A barrage of texts and local news notifications flood the display. "HEAVY SNOWFALL," one headline screams. "ALL RESIDENTS ADVISED TO STAY OFF ROADS," says another.

My heart drops to my stomach.

Snowed in? Now? With him?

In a frantic move, I rip the covers off Sean, wrapping them around myself like a makeshift toga before dashing into the living room. My bare feet hit the cold wooden floor, sending shivers up my spine as I rush to the window.

Pulling aside the curtains, I'm met with blankets of white. It's as though nature itself conspired to lock me in this cottage with Sean, pushing us into a cozy, unwanted hibernation.

I feel the breath leave my lungs, my heart pounding in my chest.

We're snowed in. Completely, utterly snowed in.

There's no escaping this, not the snow, not the cottage, and certainly not the complicated tangle of whatever Sean and I have just become.

I wrap the covers tighter around me, as if they could shield me from the reality crashing down.

"Hey, yeah, got it," I hear Sean's muffled voice coming from the bedroom. "No, no need. My mom will be fine. Yeah, I'm stuck too. Alright, thanks."

He appears in the doorway of the living room,

phone in hand, eyes catching the blanket I've wrapped around myself like a survivalist's cocoon. For a moment, we lock eyes, the silence filling with every unspoken word, every unsaid regret and hidden desire.

"So," he starts, clearing his throat awkwardly, "all my jobs are called off. Your parents called. They've offered to take my mom in until all of this settles."

I nod, still not able to meet his eyes, instead focusing on the window. The impenetrable wall of snow has turned the outside world into a blank canvas, and I'm suddenly aware of how small this cottage feels.

It's like that movie—what's it called? Oh, yeah, The Shining. Except instead of ghosts and an axe-wielding maniac, it's just regret and sexual tension.

"I slept with my brother's best friend," I mutter to myself. "The one guy I'm not supposed to want, but also kinda hate but maybe don't really hate, and now I'm trapped here like a Hallmark movie gone terribly wrong."

I'm so engrossed in my existential crisis that I barely notice him stepping behind me. I feel the blanket being lifted from my shoulders, only for it to settle back around me, this time encompassing him as well. He wraps his arms around my waist, and I find my back pressed against his chest.

Oh, great, so this is how we die—stuck in a snowed-in cottage, draped in a blanket of awkwardness and post-coital regret.

But then I feel the heat of his body blending with my own warmth, and all thoughts fizzle out like a sparkler's last glow.

"I hate you," I whisper, though the conviction in my voice is as thin as the ice we're both standing on.

"I hate you more," he murmurs into my ear, his

breath hot and tickling.

Oh, screw it.

As I lean back into him, it occurs to me that being snowed in might not be so bad after all. At least, not when you're snowed in with a man who has a body like Sean's and knows how to use it.

"Wait, do my parents know we're together? I don't mean together together, but here together? As in me and you in this house? Trapped?" The words spill out of my mouth like water from a burst dam.

He spins me around to face him, his hands firmly gripping my shoulders. "Jesus Christ, Squirt, you're hyperventilating. No, your parents don't know we're together or whatever the hell you're panicking about."

I look up and realize two things: one, he's absurdly close, and two, he's naked. Very, very naked. That's about all the brainpower I can muster before—

"OH MY GOD, YOU'RE NAKED!"

"Didn't seem to bother you last night."

I yank the blanket tighter around me and bolt for my bedroom, Sean hot on my heels. "We need clothes."

"I've heard that's generally a good idea," he mutters.

As I reach my room, I realize I'm actually racing a naked man for clothes. What's become of my life? I snatch a pair of jeans and a hoodie from my dresser, throwing them onto the bed.

"Out! Out, out, out!" I shriek, ushering him towards the door.

He rolls his eyes but steps outside. "Fine but hurry up. You act like you haven't seen—"

"I've seen enough, thank you!"

Oh, and what a sight it is.

The door slams shut, and I hurriedly get dressed.

There's a knock just as I'm pulling my hoodie over my head. "You decent?"

"Depends on who you ask, but yeah, come in."

"Better?" he asks, still stark naked.

"Marginally."

"Good. What now, your highness?"

"We need to make plans. You know, figure out how to keep from killing each other, that sort of thing."

He chuckles. "You think we're gonna be here that long?"

I glare at him. "Aren't you Mr. Wilderness? Tell me, how long can a blizzard last?"

He shrugs. "Could be hours, could be days."

"Days?!" My voice skyrockets again.

"Oh for the love of—" Sean grabs my shoulders, forcing me to meet his eyes. "Calm. Down."

"I'll have you know, I'm very calm." I wriggle out of his grip.

"Sure, as calm as a caffeinated squirrel."

Starbucks would be amazing right now.

Concentrate, Holly.

My phone buzzes from the nightstand, another weather alert. "Heavy snowfall expected to continue. Residents advised to stay indoors."

"See! Even my phone says we're stuck. Doomed! Trapped like rats!"

"Rats?" Sean chuckles. "Don't insult us. If anything, we're like... sexy snow leopards or something."

I snort. "Speak for yourself. I feel more like a deranged penguin."

He laughs, throwing his head back, and just like that, the tension breaks.

"We're fine," he says, softer now. "We're more than fine. We have food, heat, and hey—" his eyes darken, turning that delicious shade of *we-shouldn't-but-we're-going-to-again*—"we've got each other."

I consider this, looking at the blizzard outside, then back to Sean again.

"God help us," I mutter under my breath, walking into the living room. I snatch a notebook and pen from the coffee table. Nothing soothes the anxious mind like making a good old-fashioned list.

He arches an eyebrow as he watches me. "What are you doing?"

"Making a list. Lists make me feel better."

He leans against the wall, arms crossed. "Okay, what's first on this list of yours?"

I glance up, pen poised above the paper, and my gaze meets—oh God, not-so-little-Sean. And he's doing very little to hide his interest. I avert my eyes, but it's too late. Now we're both aware that I'm aware, and the room somehow feels ten degrees hotter.

I clear my throat, trying my best to ignore the flush coloring my cheeks. "Uh, you need to get dressed."

He looks down. "I am dressed."

"You've got a blanket…that you're holding. You're not even trying to hide yourself. More dressed. More clothes mean more dressed. That's how it works."

He laughs. "Fair point. I've got a bag with spare clothes in my truck. So, what's second on the list?"

"Hold on, cowboy," I say, scribbling *Sean needs to get more dressed* at the top of the page. "We need to prioritize. The way I see it, you getting more clothes is contingent upon us getting out of this cottage, which means we need to deal with the snow situation first."

"So, first on the list should actually be: plan a daring escape from this snow prison so Sean can retrieve his spare clothes from his truck," he suggests, smirking.

I roll my eyes but jot it down anyway. "Fine. Plan a daring escape from snow prison is now number one."

He walks over to peer at the notebook, but I quickly close it, hugging it to my chest. "Uh-uh! No peeking. This is top secret, classified information."

"I didn't know making a to-do list could be so espionage-esque."

"Oh, you have no idea. We're talking James Bond-level planning here."

He bows dramatically. "I look forward to being both shaken and stirred by your plans, Ms. Bond."

I can't help but laugh. Despite the snow, despite the crazy awkwardness of this situation, he has a way of making everything feel lighter, easier. But I shake the thought away. After all, we're still trapped in a snow-covered cottage with no immediate means of escape, and my brother's best friend—who I've just slept with—is practically waving at me with his...

I giggle to myself.

Great, I've turned into a teenage girl who can't say Sean and penis in the same sentence.

God help us indeed.

He disappears into the bedroom, reappearing moments later in the damn Santa suit from last night. The sight of him in that ridiculous outfit brings back a flood of memories that are anything but PG-13.

"You're back in uniform."

He winks. "Just trying to keep things festive."

Before I can respond, he pulls on his boots and announces, "Okay, Operation Snow Prison Escape is a go."

And just like that, he manages to climb out the window and into the wintry abyss. I can't help but wonder how he moves so fast in those boots. A few cold minutes later, he climbs back inside, now carrying a duffel bag.

I eye the bag with a mix of curiosity and skepticism. "So, do you always carry extra clothes in your truck or is that just a Sean thing?"

"Jealous, are we?"

My cheeks flush. "No! I just wondered if that's your go-to move when you're sneaking out of...other situations."

His eyes lock onto mine as he takes a step closer. "The spare clothes are for work."

"Work?" I gulp, feeling the heat of him as he advances.

"Yeah," he says, crowding me against the wall, his voice dropping to a whisper. "My job involves getting dirty."

I swallow hard, fully aware of the innuendo but not daring to acknowledge it.

"And?" I ask, my voice far too breathy.

He leans in even closer, so that his lips are just inches from my ear. "It involves me getting really, really sweaty."

I swear I almost moan out loud as a shiver rakes through me.

This is dangerous, my inability to walk away from this man when he's looking at me like he's found the Holy Grail.

He shouldn't look at me like that. I'm not sure if I want to kiss him or strangle him with some tinsel.

He runs his thumb over my lips, his other hand already working the buttons of my jeans.

For fuck's sake, Holly, it's not too late to walk away from this.

Once is dangerous. Twice is nuclear.

"Cold?" he asks as his hand slips into my panties, his finger instantly rolling circles on my clit.

Fuck it. We're going nuclear.

My eyes roll, my hands reaching out to grab his biceps. "A little."

"Well then," he says, his arm caging me in at the side of my head as his other hand works me into a frenzy. He slips a thick finger inside me, and my legs lose the ability to hold me upright. "I'm making it my personal responsibility to see that you're warmed up."

The room temperature soars. Lists, snow, and everything else momentarily fade away. My ability to think or speak coherently is officially compromised, and I don't think I'll ever run out of inspiration for my books again.

TWENTY-TWO

"You kept it," I note as my fingers trace the amateur carvings on the small wooden decoration. The edges are rough, the design slightly asymmetrical, and Holly's name is etched into it, the letters jagged from the hand of a fourteen-year-old boy who barely knew what he was doing.

Back then, things were tough. Ma and I were scraping by, and the idea of Christmas gifts was more of a luxury we dreamt of rather than a reality we lived. So, I made this. I remember the embarrassment like it was yesterday, the burning in my cheeks as I handed everyone their individual decorations, crudely crafted pieces of wood.

And now, here it is. Years later. She kept it.

The realization does something strange to my chest, like my heart's trying to fight its way out or maybe just swell to keep all these emotions inside. I'm not sure which.

Holly steps beside me then, two cold beers in hand, her presence a familiar comfort. She's quiet for a moment, her gaze following mine to the decoration. I feel her take a breath, maybe to say something, but then she stops. Even in the dim light, I can see the pink tinting her cheeks.

She shrugs, a small, sheepish move. "It was a gift," she says, her voice quiet. "And it's beautiful. In its own unique way."

I turn to her, my hand leaving the ornament to take one of the beers she's offering.

She grins, but it falters, and she looks back at the tree, at the ornament. "I've always loved it."

After a sip of her beer, she glances around the room, taking in the flickering candlelight and the fire I've managed to keep alive. "You know, you did a pretty good job with this place."

I rear back mockingly. "What's with the compliments? You sick?"

"Shut up, Sean," she retorts, but she's smiling as she says it, and that smile is enough to make me want to pick her up and carry her back into the bedroom. We've hardly left it all day, but I don't think I'll ever get enough.

Whatever dreams of mine she possessed over the years weren't anything like this. They were mundane compared to reality, and I'm afraid it's already too late. She's ruined me. I'm an addict.

We each take another drink of our beers before moving over to the couch. She sits down first and pulls a blanket over her lap, settling into the cushions. I can't help but think she's trying to put layers between us—like a simple blanket would do her any good.

That makes me smile. It's a cocky smile, and I'm aware of it, but I can't help it. Now that I've had her, no amount of blankets, physical distance, or mental barriers is going to protect her from me. Not while we're in this house. Not when we've crossed a line I never thought we'd cross, one that's shifted the ground beneath me in a way that's as terrifying as it is thrilling.

I sit down next to her, close but not touching, and it takes everything in me not to close that small gap. Our eyes meet over the rims of our bottles.

Blushing, maybe from the beer or the tension or both, she suddenly blurts out, "Let's play twenty questions."

I scoff. "What are you? Twelve?"

"It's a way to pass the time. If I leave you alone for too long, you'll try to fix something else around here. And who knows, maybe we'll learn something new about each other."

"What, like favorite colors? Yours is red by the way."

She rolls her eyes. "Oh please, like you have anything better to do."

"Fine, but maybe I should be in charge of the twenty questions. That way, at least one of us will ask something interesting."

She pouts, "Are you saying my questions would be boring?"

"Do you really want me to answer that?"

Her eyes narrow, but she's grinning, and the look is

so damn beautiful that I feel a sudden warmth that has nothing to do with the fire or the beer.

"Fine," she agrees. "You can ask the first question, but I swear, if it's something dumb, I'll throw you out into the snow myself."

"Alright," I say, leaning back and pretending to think hard. "First question: If you had to be trapped in one of your romance novels, would you prefer the brooding billionaire, the bad-boy biker, or the sensitive artist?"

She looks surprised, then amused. "Really, Sean? That's your groundbreaking first question? If I didn't know any better, which I do, I'd say you've read my books."

"Well? I'm waiting."

She sighs dramatically, trying and failing to hide her smile behind her bottle. "The sensitive artist."

I feign shock. "Not the bad-boy biker? I was rooting for him."

"I've had enough bad boys to last a lifetime." She looks pointedly at me.

I chuckle. "Duly noted. Your turn."

"Alright. If you had to wear women's lingerie for a day, what would it be? A lacey thong, a corset, or a garter belt?"

I nearly spit out my beer. "What the hell kind of question is that?"

She grins, obviously pleased with herself. "You said to make it interesting."

"Damn," I mutter. "Alright. A corset. It seems...supportive."

She nearly chokes on her beer. "Oh my god, I can't unsee that now."

"You got any?"

"Why? Are you telling me you want to try it?"

I wink at her, making her shift in her seat. "Oh, no. I want to see you in it."

"Pervert." She chews her bottom lip, her eyes bulging. "I might."

"Mmm," I hum, closing my eyes only to receive a punch to my arm.

"Stop picturing me in lingerie."

"Don't have to. I can close my eyes and see you naked."

"Oh my God." She sinks back into the cushions, laughing. "Just ask your damn question."

"What's the most embarrassing thing you've ever done?"

She hesitates, and I swear I don't think any human has ever turned a brighter shade of red. Attempting to hide it, she buries her face in her hands. "I can't say it."

"Fuck that." I pull her hands away. "You're saying it. You're not getting away that easily."

"You're going to laugh."

"Of course I am."

She throws her head back on the couch before taking a long drink of her beer.

"This was your idea, remember?" I remind her.

"It was a terrible idea. Why didn't you stop me?"

"Stop deflecting."

"Okay, okay." She gives in, but she still looks like she's about to burst into tears. "I was in college before I gave my first…" She swirls her fingers around. "You know?"

"Not a mind reader, Holl."

"My first blow job."

I was wrong before. She blushes a brighter red than she already is.

My brows almost reach my hairline. "Fuck. Could have fooled me. You learn fast."

She bites down on her lip as she smiles, shaking her head. "Thanks, but it wasn't always the case. I was young—"

"Not that young."

"Okay, I was not that young, but I was naïve, and I thought blow jobs meant that you... well... um... that you—"

My eyes almost pop out of my head. "Holly, no!"

"Yes."

"No!"

"Oh, yes. I didn't know I needed to suck and took the name blow job literally."

I tilt my head before ruffling her hair. "Oh, you're just brand new, aren't you?"

"Shut up. In my defense—"

"There is no defense."

"Let me speak. In my defense, it's called a *blow* job."

"Baby, we are not balloon animals."

She shoves me, trying not to laugh, but I can tell she is mortified. "I can't believe I just told you that. They nicknamed me Holly and the blowfish for three years."

I can't help myself, I burst out laughing, but at least this time, she joins me.

"So how does a girl that blows and doesn't suck go on to become a best-selling author of porn books?"

"It's not porn. At least not all of it. And I'm a fast learner."

Wrong answer. My jaw clenches so tight, I think I hear it pop.

She's clearly getting more amusement out of this than me because she sets her beer bottle on the floor, pulls back her blanket and crawls across the couch.

163

Hands on my shoulders, she straddles my lap.

My heart thunders in my chest, my jeans already growing too tight as she presses against me. It's the first time she's initiated anything, and it takes everything in my power not to take over.

"I think you might be jealous," she whispers, pulling her hair over her shoulder and leaning so close our breaths mingle in the air between us.

"I think you might be right."

"The mind is a powerful thing. If I can make you jealous without touching you, even in your mind, what could I do with my hands?"

She makes a deliberate show of reaching under her t-shirt to unhook her bra.

I shake my head. "Holly, what are you doing?"

She smiles and removes my beer from my hand before taking a drink of it and putting it down on the floor. "I'm going to prove to you that I'm not a total amateur."

"I think you've already shown that, but who am I to get in the way of a woman proving a point?"

I pull her closer, loving the way she fits in my arms.

She answers by sliding off my lap, kneeling in front of me, and ripping my jeans open. Her eyes lock on mine as she unzips them, sliding them down my hips.

My breath comes out in a hiss when she wraps her hand around my cock. When I see her tongue dart out to lick her lips, I thrust into her hand.

"Fuck." My hips rock faster. I want to make her feel how much I want her, but I'm having a hard time concentrating.

She leans forward, her hair covering her face, and I close my eyes, wondering what she's going to do. The second I feel her hot breath on me, I know I don't have to wonder anymore.

In one long, slow lick, she tastes my cock from the tip to the base.

Her tongue is soft and wet and fucking perfect.

"Holly," I growl. I fist my hand in her hair, knowing what it does to her. The moan she lets out only makes me want to do it again. My beautiful girl likes it rough.

She rocks from where she kneels, obviously trying to ease the friction.

"Holy shit." I grip the couch, trying to hold myself in place. It's a miracle I don't come right then. It feels like my whole body is on fire. I'm ready to explode, my muscles straining as I try to hold off.

She swirls her tongue around my tip, her fingers pushing into my thighs before she lowers her mouth onto my cock, her eyes watering. She hollows her cheeks, sucking me like she's been doing this to me for years.

I don't know about before, but she knows what she's doing now.

Point taken.

I yank her head up, using her hair as leverage as I pull her to me. Our lips crash together, her tongue finding mine before I can get a word out.

Pulling her back onto the couch, I lay her down, thanking whoever the fuck is out there that she is only wearing one of my t-shirts.

I don't have time for buttons.

"No fair," she moans. "I was enjoying that."

"You and me both, baby. But you've proved your point."

I put my hand on her cheek, then lean forward, kissing her lips before moving down. Licking a path from her collarbone to her breasts, I stop to suck one of her nipples into my mouth. She cries out loudly, her hands gripping my shoulders tightly as I lavish attention on both of her breasts.

"You're teasing me," she argues.

"Yeah, but I hope to make up for it by fucking you until you can't walk tomorrow."

"We've still got questions to ask."

"Stop acting like you don't already know the answers."

I close my mouth around her nipple again, just sucking at first.

"Yes." She sighs, her hips rocking.

"Lift up, baby. I want to taste you. I want to hear you scream my name." I nudge her shoulder, helping her move.

She slides and as soon as I can see her, I kiss a path down her stomach before pushing her legs open.

I spread her with my thumbs and stroke her with my tongue.

It doesn't take her long to rock her hips, her moans filling the room. I slide my hands under her ass to push her closer to me, loving the way she reacts to my touch.

I suck her clit into my mouth, pressing my lips against her as I move my tongue, fucking her with it. She cries out, her fingers fisting my hair. I almost come at the sound.

I love that I'm driving her crazy.

I love that she's letting me.

She's so close, so fucking beautiful, her legs shaking, her body begging for more.

I could eat her out for hours, but I'm not sure I'd survive that. I rise up, my hands on her hips, putting her exactly where I want her.

She moans as I enter her, forcing me to hold still

for a second. I love the way she feels. Her legs wrap around my hips, and I brace myself on my forearms, my hands gripping her shoulders.

She grits her teeth and presses her hands against my chest. I lean forward and kiss her, thrusting as slowly as I can manage.

"Faster," she begs, her hips rocking against mine.

I do what she asks, thrusting in and out of her. My thumb finds her clit between our bodies, and I start to motion circles around it, applying just the right amount of pressure.

"Oh my God, Sean." She spreads her legs farther, and I growl.

I don't think I'll ever tire of hearing her say my name like that.

"Harder," she cries.

"Fuck."

I want her wild and ready, her hips moving like she needs more, more, more.

Her sounds drive me crazy, her moans and gasps making me push harder, deeper. I feel my whole body burning and clenching, from my head to my toes.

"Come for me, baby. Let me feel you."

"Sean, I'm so close, I can't." She's breathless, her moans telling me she's about to break.

"Let go," I demand. Her eyes meet mine. "Now!"

Tensing around me, she lets go, her body trembling as my name rips from her throat in a strangled roar.

I feel her walls clench around me, her body shaking under mine, and I don't hold back anymore.

I thrust as hard as I can, feeling my body explode. I keep my eyes on her, drinking her in because I know the snow outside this cottage will eventually melt, and all of this will be nothing more than memories.

TWENTY-THREE

HOLLY

"What's this I hear about you and Sean getting into a public argument? Again, Holly? Seriously? Have you both not grown out of this by now?" My mother continues to scold. She's been rambling on for so long, I'm holding the phone away from my ear and mumbling my agreement every time she takes a breath.

Sean saunters out of the bathroom, hair dripping and covered in nothing but one of my much-too-small towels. It's riding dangerously low, and I resist the urge to tug it up or maybe even down.

Noticing my expression, he arches a brow at me before leaning back against the counter and crossing his arms over his chest.

Those arms.

My body is suddenly tingling, the feeling of his hands lingering on my skin like sunburn. But the only thing to soothe the burn is his touch. I keep dipping my fingers in the honey pot, never quite getting my fill. I'm afraid I never will.

I pull the phone away again, covering the speaker so my mother won't hear. "This is your fault." And I mean it in more ways than one.

He points at his chest. "My fault? What have I done now?"

"You kidnapped me and dragged me back into the bar the other night, and now apparently the entire town is talking about it."

"I didn't even hear it from my own daughter," my mother continues, but I can tell she's more nosy than angry.

"I promise I'm practicing my deep breathing exercises to avoid future Sean-related incidents in public." I cover the phone's microphone and whisper-hiss to Sean, "Go put some clothes on before you get me into more trouble!"

He shrugs innocently. "If I had known our every interaction was going to be reported to the family newsletter, I might've behaved differently."

"Just...Shoo!" I gesture towards the bedroom.

Over the phone, I can hear my mom's suspicious tone. "Holly? What was that? What's going on?"

I clear my throat, aiming for nonchalance. "Oh, you know, just talking to the...TV. I've named him Sean. Very talkative, this TV."

"Naming inanimate objects now? Oh honey, we need to get you out more." She tuts in concern.

"That's what I keep saying, but apparently blizzards and Sean Colsons are out to ruin my life."

"Are you sure that you're okay?" My mother's voice is now laced with concern. "That storm is a doozy, and being cooped up alone can't be good for your sanity. Especially if you're naming your electronics."

"Mom, I promise I'm fine. Just cabin fever setting in. Maybe a bit too much wine. And a lot of old movies."

And so much sex.

Sean emerges from the bedroom, fully dressed. Clothes are over-rated. I know I told him to put them on, but his body was made to be admired. He steps into the kitchen, returning minutes later, carrying two mugs of hot cocoa.

He mouths, "Peace offering?" holding them up hopefully.

I accept one. "You think chocolate is going to make everything better?"

He grins cheekily, whispering, "Works nine times out of ten."

As I take a sip, I'm surprised to find marshmallows and a hint of peppermint.

My mom, still on the line, hears my pleased sigh. "What was that?"

"Hot cocoa," I mumble, taking another sip. "So good."

"Are you high, child?"

I wish.

"No, Mom, I'm not high."

Sean's shoulders rattle as he suppresses a laugh. My mother's filter has worn away over the years.

"Okay, but as for this Sean situation, you both need to get it together. Next time I hear about you two, I want it to be something positive, okay?"

Yeah, it'll be a positive pregnancy test if we keep going at this rate.

"I'll do my best. Say hi to Dad and Brenda for me."

"Will do. Love you, sweetie. Stay safe and warm."

"Love you too. Bye."

I hang up and take a deep breath. "You are in so much trouble."

He grins. "Just think, without me, you'd be having these delightful conversations with your TV, Sean." He inches closer, leaning over me where I sit on the couch, his cocoa mug dangerously close to tipping. "So, am I forgiven?"

I pull the blanket back, inviting him to sit beside me before handing him the remote. "Choose the cheesiest Christmas movie and maybe I'll think about it."

So he sits, and does exactly as I ask. We fall back into a routine that's becoming dangerously familiar. We don't speak about when the snow outside will inevitably melt. We don't speak about the world existing outside this cottage. We don't touch, even when we both know we want to because we both know what happens when we do, and we're exhausted. But this white-hot tension continues to build. One of us will snap. We always do.

I try to focus on the movie, but all I can feel is the heat of him at my side. He's close, but not close enough. The cottage turns dark, the only lights coming from the Christmas tree, and maybe it's the hot cocoa from earlier or the lack of sleep, but my eyes grow heavy.

I try to keep my head upright, but it lulls to the side, every muscle feeling like lead. Sean's hand is on my shoulder, guiding me back onto his chest. I don't have the energy to open my eyes. Not when I'm enveloped in his warmth, in the scent that always makes me a little dizzy. I let out a soft moan as I'm cocooned against his body.

Pressing a soft kiss to the top of my head, I hear him whisper against my hair, "Sleep, sweetheart."

Like my brain has reprogrammed itself to follow his every command, I sleep.

I hardly wake again when he carries me to bed. Or maybe I'm only dreaming because surely it's only in my dreams that Sean gently cups the side of my face and whispers, "How am I going to let you go?"

TWENTY-FOUR

SEAN

"We should go outside and check the snow situation," I announce, pulling on my boots. "See if we can gauge when this storm is going to let up."

Holly glances up from her book, eyebrows arched. "We?"

"Come on, it'll be good for you—fresh air and all."

With a sigh that's part exasperation, part acceptance, she sets down her book and starts bundling up. "Fine, but if I freeze to death, you'll be to blame."

"Dramatic," I mumble under my breath, earning a nudge to my ribs.

We step outside, the snow crunching under our

boots. I have to admit, the world looks different under a blanket of white; serene, peaceful.

I start trudging through the snow, measuring stick in hand, heading for a clearing that would give us a good sense of snow accumulation. Holly trails behind, her boots making smaller, dainty impressions next to my larger ones.

"So, what's the expert verdict?" she asks as I plunge the stick into the snow.

"About a foot and a half," I report. "And it's still coming down. Looks like we're not going anywhere soon."

She sighs, a cloud of vapor forming around her face. "More time stuck with you. Lucky me."

Before she can react, I scoop up a handful of snow and shape it into a ball. "Very lucky," I say, launching the snowball her way.

It hits her square in the arm, and she looks at me, incredulous. "You did not just do that."

With a grin that I know is inviting trouble, I reply, "Oh, but I did."

Her eyes narrow, and then she's diving for her own handful of snow. Within seconds, a full-fledged snowball fight erupts. We're both laughing, dodging, throwing—our past tensions momentarily forgotten.

It's during combat that I can't help but appreciate the way her eyes light up when she laughs, the way her hair frames her face like a halo, touched by snowflakes. A realization crashes into me with the subtlety of a sledgehammer: Holly with the sharp tongue is dangerous, but this Holly, the carefree woman laughing until her legs buckle, she's fucking lethal.

A snowball lands right in my face, snapping me out of my reverie.

"Game on, baby."

I spot her hiding behind her car, probably plotting her next move. I tread quietly through the snow, each step calculated. She senses me just before I get there, screaming as she starts to run, but her shorter legs are no match for my stride.

In two steps, I catch up to her, and with a fluid motion, I scoop her up in my arms as she squeals. We both lose our balance and tumble to the ground, falling into the snow. My hands catch me just in time, preventing me from crushing her as I land on top of her.

And there we are, me hovering above her, our faces inches apart. The laughter fades, replaced by a tension so thick I can hardly take a breath. Both of us are aware that we've crossed into territory far more dangerous than a simple snowball fight.

I hold myself there, suspended above her, and the world seems to pause.

I look down, her winter layers separating us like a fortress wall, and groan. "You've got way too many fucking layers on."

The corner of her lips curl, and then she reaches for the zipper of her coat. She slides it down slowly, her eyes never leaving mine. We stay like this for a long minute, eyes locked on each other.

With a smirk, she says, "That better?"

I can't even form words as I take in the sight of her. Her creamy skin glows, her curves are accentuated by nothing but a thin black tank top that hugs every inch of her body. My mouth is suddenly dry as my desire for her grows stronger by the second.

Without warning I press my lips against hers. The snow around us forgotten as we move together in sync.

I grab hold of one of her legs and wrap it around me before carefully rolling us over so she is now on top. I feel the heat radiating from between our bodies as she grinds against my hard cock, knowing exactly what she's doing to me, teasing me just enough to make me go crazy with need.

But before I can lose myself completely to pleasure, common sense kicks in, and I pull us back up on our feet. Taking her hand in mine, I lead us inside where it's warm again before turning to look at her with an expression that conveys just how much heat we both feel radiating between us.

"We need a shower," I say softly as my hands run along the length of her arms until they rest on either side of her shoulders.

She nods, her eyes now glassy. We both walk towards the bathroom in a trance-like state, our hands still intertwined.

Once inside, I turn on the water and let it run hot until it creates a thick steam around us.

My hands glide effortlessly over her wet skin, exploring every inch of her body as if for the first time. Just touching her ignites a fire within me that can only be quenched by being inside of her.

Wordless, I grab her waist, lifting her around mine and press her back to the wall.

She cries out as I enter her in one swift motion, my hands now gripping her hips tightly to keep us connected. I grind against her, filling her with an intensity that builds each time we meet.

It doesn't take long for us both to find our release.

I bury my head into the crook of her neck as I try to catch my breath, and allow myself just a minute to lose myself in the feeling of her arms wrapped around my shoulders.

It's in that minute I forget that this can't last forever.

TWENTY-FIVE

HOLLY

Wrapped in a soft, fluffy towel with my hair still damp from the shower, I remove a lasagna from the fridge to put in the oven. The warmth from the hot water has barely faded, but a different kind of warmth floods over me as I hear Sean's voice drifting down the hall.

He's on the phone, speaking with a gentleness I've come to know but rarely hear so openly. It's that same tenderness he hides behind jokes and jabs. But right now, there's no hiding.

"Yeah, Ma, I promise. As soon as this snow lets up, I'll come get you...Yeah, I know...I know, you've told me that recipe a hundred times...Yes, Ma, a hundred and one now."

The corners of my mouth pull into a smile, a picture forming in my mind of Sean's mother, of how her eyes must crinkle like his when she laughs. His relationship with her is filled with the patience and love that people don't always associate with him at first glance. But I know better. I know the real Sean, the one that's been revealing himself little by little.

I hear him end the call with a warm, "Love you too, Ma," before his footsteps grow louder, signaling his return to the kitchen. As he enters, his eyes meet mine, and there's a moment where the world narrows to just the two of us. His eyes search mine briefly, as if double-checking that the emotional intimacy from earlier hasn't vaporized.

Pushing aside those thoughts for now, I turn to the oven, sliding the dish inside. The savory aroma begins to fill the space, mingling with the lingering scent of our shower.

"You're good with her," I say without turning around, focusing on setting the oven timer.

Sean taps his knuckles against the kitchen counter, a thoughtful look on his face. Running a hand through his still-wet hair, he finally says, "Yeah, thanks."

"You're worried about her?" I can't help but ask, sensing there's more to his emotions than he's letting on.

His gaze drops away. "I'm worried about what being in a different environment will do to her. She's not used to change."

Just as I'm about to reply, my phone pings from where it sits on the counter. I pick it up and see a picture from my mom. In the photo, Brenda is sitting in a chair by the Christmas tree, a blanket draped over her lap, and a mischievous smile on her face as she holds one of my books.

I bite back a smile, turning my phone screen toward Sean. "She seems pretty comfortable to me."

He glances at the screen and then throws his head back, groaning. "Jesus Christ, is that one of your books? The one with the—"

"Don't even say it," I interject, cutting him off.

"Too late. The image is burned into my mind. My mother is reading your...your..."

"Sexy literature?" I supply helpfully, unable to keep a straight face.

"Jesus Christ," he repeats, making a beeline for the front door.

"What the hell are you doing?" I call after him, genuinely puzzled.

He returns a minute later, lugging his heavy toolbox into the house. "Fixing something. Anything is better than thinking about you corrupting my mother with your...*sexy literature*."

The idea is so absurd and his reaction so over-the-top that I burst into laughter. "Oh my God, you're serious. You'd rather play handyman than consider the fact that our moms are adults who can read whatever they want?"

"Damn straight," he says, heading for the guest bedroom. I haven't really touched it since I moved in, but I'm sure it will be perfectly functional by the time Sean takes his frustration out on it.

The sound of a drill starts up from the other room, drowning out my continuing laughter. After a moment, his voice echoes from the spare room, "Hey, where do you keep your nails?"

"If I had any, I would keep them in the bathroom,

like any other woman," I shout back, still laughing.

"That's not what I—never mind!" he yells, followed by the sound of what seems like a whole shelf crashing down.

"Everything okay in there?"

"Perfectly fine," he yells back, but his voice cracks, making me laugh even harder.

TWENTY-SIX

Cabin fever is a thing. A very real, very annoying thing. I didn't think it was possible to get tired of doing nothing, but as the daylight starts to wane on yet another day, I realize I need to find something else to do other than Sean. I've tried distracting myself with writing, but his presence in this cottage has proved too inspiring. Apart from some finishing touches, I've all but finished the book.

We've already gone through a series of board games, indoor mini-golf with some improvised putters, and some terribly cooked meals courtesy of Sean, who claims he "doesn't do kitchens." But he wanted to practice and seeing him so domesticated in my kitchen is delicious.

There's a battle going on inside me. I'm too stubborn to let go of all the hard feelings we've built up over the years. Yes, most of it was trivial, but it's how we are. How do we change it now?

Yet, having him here has shown me just how lonely I am. Is loneliness all this is? Am I craving touch so much I'm willing to find it in Sean? The pounding under my ribcage tells me it's something completely different. It's something scary. It's something my body is already growing accustomed to. It's something I not only like, but love. I love having his hands on me. I love the relief that washes over my body when he touches me. And it's confusing because I went into this knowing what it was. Sex. Simple. I can deal with that. It has clear lines. But those lines are beginning to blur. I'm not sure where I stand any more. Especially when he fucks me like a man starved but touches me like I'll break.

It's in those simple touches, I'm losing myself.

But none of it matters because he's also Mark's best friend. My brother can never find out about this because it would gut him, and I never want to get in the way of their friendship. The only person who knows and loves my brother as much as I do is Sean. There's no choice to make, and I wouldn't ask him to.

Blowing out a long breath, I head to the storage closet for some more scented candles and almost trip over a box of old photos. I pull it out, sit cross-legged on the floor, and start flipping through the pictures.

"Whatcha got there?" Sean asks, appearing in the doorway. A trail of sweat creeps over his bare chest, and I remind myself breathing is necessary if I plan on getting out of this storm alive.

Those hands might have been carved from years of hard work, but his body is the man's temple. He works on keeping it in the shape it's in. I'm just the lucky benefactor of getting to watch him workout in my living room.

Speak, Holly. Stop staring.

"Old memories," I reply, holding up a photo of a

younger version of us at a water park. Mark is there too, of course. We're all grinning like idiots. "Remember this?"

He squats down next to me, his eyes lingering on the picture. "Ah, yes. The summer Mark tried to do a backflip off the high dive and belly-flopped instead. He was red for days."

"He couldn't sit properly for a week. Mom had to buy him a floaty ring to sit on."

He picks up another photo. It's of the three of us at my high school graduation. "We were so young."

"Yeah," I agree, a softness creeping into my voice. "So full of dreams."

He meets my eyes. "But you're living your dream."

A small smile tilts the corner of my mouth as he looks down and plucks a photo from the box. It looks like there's a thousand memories playing behind those dark eyes. I shimmy closer to him to get a better look.

It's an old polaroid, the caption handwritten: *New Years Eve, 2014.*

I'm sitting on the edge of the kitchen counter in Sean's childhood home, looking a little worse for wear. I hardly remember that night. I prefer not to remember because it still makes me cringe. Me and alcohol are not friends. But his hand is under my chin, tilting my head back, and we're both laughing. We look carefree. It's an intimate moment between two people who look like the younger version of who we've been over the last couple of days.

My heart thumps in my chest as his thumb gently moves back and forth over the picture. I feel like I'm looking at a jigsaw puzzle but missing the last piece. He looks…sad?

"You were always so beautiful, Squirt." He smiles,

but it doesn't reach his eyes.

I know I'm fucked because I don't even mind that damn nickname anymore.

"Do you remember who took this?" I ask, unable to keep my eyes off how the muscles in his jaw tense, pulsing in and out.

"I think it was Jackie." He doesn't look up from the photo when he adds, "You left for the city soon after this."

"Sean?" I breathe, needing to meet his eyes, but he shuts them as he inhales a steadying breath.

"Don't, Holl," he whispers, raising his head to look at me.

The atmosphere changes, becoming more intimate, more vulnerable. For the first time, I feel like we're not just looking at each other, but seeing each other.

And it hits me. What I recognize in that photo is the way he looks at me. It's how he's looking at me now. It's probably how I'm looking at him. But it's also how I looked at him for years when I was a teenager and convinced myself I was in love with Sean.

But that can't be right.

"You okay?" he asks, his voice strained.

I nod but don't meet his eyes. "Yeah. Just memories, you know?"

He takes my hand and presses a soft kiss to my palm. "Memories can be a double-edged sword."

Silence settles between us, but it's not uncomfortable. It's the kind of silence you share with someone when words are unnecessary.

"You need to keep these...For old times' sake," he finally says.

We fall into another silence as he goes through more recent photos, filling in the gaps of the years I was away.

"Proud of you, you know?" He's staring at a photo of a book launch.

My book launch, to be precise.

I raise an eyebrow, a little taken aback. "You are?"

"Of course. You said you were going to do it, and you did."

I smile, touched by his words. "Thanks." I feel a blush creep up my cheeks as I nudge him playfully. "Proud of you too."

"God, that must have killed you."

I rub my throat. "I think I'm choking. Those words burned a little." He flashes me one of those full smiles and my breath gets stuck in my lungs. "No, really. You've built a successful business from the ground up. You should be incredibly proud."

For a moment, the playful, cocky Sean I've always known is gone, replaced by a man who's seen his share of struggles and has come out stronger.

The air between us thickens, brimming with an intensity that could be sliced through with a knife. When his lips finally meet mine, it's like a match to gasoline, igniting a blaze that radiates warmth from the pit of my stomach to the tips of my toes.

His lips are soft, a paradox to the firm grip he has on my waist. The kiss starts slow, almost a question, as if testing the waters. But when my mouth parts, allowing him to deepen the kiss, all hesitation vanishes.

"You're still an asshole," I manage to whisper against his lips.

"And you still drive me insane," he replies, voice husky and tinged with a promise of things to come.

It's a kiss that says what words can't: that despite everything, there's a connection here that runs deeper than we're willing to acknowledge.

As we finally pull away, both of us gasping for air but not wanting to let go, it's as though years of pent-up tension and emotion have been released, leaving us in a state of exhilarating vulnerability.

"We're ruining the status quo, aren't we?" is all I can muster.

"We ruined the status quo the minute you let me inside this cottage."

∞∞∞∞

"Sean?" My voice is a whisper, barely disturbing the serene silence of the bedroom.

The room is dark, save for the sliver of moonlight that sneaks through the curtains, casting a gentle glow over the tangled sheets that cocoon us. His breathing is deep and even, one of his arms tucked under the pillow while the other lazily drapes over my waist, a connection he seems to need even as he drifts off.

"Yeah, baby?" he mumbles, the words a warm hum in the darkness.

My stomach does that familiar flip, the one I've come to recognize as the 'Sean-effect'. I love it when he calls me that—as if I'm something precious, something cherished.

"Can I ask you something?"

"Sure." His response is automatic, the word drawn out and coated with sleep.

I hesitate, biting my lower lip. Ever since I accused him of cheating on Ashley, curiosity has gnawed at me. I did some social media stalking, but it did little to help, offering tidbits of Ashley's life post-Sean. They ended things three years ago. Later that year, she got married to someone else, but the shiny images turned to dust, ending in divorce. I can't help but wonder about the story untold, the pieces that don't fit together.

"You don't have to answer me, but what really happened between you and Ashley?"

There's a pause, and for a moment, I think he might have drifted off to sleep. But then his eyes open slowly, a little more alert, a little more present.

He lets out a long breath and laughs lightly, the sound almost sad. "You really need to work on your pillow talk."

I remain silent, my heart pounding slightly, not expecting him to answer, but desperately hoping he will.

He sighs, his gaze fixed on some distant point, perhaps lost in the memories. "Ashley came from money. A lot of it. Her family...they were high society through and through." He pauses, but there's no tension there. Not anymore. "They didn't approve of our relationship. I was working on getting the business off the ground back then, and things were tough to begin with. They wanted her with someone...more on her level."

My heart aches for him, the unfairness of it all pricking my eyes. How is that even possible? He's built a successful business from the ground up, he's funny, charming, ridiculously hot.

Ashley is an idiot.

"I'm sorry," I whisper.

His hand reaches out, fingers stroking my cheek sleepily. "Don't be sad for me, baby," he murmurs, his voice a soothing balm. "Truth is, she did me a favor. We'd grown apart long before her family ever got involved. I wasn't in love with the woman she'd become."

He places a brief, soft kiss on my forehead, a reassuring promise, before his arm tightens around my waist, pulling me closer into the safe harbor of his body.

"Now, sleep," he whispers against my hair, his breath warm and comforting.

The rhythm of our hearts, so closely entwined, lulls me into a distant sleep, but his arms...they never let me go.

TWENTY-SEVEN

I wake up to the sound of someone moving around in the house. My eyes blink open, and for a moment, I'm disoriented. Then I feel Sean's arm draped around me, and last night comes flooding back. There was a switch flipped. We woke in the middle of the night, our bodies immediately finding each other.

And it was...different.

It was the look in his eyes, never leaving mine, as if he was committing every feature to memory. His hands explored, his body commanded, and I responded with an intensity I didn't even know I had. It was pure, raw emotion, as if the barriers we had built over the years were suddenly crumbling away.

His lips met mine, soft and hesitant at first, but the kiss deepened as if drawn by a magnetism we couldn't resist. We had kissed before—stolen moments wrapped in anger and confusion, each trying to get the upper hand. But this was something else entirely. There was an intimacy, a vulnerability, neither of us was prepared for.

But it was that very vulnerability that scared me. We were in uncharted territory, exposing parts of ourselves that we'd never shown anyone. I felt bare, stripped of my defenses, and it was both exhilarating and terrifying.

He seemed to understand, pulling me closer, holding me like he was trying to shield me from the world, from my own fears. We didn't speak. Words would have been superfluous, a mere distraction. Instead, we communicated in caresses, soft sighs, and the shared rhythm of our hearts.

The pace was unhurried, as if we had all the time in the world. Each touch was a question, each response a confession. He was gentle, reverent, treating me with a care I hadn't known I craved until that moment. It was as if, in acknowledging the depth of what was growing between us, we were reshaping the very foundation of our relationship.

As the night wore on, we clung to each other, taking solace in the warmth and the newfound intimacy. It was a connection that went beyond the physical—souls intertwining, searching for a bond that had always been there, just hidden beneath layers of resentment and misunderstanding.

Despite the whirlwind of emotions, sleep eventually claimed me again. My last memory before drifting off was of Sean kissing my forehead, his voice a soft whisper in my ear, "We'll deal with it tomorrow."

Well, here we are.

It's tomorrow.

I just don't want it to be.

I'm about to nudge Sean awake when my brother's voice echoes through the house. "Holls, you okay? The roads are clear, just wanted to check on you, but it looks like Sean got here first."

Shit.

His truck is outside.

My eyes widen, meeting Sean's, who's now awake and looking just as panicked.

"Fuck," we both mutter simultaneously.

We scramble for the sheets, for our clothes, for any semblance of decency, but it's too late. The bedroom door bursts open, and there stands Mark, his eyes going from Sean to me and back again. His expression morphs from concern to disbelief to outright anger within seconds.

"What the actual fuck?" Mark explodes, his eyes burning holes through his best friend.

"Listen, it's not—" Sean starts, but he's cut off.

"It's not what? It's not what it looks like? Because it looks like you're in bed with my sister!" Mark's voice is a dangerous octave higher than usual.

"I need to talk to you. I'll explain," Sean insists, but he's struggling to find the right words, his face flushed with a mix of embarrassment and guilt.

"Explain? How the hell are you going to explain this, man? You've known her since we were children!"

Oh shit. Oh shit. Oh shit.

"And I've known you since we were even younger," Sean counters, trying to keep his own temper in check. "Don't you think I know how serious this is?"

"Obviously not serious enough to keep your hands off her."

"Mark," I finally interject, unable to bear the tension any longer.

"You jumping into bed with just anyone now, Holly?"

I swear my heart splits in two.

"Hey," Sean roars, his eyes murderous. "Watch your fucking mouth."

This is everything I feared.

"Stop," I plead. "Mark, we're both adults here. We made a choice—"

"A damn stupid choice." He cuts me off, but his eyes are still locked on Sean.

"Look, I get that you're pissed, and you have every right to be," Sean says, finally pulling on a shirt. "But this isn't just something that happened. There's more here, and we need to talk about it—"

"Talk about it?" Mark scoffs, throwing his hands up. "Oh, we're going to talk."

He turns to me, his anger morphing into disappointment. "You're just another notch on his bedpost, Holl. You know that, right?"

My heart splinters into pieces because a part of me already knew that, but it's Sean's lack of response that confirms it.

What did I expect? I knew what this was. But there's still a part of that naive little girl that had a crush on Sean as a teenager that still lives somewhere in me, that ignited that flame in my belly.

I was too blinded while we were cocooned here in our own bubble that I forgot that there was an entirely different world outside of it.

It's my turn to look at Sean, but the heat I've grown accustomed to over the last week is nothing but ice now and it's cold to my skin.

Say something.

I wait, but nothing comes.

I feel another crack in my chest.

Mark doesn't wait for a response. He gives Sean one final glare before turning on his heels and storming out of the bedroom. The heavy thud of the front door closing echoes through the house, reverberating in the awkward silence he leaves in his wake.

Sean finally looks at me, but his eyes are unreadable, a guarded wall I can't penetrate. The tension in the room is stifling, suffocating, as if the air itself is holding its breath, waiting for someone to speak. I suddenly feel bare, and not just because of my state of undress.

"Sean," I begin, my voice wobbling despite my best effort to keep it steady, "Say something. Anything."

He opens his mouth, hesitates, and then closes it again. The weight of Mark's accusation hangs between us, a physical entity that neither of us can ignore.

Finally, he speaks, but his voice is low, almost a whisper. "I never meant for any of this to happen. Not like this."

"Is that all you've got? You never meant for it to happen? That's your grand explanation?"

"I don't know what you want me to say," he confesses, looking lost for the first time since I've known him. "I never intended to put you in a position where you'd be caught in the middle of whatever this is."

"And what is *this*? Because if I'm just another notch on your bedpost, like Mark said, then you better tell me now."

"I don't know," he admits, his face etched with a mixture of regret and indecision. "I honestly don't know. Last night, this morning—they felt different, but now...I just don't know."

The raw honesty in his voice does little to comfort me. Instead, it deepens the ache in my chest, the searing pain of reality cutting through the warmth that had enveloped us just hours earlier.

"You don't know," I repeat, tasting the bitterness of each word.

"For fuck's sake, Holly," he says, getting to his feet. "What did you think this was? What do you want?"

What do I want?

I don't know because I haven't had time to think about anything beyond being snowed in with him in this cottage.

Do I want something more?

That thought would have been laughable a week ago, but now? Now I'm not so sure, and he sees it in my eyes. His head falls between his shoulders before he kneels on the bed and takes my face in his hands.

The sting of tears prickles the corners of my eyes, but I force them back. I won't cry. Not here, not in front of him.

"You know me. I don't do..." He struggles for words. "Whatever you think this is," he says, and even though his voice is icy, there's a catch, a little break that betrays him.

I let out a bitter laugh. Sean doesn't do relationships, doesn't do the morning after. For as long as I've known him, he's had one serious relationship, and he admitted last night that he didn't even love her. Not really. Was I really stupid enough to think that maybe, just maybe, I'd be the exception?

"I'm not what you want," he adds, still avoiding my gaze. "I'll get bored. Move on. It's what I do."

"You're really selling yourself here." The acid in my words cover up the crumbling facade of my bravado.

"I'm trying to be honest with you," he says, finally meeting my eyes.

"Honesty, at this point, seems like a slap in the face, don't you think?"

"What do you want me to say?" His voice rises, losing his own facade of cool detachment.

"I don't know. Maybe something that doesn't make me feel like a whore or that all of this was a mistake."

"Don't ever, and I mean ever, call yourself a whore. And this wasn't a mistake," he says softly, contradicting everything he just told me.

"Then what was it? Because right now, it feels like it was just a lapse in judgment. For both of us."

His eyes search mine, and for a moment, I think I see a glimmer of something more, something real. But then he looks away, putting that insurmountable distance between us again.

"Maybe it was," he admits, his voice barely above a whisper. "Or maybe it was inevitable. I don't know."

"You don't know," I echo, the words thick and bitter in my mouth. "Seems to be the theme here."

He opens his mouth as if to say something else, but then closes it, nodding slightly as if agreeing with my last statement.

I finally break away from his touch, my skin still tingling where his hands had been.

"You're right," I say, my voice shaky but resolute. "You're not what I want. Because what I want is someone who knows what they want."

With that, I slip out of the bed, gather my clothes, and leave the room, each step feeling like a mile. I don't look back. I can't. Because if I do, I might just see something in his eyes that makes me want to stay. And that's the last thing I need right now.

TWENTY-EIGHT

I walk into Jackie's apartment, the scent of cinnamon and vanilla hitting me immediately. The twinkling lights from her Christmas tree catch my eye, and I can't help but laugh. It's the most pathetic excuse for a Christmas tree I've ever seen. Bare branches with the occasional sparse needle, drooping under the weight of mismatched ornaments.

"Jackie, your tree looks as miserable as I feel," I announce as I kick off my boots and hang my coat on the rack by the door.

She chuckles from the kitchen where she's pouring two mugs of hot cocoa. "Don't insult Harold. He's been with me for ten years, and I just can't seem to part with the fucker."

I take a seat on her comfy sofa, glancing again at Harold. "Ten years? Are you sure it's not a twig you just dressed up?"

"Harold has sentimental value," she defends, handing me a steaming mug before sitting next to me. "So, what's got you looking like you want to join

Harold in the sad Christmas corner?"

I take a sip of cocoa, relishing its warmth before delving into what's been bothering me. "Sean and I... um... we..." I struggle to find the right words, but Jackie has enough for both of us.

"You had sex? Fucked? Boned? He threw his sausage up your alley?"

"Jesus."

"HA!" She throws her head back. "I knew it."

"He was there when the storm hit, so we've been snowed in together all week long."

"And let me guess, you both didn't exactly weather the storm as enemies?"

The tears welling in my eyes is all the answer she needs. "We made it complicated."

"Girl, I would hope so." She leans forward. "I mean, Sean? Really? Tell me everything. And don't skimp on the details."

"Do you want the PG version or—"

"R-rated, Holly. R-rated!" she insists, setting her mug down with emphasis.

I go on to recount the last few days, from the awkward start to the emotional roller coaster it turned out to be.

Jackie listens intently, alternating between laughter and gasps of disbelief. When I finish, she takes a deep breath and says, "Damn."

"I know. And now, I don't know what to do. One moment it felt like there was something real, something more, and then the next thing, it's like we're strangers."

"Do you like him? Like, really like him?"

I shrug, still in denial. I saw a side to him in the last few days that I've never seen before. The man who held me while I slept and kept me there until my eyes opened in the morning. The man who breathed kisses down my neck while I was writing for no other reason other than he could. The man who had me doubled over with laughter until I could hardly breathe, and then kissed me until I was silenced.

"If you think it's just cabin fever or holiday loneliness," she continues, "then girl, you better run."

"That's the thing. I don't know. But what I do know is that I can't stop thinking about him. About us." I laugh but it's humorless. "I can't believe there even is an *us*. It's Sean and me. Sean who's had a longer relationship with his underwear than any woman."

"Don't take that personally. Men tend to hold onto underwear for too long." She sips her drink. "But wait. What about Ashley?"

I press my palm against my forehead. "Ashley, right. I always forget about her."

Jackie blows out a breath and sits back into the cushions, but my mouth keeps rambling on.

"And I'm not even going there with my brother. He's his best friend. For all I know, we could have ruined that friendship. They're like brothers."

"Then they'll fight like brothers." She offers me a small smile. "And they'll make up like brothers too. Your brother or even Sean for that matter isn't my concern here. It's you. You've already got a lot on your plate with the book, the move, and Adam, and now Sean. Give yourself a break."

At the end of the day, it doesn't matter because Sean doesn't want me. Not now. Not in the future. He wanted a fling. Something to keep him warm and occupied while he was stuck inside. I was that.

"God, I'm such a fool," I sulk, sitting back into the

chair and wrapping my hands around the warm cocoa.

"Yeah, but you were a horny fool. You won't get any judgement from me."

"I love you."

"I know. Love you too."

Inhaling a deep breath, I try to shake off the emotional haze that's enveloped me. "Alright, enough about me and my tragic love life, or whatever this is. Distract me. I want all the sordid details of what's happening in your world. Spill."

She grins. "Well, you're in luck. I've been seeing someone."

My eyes widen, and I sit up so quickly that I almost spill my cocoa. Grabbing a pillow, I fling it at her with mock indignation. "How have you not told me this?"

She shrugs, catching the pillow and placing it neatly back on the sofa. "It's nothing serious. On and off for a little while, and besides, you were preoccupied being snowed in with a Greek god."

"A Greek god who moonlights as a jerk," I retort, rolling my eyes.

"Well, even Zeus had his flaws," Jackie says, winking. "But honestly, I didn't think you'd want to hear about my fling when you were living a rom-com fantasy—minus the rom and with a dash of com."

"Okay, I want to hear everything," I demand, "Who is she? How did you meet? And why is it nothing serious?"

She leans back, clearly relishing the attention. "Her name is Erica. We met at a charity event a few months back, and we just clicked, you know? But we're both busy people. She's in finance and travels a lot for work, and I've got my hands full grading papers and planning lessons, so we just haven't committed to making it a thing yet."

"Busy people? Jackie, you're a school teacher who complains about having to wake up before 10 a.m. on weekends. You have time," I tease.

She snorts. "Speak for yourself, Miss Bestselling Author who's been cooped up in a cabin, too busy to even return my texts."

"Okay, okay, you've got me there," I admit, feeling the heaviness in my chest lighten ever so slightly.

"So," she says, leaning in with a mischievous glint in her eye, "Are we both just tragically terrible at relationships, or what?"

I let out a laugh, this time a genuine one. "Speak for yourself. I was tragically terrible at something that wasn't even a relationship. You, at least, have something going."

"Fair point."

We both sip our cocoa, letting a comfortable silence settle over us. For the first time today, I feel like maybe, just maybe, things might eventually be okay. Not today, perhaps not even tomorrow, but someday.

"So, what now?" she finally asks, her tone softening. "What are you going to do?"

I sigh, staring down into the cocoa as if it holds the answers. "There's nothing to do. I'll have to speak to him again because this town isn't big enough for both of us."

She reaches over and squeezes my hand. "Whatever you decide, you know I've got your back, right?"

I look up, meeting her sincere gaze. "I know. Thank you."

"We could always go out and get drunk…or stay in and get drunk?"

I laugh. "I'm not quite at that stage just yet. Give

me twenty-four to forty-eight hours."
 "It's a date."

TWENTY-NINE

After leaving Jackie's place, my mood is only slightly improved. She always has a way of lifting me up, but some weights are just too heavy to fully shake off. As I sit in my car, keys in the ignition but not yet turned, I take a moment to just breathe.

I finally muster the courage to glance at my phone. My eyes immediately dart to the notification screen. Several text messages and missed calls, all within the span of a few hours. But not one from Sean. Instead, it's my family—mostly my father and Mark. My heart leaps in a strange blend of relief and worry. Relief because, in this fragile state, I don't think I can handle any more interactions with Sean; worry because multiple missed calls from family usually mean bad news.

I tap to call my father back, my fingers shaky as they touch the screen. The phone rings twice before he picks up.

"Holly? Where have you been? I've been trying to reach you."

His voice is tinged with a sharp anxiety I don't often hear. My stomach sinks.

"Dad, what's wrong? What happened?"

"It's Brenda," he pauses, taking a deep breath as if bracing himself for the words he has to say next. "She had a fall when Sean came to pick her up. She's in the hospital."

My heart drops into my stomach, making it churn. Despite everything that happened with Sean, Brenda has always been a constant, a source of warmth and kindness in my life. I can't imagine her in a hospital bed.

"Which hospital is she in? I'm going there right now."

"St. Michael's, room 237. But Holly, she's going to be fine. You don't have to—"

"I'm going, Dad. I have to see her."

I don't wait for his reply, hanging up and jamming the keys into the ignition. As I navigate through the streets, my thoughts are a messy swirl of worry for Brenda, guilt over my unresolved tension with Sean, and frustration at how complicated everything has become.

Pulling into the hospital parking lot, I take a few shaky breaths to steady myself before heading inside.

I make my way to her room. The door is slightly ajar, and I hesitate, my hand hovering over the doorknob. Taking a deep breath, I gently push the door open and step inside.

The room is empty, save for Brenda lying there, hooked up to an array of machines. She looks so fragile that my heart constricts. But when she turns her head and sees me, her face brightens.

"Holly! What a lovely surprise."

Despite her situation, her eyes are as warm as ever. They hold a glimmer of relief, as if my presence has lifted a weight off her shoulders. I approach her bedside and take her hand gently.

"How are you feeling?" I ask.

"Oh, I've been better," she chuckles softly. "Come sit."

As I take the seat next to her bedside, I can't help but notice how much she's changed since the last time I saw her. Her once-vibrant red hair has faded into a soft, muted shade, peppered with streaks of silver. The skin on her arms appears thinner, more translucent, like delicate tissue paper. There's a sort of frailty in her presence, one I've never seen before. But despite these changes, her eyes are still the same—warm, comforting.

"What happened?"

"It was only a wobble. I hit my knee, but my son is dramatic and demanded I come to the hospital."

"Did you slip on the ice?"

"Please," she scoffs. "I could run on that ice since I was a little girl. I fell in your parent's house, who were so good for looking after me. My balance just kind of…went."

She's so vulnerable looking back at me. Far from the feisty woman I remembered. I know her and Sean struggled throughout the years, but she was always kind to me. I still remember when she braided my hair every time I went by to see her. I realize now that the smell on her breath was Vodka, but as a child, I was none the wiser.

"It's so good to see you," she says, her voice tinged with affection. "Sean will be so happy you're here too. He's just busy talking to those damn doctors."

A lump forms in my throat, tightening its grip with each passing second. "Those doctors are here to help you."

She snorts softly, her eyes narrowing. "Help? All they do is poke and prod at me, telling me I need more tests, as if I'm some sort of lab rat. I'll tell them what I need."

I smile at her spunk. "I know it's frustrating, but they're just trying to make sure you're okay."

She waves her hand dismissively. "Oh, I know. I'm just not the most patient patient." She looks at me closely, a nostalgic glint in her eyes. "So, how's college going? Have you picked a major yet?"

My heart sinks. I haven't been in college for six years. I take her hand and meet her eyes, offering her a gentle smile. "Actually, I graduated a while back. I write books now. That's my job."

There's a glimmer of confusion crossing her face, muddling with the warmth in her eyes. She waves it off with a soft chuckle. "My memory isn't what it used to be it seems. But that's wonderful. You always had a notebook strapped to your side. I'm glad you're still writing. Sean has a business of his own, you know?"

"Yeah?" I ask, fighting the sting behind my eyes as she squeezes my hand. For the first time her gaze lights up with nothing but pride.

"He's a good boy. He takes good care of me, even if he's always trying to get me to a doctor. He has no patience with them either."

"Like mother, like son, right?"

"Exactly."

For the next while, we just talk. We reminisce about the good old days, laughing over the antics we all go up to as kids. I'm reminded of summers spent climbing trees and the one disastrous attempt at a homemade go-kart that ended in all of us being grounded.

"Do you remember the time you all tried to bake cookies and ended up turning my kitchen into a flour war zone?" Brenda asks, chuckling at the memory.

"How could I forget? Sean kept blaming me for the mess, but he was the one who started it."

Eventually, I steer the conversation back to a topic I know we can't avoid. "I know you don't like it, but the doctors are really here to help. Please, let them do their tests. For Sean, if not for yourself."

Her face tightens. "I've lived a long life. I know my body. These doctors, they're so young. What could they possibly know?"

"They know medicine. They've seen countless cases, probably some exactly like yours. If there are treatments that can help, wouldn't you want that?"

She sighs, her eyes meeting mine. They're filled with a complex mixture of stubbornness and vulnerability. "You remind me of my Sean. Always wanting to fix things, make them better."

I squeeze her hand, my voice soft but insistent. "Then let us fix this. Let us help you get better."

After a long, heavy pause, she finally nods. "Alright. I'll cooperate with the doctors, go through their tests."

Just as I'm feeling the weight of the silence settle in, the door creaks open and Sean walks in. He stops at the threshold, his eyes locking onto mine as he stands there. The world seems to pause, a still frame capturing the tangled web of emotions between us. The twinge in my chest breaks the spell, and I drop my gaze.

Oblivious to the undercurrents of tension, Brenda's voice cuts through. "Ah, there you are, son. Look who's here. Holly came to visit. Isn't she beautiful?"

His eyes land on me again, holding my gaze as he answers, "She is, Ma. She really is."

Brenda continues, unaware. "So, are you just here for the summer, Holly?"

"It's Christmas," he tells her, going to her side to fix her pillows.

Her eyes widen. "It is? Oh, Sean, there's so much I need to get."

"Don't worry about it." He leans down to kiss her forehead. "Whatever you need just tell me and I'll sort it."

She holds the side of his face, affection in her eyes before she turns back to me. "Just home for the holidays then?"

"Actually, I'm here to stay," I say, trying to ease the tension with some news. "I bought a cottage here in town. Sean helped renovate it."

Her eyes widen. "You two were in close quarters and didn't kill each other?"

No, what we did was far worse than murder. We complicated everything.

Before I can respond, a doctor steps into the room, clipboard in hand. "Mrs. Colson, it's time for your MRI."

I stand, leaning down to kiss Brenda's cheek. "I'll be back to visit soon."

Sean tenses beside me, his body rigid as he braces for his mother's usual defiance. But instead of fighting the doctor off, she simply winks at me.

As I move past Sean to leave the room, he finally breaks his silence. "What did you say to her? She's usually screaming bloody murder when the doctors come in."

Shaking my head, I try to muster a smile but fail

miserably. "Nothing. We just talked."

He looks pained, his dark brown hair disheveled in a way that, against all odds, doesn't make him look a mess. It's endearing, really, and I'm disarmed by how much I care, by how much I recognize this agony in my chest as something so much more than the aftermath of casual sex, and how much I refuse to acknowledge it right now because when I do, I'm going to break. His eyes, tired and a shade darker than I remember, seem to carry the weight of a thousand unsaid words between us.

For the first time ever, ignoring the rational part of my brain, I just want to give him a hug. So I step into his space, granting myself this fleeting moment of comfort. I wrap my arms around him, my face pressed against the soft fabric of his shirt.

He only stills for a split second, shocked by the sudden intimacy. Then his hands find my lower back, pulling me closer, breathing me in like a man starved of air.

"Take care of her," I whisper, my words muffled against him but piercing in their sincerity. "If she needs anything, you know where to find me."

Reluctantly, I pull away, meeting his eyes just briefly, a mosaic of emotions neither of us is willing to decipher at this moment.

"See you around." I turn to leave, my feet carrying me away, but my thoughts are anchored in that room, in that moment, with him.

And then a part of my heart shatters when I hear him reply, "See you around, Squirt."

THIRTY

SEAN

I watch her leave, my chest tight, my hands clenched into fists at my side. That hug—unexpected and heartbreakingly brief—felt like a sip of water to a man dying of thirst. I don't know why she did it, but the fact that she reached out to me is enough to have my mind racing.

"Holly's such a sweet girl," Ma says from the hospital bed, her voice pulling me back into the room. I look at her, noticing the frailty she tries so hard to hide. "You always liked her, didn't you?"

I walk over to sit in the chair Holly just vacated, still warm from her presence. "I did, Ma," I admit quietly.

"I still do."

She smiles at me, eyes bright yet clouded with a layer of tiredness that scares me. "Then why'd you let her walk away? Life's too short."

I rub my forehead, feeling the weight of regret settle on me. "It's complicated. Besides, it's not just about me and Holly. There's a lot going on."

The doctor walks in before she can respond, effectively cutting off the conversation. I'm grateful for the interruption, but I can see the disappointment in her eyes. It's not just about her condition; it's about a life left unlived, words left unsaid.

After discussing my mother's situation with the doctor, I step out of the room. My phone buzzes in my pocket, and I pull it out, half-expecting, half-hoping it's Holly. But it's a text from one of my employees about an issue at work. I deal with it quickly, my thoughts still on Holly, on that hug, and on the confusing tangle of emotions that has wrapped itself around my heart.

I find myself walking down the hospital corridor, my feet carrying me towards the exit. I need air, space to think. The chill hits me as I step outside, but it's a refreshing contrast to the stuffy hospital atmosphere.

For a brief moment, we became something more. Now, I'm not sure what we are. My thoughts drift back to the time we spent together. The way her eyes sparkled when she talked about her writing, the way her laughter filled the empty rooms, turning them into a home. I thought I was only helping her with a place to stay, but she filled the gaps in my own life, spaces I didn't even realize were empty.

I'm standing outside, leaning against the wall of the hospital, lost in thought when I spot Mark striding purposefully towards me. My heart tightens; given what he walked into earlier this morning, I half-expect him to punch me. And honestly, I'd deserve it.

He's been more than just a friend. He's a brother in every sense except biology. He's been there through thick and thin, especially when it comes to my mother. We've shared the weight of each other's worlds without asking for anything in return. As teenagers, when we should've been out causing mayhem, he stayed with me on nights when my mother was too drunk to see straight. She's like a second mother to him, just as his mother is to me.

"About earlier—" I begin, but he cuts me off before I can get another word in.

"You were right. You're both adults. I have no right to interfere. But she's my sister, man. And she's one of the good ones. I won't stand by and let you use her."

His words slice through me, because deep down, I know he's right. Whether it's the raw sincerity in his eyes or the simple, irrefutable logic of what he's saying, it hits home.

"That's not what it was."

"Then if it's something more, don't string her along. And if it's not, then end it."

His gaze holds mine, unflinching, and I know he means every word.

Leaning closer, his eyes narrow, dead serious. "Break her heart, and I don't care if you're my best friend, I will kill you."

I breathe out a laugh, the tension between us easing just a bit. "I'd be disappointed if you didn't," I reply, fully aware that he means every word he says. We've been friends for too long, shared too much for me to doubt him on this.

He puffs out his chest, inhaling deeply as he closes

his eyes and counts backwards from ten.

"What the fuck are you doing?"

"Taking a minute to separate the fact that she's my sister before I ask how the fuck all of this happened?"

I grimace. "You don't want the details."

He might really punch me now. "No, dickhead, I don't want the details. You were obviously there when the blizzard hit, but what happens now?"

"Have you forgotten she's your sister yet?" I ask cautiously.

"A little, depends on what you say."

"I left things in disaster."

"Ah," he drawls, leaning against the wall with me. "You pulled a Sean."

"I pulled a what?"

"A Sean," he repeats. "You know, where you get scared and you bolt. You retreat into yourself, man. It's what you've always done."

I wince at the accuracy of his observation, my own shortcomings reflected back at me through the eyes of someone who knows me better than almost anyone. It's a behavior pattern I've struggled to break, a cycle I've never managed to escape.

"Yeah, well, maybe you're right. But this is Holly we're talking about. And I—"

"You what?" he interrupts, pushing off the wall and taking a step toward me. "You've both hated each other for most of your lives? You—"

"I never hated her," I cut him off sharply.

"I know that too, you idiot. You've looked out for her when I couldn't, even if she wanted to kill us for it. That our job. So, what, you're afraid of screwing it up? News flash, man, you've already screwed up. Question is, what are you going to do about it?"

What am I going to do about it? Holly isn't just someone I can run away from. My eyes flicker to Mark, seeing the concern mixed with frustration there.

"I don't know," I confess. "But I'll make it right. I promise."

"Don't promise me anything. I'm not the one who needs to hear it."

We get caught in a silence, filled with unspoken understanding and years of friendship. Mark breaks it first.

"I should go in and see how Brenda's doing. You comin'?"

"Yeah," I say, pushing off the wall. "I'm comin'."

∞∞∞∞

After Mark leaves, my mother seems brighter for the visits, but her eyes are hallowing, the dark rings almost engraved around her eyes. She stares at the wall aimlessly just like she does at home.

Sometimes I want to crawl inside her mind so I can know where she is all day when her memory evades her. I want to see what day she's reliving. I want to understand, but mostly, I'm terrified of what I will find. I've tried my entire life to bury those memories. I don't want to live them from her point of view too.

I run a hand through my hair, pulling at the tips before stretching my neck, these hospital chairs and this morning's tension coiling around my joints.

Her hand is tiny when she takes mine, the skin wrinkled. She looks older than her sixty-five years.

"You should go home, son." She smiles but her eyes are already heavy as she looks up at me.

"I'll wait, Ma. I don't mind. Let's see what else the

doctors say."

"Those fucking doctors."

I suppress a laugh. My mother never cursed when I was growing up. My only memory of her using language was when she got wasted…which was regularly, but she always muttered them under her breath.

"You know, you're getting quite a tongue on you lately."

She shrugs her narrow shoulders. "Fuck it."

I burst out laughing.

She smiles before it falters. "I'm sorry, Sean." My eyes widen watching as tears brim in hers. "For everything. I know I wasn't a good mother—"

"Stop it, Ma. I just want you to get better."

She glares at me like she used to when she was scolding me as a child. "How about you have manners and let your mother speak."

I dip my chin and take her hand.

"You're a good son. Better than I deserve. I'm so proud of you." Her voice cracks on the words. "I just wanted to say thank you."

A sticky lump forms in my throat, but I swallow around it. I could tell her how I'm only giving back what she gave me. We both did our best with what we had. But I know she wouldn't accept it, so I press a kiss to her cheek. "Welcome, Ma."

She pulls at her blanket, her cheeks flushing. "I know my memory hasn't been right for a while, and it can't be easy on you looking after me all the time. Especially when I'm a little over the top." I scoff and she darts another glare my way before she adds, "Let's see if these doctors are any good."

I'm stiff as I move in the chair, but relief floods me.

"Has this anything to do with Holly's visit or is it the young doctor I seen come in here earlier?"

Her mouth falls open but there's a glint in her eyes. "It does help to have something to look at while you're in this dreary place." She presses her fingers together like she's squeezing something. "And he did have a rather nice backside."

"Jesus Christ." I throw my head in my hands and laugh. It's good to see her like this, joking, remembering shit.

"It was good to see Holly too," she adds. "God, she's a beauty, isn't she?"

Guilt swells in my chest as I nod in agreement.

"And you, son," she takes my hand, "are a complete fool."

What the fuck?

"Don't look at me like that. Like a complete moron. You're smart, but sometimes you are utterly stupid."

"Jesus, thanks. Please tell me what I did this time?"

"I might be struggling with my memory, but my eyesight is just fine."

She stays silent as if waiting for me to catch on. I arch a brow.

I'm clueless.

"Holly. The way you look at that girl. The way you've always looked at her."

My heart thuds, and I'm momentarily speechless. "Ma, you're imagining things."

She rolls her eyes, a grin pulling at the corners of her lips. "I may have not been the best mother, but I know my son. And I can still recognize the tension between two people. You practically burn holes in each other with those glares."

"So, what are you saying?" I chuckle nervously,

trying to divert her from the road she's traveling down.

"I'm saying that sometimes the line between love and hate is very thin. So thin that you could cross it without even realizing. It's like you're both a powder keg, just waiting for the right spark, the right moment. And then—boom!—everything changes, and all that tension turns into something far more volatile...or something far more beautiful."

I look into her eyes, and it feels like I'm the one who's been seen, like she's looking into the very depths of my soul. It's both comforting and disconcerting.

"You're talking like a poet."

She squeezes my hand. "You two might have your differences, maybe even deep grudges, but sometimes those passionate feelings can flip into something else, something you might not be ready to face but perhaps should."

My mind goes back to last night, to the feel of Holly's lips on mine, the way her body melded into mine, and then how she looked at me with her stormy eyes afterward.

My mother gives me a knowing look. "You don't have to lie to me. But whatever is going on, don't mess it up. Don't let your fears dictate your actions. If there's a chance for something real with her, don't let it slip away. You might regret it for the rest of your life."

I swallow hard. I've had my fair share of regret, and the thought of adding Holly to that list terrifies me.

I don't say anything, but she knows I understand.

She smiles, her eyes filled with a blend of mischief and wisdom that only a mother could muster. "Good. Now, let's see if these doctors are any good."

THIRTY-ONE

HOLLY

"Jackie, for the love of God, we are not buying inflatable elves for the lawn!"

"Why the hell not? They're cute, festive, and they'll make your Mom's house the talk of the town." She pouts while holding up two ludicrously large inflatable elves, each grinning as if they know a secret you don't.

"Those things are the stuff of nightmares." I try to navigate around a mountain of tinsel that someone abandoned in the middle of the aisle.

My mom, ever the diplomat, chimes in, "How about we compromise and just go for some extra lights instead?"

Jackie considers this, deflates a little—much like I hope those elves will—and then nods. "Fine, but I'm holding both of you responsible if we lose the unspoken but intensely serious neighborhood Christmas decoration war."

"It's a burden we'll have to bear."

We're at Gary's Seasonal Wonderland, the all-year-round holiday store that has somehow managed to stay in business in our small town for over a decade. I've always loved this store, but my feet are aching after a morning of gift shopping.

"Oooh, look at these scented candles!" Mom exclaims, picking up a jar and sniffing it. "Frosted Cranberry, sounds exotic."

Jackie raises an eyebrow. "If by exotic you mean it smells like my grandma's potpourri had a love child with a fruit salad, then sure."

Ignoring her, my mom puts the candle in our already overloaded cart.

"Mom, your house already looks like Christmas threw up on it. Why do you need more decorations?"

"These aren't all for me. Brenda is allowed to come home in two days. God knows Sean is already working himself ragged." I ignore the slight spasm in my chest at the mention of his name. I haven't seen or heard from him since the hospital last week. I try not to dwell on it, try not to feel the slight ache in my ribs, but it hurts. I can admit that much.

The cottage still faintly smells of him. The silence from him is unsettling, and my thoughts drift dangerously towards the man-shaped void he's left in my life.

It's so ridiculous, but my heart has severed all connection to my brain on this one. I'm walking aimlessly into unknown territory.

It's just a little crush. I haven't been home in so long, I'm clinging to something familiar, particularly after the breakup with Adam.

Adam!

It's the first time I've thought about him since the dress up party at Molly's.

"I was thinking we could clean the place up and put out some decorations for when she gets home," my mother continues, knocking me out of my reverie.

"That's really lovely, Mom. Count me in."

Jackie leans over. "A chance to invade Sean's domestic territory? Count me in too."

"He doesn't even live there anymore. Mountain man's got a cabin," I tell her, the words sounding more acidic than I meant them to.

My mother turns to me, her eyes a little wide. "Have you seen it?"

Jackie crosses her arms over her chest, blowing a curl from her face. "Yeah, Holl. Have you seen it?"

I discreetly flip her the finger while smiling at my mother. "No. Mark told me Sean built the place a couple of years ago."

"You should see it. It's amazing. Ask him for a tour. I'm sure he won't mind."

I would rather pull my eyelashes out, but now I'm more curious that I should be.

The thought of being in Sean's space, among his things, is both terrifying and intoxicating. My imagination runs wild for a second. I bet it's all rugged and masculine, filled with leather and wood and...

God, stop it, Holly.

I shake myself back to reality, double-checking to make sure I haven't actually drooled on myself. That man might be the death of me.

THIRTY-TWO

We're nearing the finish line at Brenda's house, each of us taking on a different domestic battlefield. Mom tackled the kitchen, transforming it from a dull cooking space into a culinary winter wonderland. She even managed to hang mistletoe in the doorways, because according to her, "You never know when you'll need a smooch." Jackie took on the living room, strategically placing tinsel in all the wrong places and managing to erect a Christmas tree that leans precariously to one side. I was left with the bathroom, and let me tell you, tinsel does not belong there. Yet here we are.

"You guys, we're almost done. Do we have any of those pine-scented air fresheners left?" I call out as I finish placing some Christmas-themed towels next to the sink.

"I used the last one to make the trash can smell like a forest," Jackie announces from the living room, sounding absurdly pleased with herself.

"I think we've managed to turn Brenda's house into the North Pole's southern annex," Mom says, stepping back to admire her handiwork in the kitchen. "Wouldn't you say?"

"I'd say it's Christmas on steroids," I reply, giving a nod of approval. "If Santa ever needed a vacation home, this would be it."

Just then, Jackie trots in from the living room, holding a string of lights that blink so erratically they could induce a seizure. "I found these in the garage. Think they're too much?"

Mom and I exchange glances before bursting into laughter. "At this point, what's too much?"

"Great! Then I'm going to go hang these over the fireplace," Jackie says, trotting back to the living room. "The more, the merrier!"

Mom turns to me, wiping her hands on a festive dish towel. "Brenda is going to love it."

"Or have a heart attack from sensory overload," I add, examining a candy cane I find in a dish on the coffee table.

"You think Sean will like it?" Mom asks, almost as if reading my mind.

"How would I know what he thinks?" I say a bit too quickly, averting my eyes.

She just smirks, a look that says she knows me far better than I care to admit. "Oh, no reason. He's just been worried about his mom, that's all. I thought the festive atmosphere might lift his spirits."

"I think the only thing that could lift his spirits is if the woods came alive and started serenading him with nature songs." I immediately regret opening my mouth as her eyes narrow a little.

Uh-oh.

"You haven't been very fair to him, you know," she says softly, not pushing but making a point.

"This is about Brenda, not Sean. Can we focus, please?"

What is it with mother's and always being able to see through the bullshit?

I step away from the kitchen, wielding my duster like a wand as I move to the bookshelves that line one wall of Brenda's cozy den. This was always my favorite spot in her house growing up—a sanctuary of stories. She always had a book to recommend, whether I was dealing with teenage angst or a difficult math problem. Somehow, literature had all the answers.

Taking my time, I begin dusting each book, pulling some out slightly to wipe down their covers. I get lost in the titles, some classics, some modern, many with worn edges and cracked spines that speak to how well-loved they are. But then, as I reach the middle shelf, my heart catches in my throat.

There, stacked neatly together, are the books I've written. Every single one of them, from my first self-published novella to my most recent bestseller. I pull them out, holding them like fragile artifacts, each a piece of my soul laid bare. My heart pounds as I open the front cover of the first book I ever wrote. Inside is a small Christmas card from Sean to his mother.

"She's doing it, Ma. Merry Christmas. Love, Sean."

I can't help but cover my mouth as I read it, my eyes stinging. Sean has been collecting my books for his mother.

I quickly flip through another, pulling out a Christmas card that reads: "Ma, this one is about a spy who falls in love. It's a little far-fetched, but I'm sure you'll love it. Merry Christmas. Love, Sean."

I reach for my most recent book, my hands trembling. This was the one that made it to number one on several bestseller lists. I carefully open it, afraid of what I might find but unable to stop myself. Inside is another card: "Our girl did it, Ma. Number One. Merry Christmas. Love, Sean."

I close the book softly, putting it back on the shelf, my hands lingering on the cover. I feel like I've intruded on a private moment, on something intimate and sacred between a son and his mother. Yet, at the same time, I can't shake the sense of warmth that fills me, chasing away the residual cold I've felt for too long.

Upstairs, I check each room, but my eyes are drawn to a door across the hallway. It's Sean's childhood bedroom. A forbidden place during our teenage years, and even more so now. But something pulls me towards it, some mix of nostalgia and a burning curiosity.

I press my hand lightly against the door and slowly push it open. The room is bathed in a soft afternoon light. The walls are painted a muted shade of blue, with faded band posters and sports memorabilia dotting the shelves. A worn-out rug with intricate patterns covers the floor, and a wooden desk sits in one corner, cluttered with old notebooks and a dusty desktop computer. There's a shelving unit filled with trophies, mostly from soccer and basketball.

Moving closer to the bed, I sit down on its edge, feeling the softness underneath. My fingers absently trace the objects on the nightstand—a leather-bound journal, a vintage alarm clock, and an old black and white photograph of a younger Sean with Brenda, both smiling. There's also a dog-eared copy of a book I recognize. It's one of mine. The realization makes me smile, mixed with a twinge of embarrassment.

I remember all the whispered rumors from high

school. How every girl used to fantasize about what it would be like to be in Sean Colson's bedroom. Back then, he was the guy every girl either wanted to date or wanted to be. He still is. The mysterious, bad boy allure he radiated made this room the epicenter of most teenage daydreams, including my own.

I lie back, sinking into his bed, staring at the ceiling.

My head hurts from trying to reconcile the man I thought I knew to the man who spent days in my bed and kept a close eye on my career.

Somehow, I feel like I know everything about him while knowing nothing at all.

There's a faint noise downstairs, muffled voices. I assume it's just Jackie and Mom, probably locked in another debate about where the furniture should go. But when the door creaks open, my heart stalls in my chest.

For a split second, he doesn't notice me. He's a bit rough around the edges with his hand running anxiously through his tousled hair and then down his face. His jaw is tense, and there's a weariness in his posture.

But then, he turns.

Our eyes lock. The world falls away, replaced by a visceral connection so intense it steals my breath. The surprise in his eyes is quickly replaced by a look I can't quite place—pain, longing, and an undeniable heat. There's a vulnerability in that gaze, and it's directed at me while I lie sprawled out on his childhood bed.

The weight of the moment hangs heavy between us, charged and electric. Neither of us moves, caught in a silent dance.

I think about getting up, but I can't move. I'm pinned under the weight of his stare. Then he walks over to the edge of the bed, staring down at me. I swear I forget how to breathe.

He looks tired, and for once, I don't want to tease him about it. I want to reach out and ease away the line between his brows with my fingers.

He tips his chin. "Move over, Squirt."

My eyes go wide before his words register, and I move over on the bed. He flops down, his forearm resting over his eyes. The mattress dips and my body presses to his side.

Minutes pass, neither of us speaking. I think he's fallen asleep just before he speaks up. "Thanks for getting the place ready. Your mom is showing her around. She loves it."

I swallow the urge to reach out and touch him. "It's no problem. How is she doing?"

He shrugs. "Doctors still need to do some tests, but it's definitely her memory. At least now we can get the help she needs."

"I'm sorry, Sean."

He doesn't reply but drops his hand and stares up at the ceiling. His fingertips brush mine. I try my best not to react to the burn.

His eyes are on my face, but I refuse to look at him. I can't. I'm too afraid of what I'll see. I even try to resist when he takes my chin and tilts my face to the side. I keep my eyes on the ceiling.

"Look at me, Holl."

Inhaling, I hold my breath and look at him. I keep looking. We still don't speak.

I wait for him to say something, but he doesn't. I wait for him to acknowledge that things have changed and we're the only ones to blame, but he doesn't.

A part of me wants to shout at him. A bigger part

of me wants to feel his mouth on mine again.

I know we only have minutes if we're lucky before the bubble we've created pops.

It's probably best to do it now so I know when it's coming. "I should go."

His eyes drop to my lips. "No, you shouldn't."

Before I can process the weight of his words, his fingers tighten gently on my chin, pulling my face closer to his. There's a hint of desperation in his eyes, a silent plea for understanding, for connection. But there's also that familiar fire, the one that always danced between us, threatening to consume everything in its path.

His breath ghosts over my face, and for a split second, the world outside this room ceases to exist. As our faces inch closer, the tension becomes palpable, a tangible force pressing on my chest, making it hard to breathe.

His breath is on my skin, his warmth seeping into me like a drug. My body is screaming at me to stay, to give in to the temptation. But my mind is telling me to run, to get out of here before it's too late.

"We can't do this."

"I know," he replies but he's getting closer. "I fucking know we can't."

He kisses me anyway, my objections quickly forgotten as his mouth finds mine. It feels foreign and familiar all at once. It's the most delicious burn.

We're both drowning in a sea of emotions, an undertow of need and desperation pulling us further in. His hands cup my face, holding me still, as if he's afraid I'll pull away. But there's no chance of that. Not when every cell in my body is gravitating towards him, not when every past grievance seems insignificant in comparison to this moment.

His lips are soft but demanding, tasting faintly of coffee and a hint of mint. They move over mine, coaxing, teasing, until I'm completely lost in the sensation. There's no thinking, no analyzing, just pure, raw feeling. His tongue sweeps into my mouth, deepening the kiss, and I groan in response, letting go of all restraint.

His hands leave my face, traveling down to my waist, pulling me closer to him. I can feel the hard planes of his chest against mine, the rapid beat of his heart matching my own. My fingers clutch at his shirt, needing something to anchor me, to ground me, because everything feels so overwhelmingly intense.

But as quickly as the moment escalated, reality crashes back in. The weight of the situation, the consequences of our actions, everything he said, and everything he didn't. It all floods back. I pull away first, gasping for air, my eyes wide as they meet his equally dazed ones.

"We can't," I whisper again, my voice shaky.

Sean nods, his face flushed, eyes clouded with lust and confusion. "I know. I'm sorry."

"It's not just you," I admit, my fingers touching my swollen lips, the heat of the kiss still lingering.

His eyes follow the movement of my fingers before he looks away, his hand rubbing at the back of his neck. "I know. I'm sorry," he says again, the words sounding like a broken record.

I want to tell him it's okay, that we can forget about it and move on like nothing happened. But the reality is, we can't.

"I should go." The words feel like a punch to the gut.

He nods, not looking at me. "Yeah. You should."

I get up from the bed, my legs feeling like jelly. I want to say something, to make this situation less awkward, but my mind is blank.

I've been such an idiot. A couple of days with him, and I've allowed him to get under my skin. He wasn't even gentle about it. He clawed his way in and made his mark.

I leave, wishing he would call me back. Wishing he would say something, anything.

But he doesn't.

THIRTY-THREE

Just over a week to Christmas and I'm sitting at my parent's table trying not to choke on my mash potato while simultaneously holding myself back from stabbing my brother with a fork.

He glares at me from where he sits. Rachel obviously knows what's going on. Why wouldn't she? She's his wife. But her gaze is ping ponging between me and Mark like she's preparing for a war to break out.

He's judging me. My brother. I'm three seconds away from reminding him of how much of a whore he was in college, but I won't do that to Rachel.

My parents appear oblivious to our staring contest, arguing back and forth about the strategy for the Christmas games.

Rachel leans forward. "Will you two stop it? This is ridiculous. You're siblings. It's Christmas. And Mark," she whispers, turning to him. "Holly is a grown woman. She can do whatever…" Rachel winks at me. "Or whomever she wants."

My face flushes a furious red, a mix of anger and embarrassment.

"And Holly," she continues. "You have to understand, your brother is hurt. It was a shock…to all of us."

I shrink back in my chair, feeling like a child getting in trouble for coloring on the walls.

"Anyone for dessert?" My mother speaks up, still completely unaware.

I never thought I would say this but thank God for the Christmas games. They always keep her distracted.

"I'll get it." I willingly volunteer, maybe a little too enthusiastically because she's eyeing me like I'm ill.

"I'll help," Mark says, getting to his feet with a fake ass smile.

"Lovely," Mom mumbles, confused. "Trifle is in the fridge."

I'm two steps into the kitchen when I feel Mark hot on my heels. I spin around, my frustration finally bubbling to the surface. He's always been like this. I get it. He's my big brother, he sees it as his job to look out for me, but in this instance, I don't need him to. Rachel was right. I'm an adult.

"What?" I hiss.

His face is flushed now too, his hands clenching at his sides. "My best friend. Really? What happened to you hating each other?"

"We do hate each other," I fight back, but my voice fails to carry the heat it once used to when I uttered those words.

I don't hate Sean. Not anymore. Truth is my heart is breaking. The sharp shards have broken away and are clawing at my flesh. This hurts, and I hate that it does.

"Really?" He leans back against the counter, those judgy eyes of his never leaving mine. "Didn't look that way when I walked in on you in bed together. What's next? You going to tell me it was just a hug?"

I pull him further into the kitchen, checking that no one heard. "Will you hush?"

There's so many emotions swirling in my chest, I'm not sure which one will win.

"Why?"

I know he's not talking about why I want him to be quiet. He wants to know why I did it. It's a reasonable question. It's also one I wish I had the answer to. The only answer I have, I'm pretty sure my brother won't want to hear.

What am I going to say? It started because I was horny, and Sean is really hot.

That answer is insulting even to me. It wasn't some one-night stand with a guy I'd never see again.

It was more.

It was so much more.

Yet, I can't put my finger on it. It's too much. How do I explain to my brother that Sean makes me feel like all the pieces of myself I had lost, all those pieces that were broken and scattered around… Sean helped me find them, and I felt more like myself with him than I have in a long time.

I can't stand to see the hurt in his eyes, so I turn around like the coward I am to grab the trifle out of the fridge.

"You're not walking away from this." He hurries to my side, nudging me to grab the bowl out of my hand.

And then it happens.

He drops the bowl on the counter with too much force and the lovely, smooth cream that my mother worked so hard on, splatters… All. Over. Me.

I gasp, standing back, but it's too late. I taste it on my tongue, see it dangling from my hair, and don't get me started on my clothes.

"What the actual fuck is wrong with you?" I've lost all notions of keeping my voice down.

War has broken out in the Winter household.

Mark's eyes widen in shock, a mixture of horror and an attempt to suppress laughter evident on his face. "Holly, I... I didn't mean to—"

But I'm already scooping a generous handful of the ruined dessert, the sponge soaking in jelly, and with a wild swing, I fling it right at him. It splatters across his face and chest, the red jelly dripping down his shirt.

"Oh, it's on." In seconds, he retaliates with a spoonful of the creamy mess, which lands with a splat right in the middle of my forehead.

The next few minutes are a blur of flying trifle and escalating voices. We're both drenched in layers of cream, custard, fruit, and sponge cake, the kitchen looking like a battlefield of dessert carnage.

Suddenly, the door swings open, and our audience expands beyond just Rachel. Little Mia laughs her little head off before scooping some cream off the floor and eating it. Our parent's gape at the scene, their expressions ranging from amused to shocked.

"Holly! Mark! What in heaven's name—?" our mother gasps, her eyes wide as she takes in the chaos. She rushes forward, trying to play referee, but unfortunately, she's caught in the crossfire, and a blob of custard lands comically on her cheek.

"Mom!" we exclaim in unison, our food fight coming to an abrupt halt.

She wipes the custard off her face. "Enough! Both

of you, into the living room, now!"

We're scolded and ushered out like two misbehaving children, leaving everyone behind bewildered and a kitchen that's seen better days. Our mother follows us, grabbing each of our arms, not hard, but enough to let us know she means business.

Forcing us into the living room, we face each other but avoid eye contact.

She stands, hands on her hips "I don't know what's gotten into you two, but you're adults, not bratty toddlers. Sort out whatever this is. You're siblings. You're supposed to have each other's backs, not throw food at each other. And for the love of God, don't sit or touch anything."

We both mumble apologies, still not meeting each other's eyes.

"I'll be back, and we will clean up the kitchen together," she warns before leaving the room.

Silence envelops us, punctuated only by our heavy breaths. I steal a glance at Mark, and despite the mess, there's a vulnerability in his eyes I haven't seen in years.

"I'm sorry," I breathe, feeling the sting of tears as I drop my gaze to the floor.

"I'm just confused. Last I heard, Adam was in town trying to win you back. What happened there?"

I knew I would need to have this conversation sooner or later. I just preferred later. "Why can't this family accept that me and Adam are finished?"

"But why? You were ready to walk down the aisle to him. It was overnight and everything finished, and you decided you were moving home. There was no explanation."

"What's got you all defensive for Adam? You never even liked him."

"You're right. But you did. You loved him, so I chose to accept it."

A hard lump lodges in my throat, and no matter how hard I fight to swallow around it, nothing works.

"Holly?" he pleads, his voice booming.

"He cheated on me." I suck in a breath like I haven't inhaled pure air in months. It feels oddly satisfying to say it out loud.

Mark simply blinks at me, his face slowly morphing from shock to something more lethal. "Excuse me?"

I've started. No point in stopping now. "I forgave him the first time. He promised he would stop. That it was a one-time thing. He was nervous about the wedding. He was under pressure at work. There are more excuses I can't think of right now, but he used all of them. I became his entire world for a while. But every time he left, I would get this knot in my stomach, and I felt like I couldn't breathe until he was back again. He would hug me, and I would instinctively wait for the scent of another woman's perfume. And then the same warning signs came back. He stayed late at work. Lipstick on the collar. All the cliches, they were there, and he didn't even try to hide it. I was expected to be the good wife and put up with it. After all, I was the woman he was coming home to. But I couldn't do it. He was doing it long before he was caught, and long after. There were so many women." I throw my hands out. "You're right. I chose him. I was willing to spend the rest of my life with him, and only him. Only he wasn't willing to do the same for me."

I'm surprised that my eyes are dry when I finish. Maybe I'm cried out.

"Holly," he breathes out, his hands balling to fists before he runs his fingers through his hair. "I'm going to fucking kill him."

"No, you're not." I shake my head. "Besides, Sean got there first. He broke his nose."

Mark nods, not surprised.

"Whatever it was between me and Sean is finished. I won't let it get between your friendship. I know he's like a brother to you."

"And you're my sister," he cuts me off before I can continue, his voice softer.

"I'm sorry," I repeat.

"You have feelings for him."

It's not a question, and my heart thunders in my chest so hard I stumble back. "No."

"Don't lie to me. You never could so don't try now."

"I'm not a little girl anymore. I don't need your protection."

"No, you're not a little girl. But you're my little sister, and I will always look out for you first. I've taken pride in that job since Mom and Dad brought you home from the hospital almost twenty-eight years ago. Don't take it away from me now."

A stray tear falls, and I let it.

Thankfully, he softens at the sight of it and pulls me into his arms. "You're my best friend," he mumbles against my head.

I look up at him. "What about Sean?"

"Okay, you're my best female friend."

"Rachel?"

"Oh, for fuck's sake. Don't ever tell her I said that. She'll have my balls." I hold back a laugh. "You're my favorite sister."

"I'm your only sister."

"Exactly, so best friend is built in. It's been me and

you since day one. And I do love Sean. He's my brother. I won't choose sides. You've made it clear that you're both adults, so you both need to figure it out." He looks down at his ruined clothes. "In a more civilized way than we did."

I grimace, still tasting trifle on my tongue.

It's good.

Well done, Mom.

I throw out my hands. "We've already figured it out. Sean knows what he wants, and it isn't me."

Mark arches his brow, looking at me like I'm stupid. "Really?"

"Yes."

"Open your eyes, Holl."

"What?"

"You're playing blind. Sean will push you away. It's what he does. But I've never met anyone more equipped to push back. You're both pros at it." If he's trying to save my feelings, he shouldn't. "Sean can be complicated."

"Tell me about it."

He rolls his eyes. "What I was going to say is that he took it on himself over the years to look out for you too. And somewhere along the way, I saw something change in the way he looked out for you."

His gaze is sincere, and for a moment, I see the protective big brother who used to check for monsters under my bed. "I mean," he pauses, choosing his words carefully, "Sean's always been there, right? Always around, always annoying, always...Sean. But a while back, it started to feel different. How he talked about you, how he looked at you, how he got all weird when other guys were mentioned around you."

I frown, trying to decipher his words.

"He has grown up thinking he's not good enough for much. That shit doesn't leave you." I think back on my conversation I had with Sean about Ashley, and my heart breaks. "I'm saying maybe he's been pushing you away because he's scared. Scared because his feelings for you changed. Because you're not just his best friend's little sister anymore. You're you."

Then I think back on everything he said, and everything he didn't. Sean has never been one not to go after what he wanted. If he wanted me, he would have said it.

For now, I push it to the back of my mind. It's a problem for tomorrow.

I blow out a breath, feeling a headache bloom behind my eyes.

"And us?" I ask, smiling weakly.

"Will always have each other. That won't change. I was just...traumatized."

I can't help but burst out laughing. "Traumatized?"

"I knock on all doors now. Lesson learned."

THIRTY-FOUR

I'm moping. It's sad. I'm miserable to look at. My hair has seen better days, there's mascara under my eyes that I continue to clean, but somehow always reappears, and these flannel Christmas pajamas remind me of Sean, but they're comfy.

The saddest part of all: I'm sulking because of him.

The annual Christmas Games are today, but I feel myself coming down with a make-believe flu, so I texted my mother to let her know I won't make it.

My beautiful little cottage feels empty. I wouldn't have noticed if he had never occupied it. His presence, his stature, his personality, it was all too big and filled the days and nights completely. It's impossible not to notice his absence now.

I miss him, and it's stupid.

There's an echo of silence. Not the usual serene quiet of Pine Falls, but a deafening silence that screams of loneliness. The walls are familiar, but they're also witnesses to memories I'm trying to escape.

Every corner, every shadow, whispers of him.

And just like the cottage, my heart feels more hollow. It's an emptiness I didn't anticipate, a void I hadn't known existed. It feels as if a part of me is missing—a part I didn't even know I'd given away.

I miss him, and it's stupid.

I curl up on the sofa, wrapping the blanket around me, as if trying to shield myself from my own feelings. A part of me wants to scream, to let out this frustrating pain. Another part just wants to forget, to move on, and pretend as if Sean Colson never happened.

But deep down, buried beneath layers of pride and stubbornness, I know one undeniable truth: I've fallen for him, and there's no turning back.

Bang. Bang. Bang.

There's a knock on the door.

I freeze, staring at the wooden barrier between me and the world outside.

Another knock, more urgent this time.

Sighing, I push myself off the couch, shuffling towards the door. Pulling it open, I'm met with the last person I expected—or wanted—to see right now.

Sean.

Of course.

He looks... different. Not in a bad way, but there's a shadow behind those familiar whiskey eyes. And when he scans my appearance, his gaze heating with that usual intensity, it falters for a moment, replaced by a hint of pity.

Pity?

From him?

Before he can utter a word, I cross my arms defensively. "Don't credit yourself for my delightful appearance. I'm sick," I declare, followed by a very convincing fake cough.

241

He doesn't smile, doesn't mock. Instead, he closes his eyes and takes a deep, measured breath. As if seeing me like this hurts him. As if every inch of him wants to say something but he's holding back. When his eyes open again, they're soft, vulnerable.

"You're not sick, Squirt," he whispers.

I shiver. The cold air from outside wraps around me, curling its fingers into the warmth of my living room and dragging it out into the frosty afternoon. I wish I could close the door and the void that he brought with him, but I'm glued to the spot, trapped by the gravitational pull.

"What are you doing here?" My voice quivers, sounding far more vulnerable than I intended. "Because I've already got some emotional whiplash. If you're here to give me more, please don't bother."

His jaw tenses. The sharp cut of it is even more pronounced, and in that second, I can't read him. Is he angry? Frustrated? Or does he want to correct me like a child?

"For fuck's sake," he mutters, more to himself than to me. "Get dressed, Holl."

I cross my arms tighter over my chest, attempting to summon some semblance of defiance. "No. I'm not going anywhere. I've got spiced rum ready to go into my hot cocoa. I'm good for today."

His eyes darken, and there's a subtle shift in his demeanor. "The Christmas Games are on today."

I tilt my chin up, refusing to be cowed. "Great. Have fun. I'm sure I'll hear all about it."

His patience, already thin, seems to snap. He runs a hand through his dark hair, leaving it in a disheveled mess. The sight of it —a Sean not in control—is oddly satisfying. "Get. Dressed. Holly. You're going to the games."

My temper flares, heat rising in my cheeks. "Fuck you. Who the hell do you think you are?"

He's on me in two strides, his hands pressing into the door frame on either side of my head, effectively trapping me. His face is mere inches from mine, close enough that I can feel the warmth of his breath and see the fire in his eyes.

"I'm not fucking worth whatever it is you're doing to yourself," he rasps, his voice rough and filled with an emotion I can't place. "Get. Dressed."

I blink, trying to process his words and what they mean. Why does he care so much? Why can't he just let me be?

The ball is in my court now. I can slam the door, or I can face the chaos.

Please, I'm not facing anything in these pajamas, so I shut the door and walk away.

I'm three steps in when the door swings open again. I spin around, my hands balling into fists.

"I knew not fixing those locks would come in handy." He smirks at me, and I suddenly feel like weak prey in a lion's den.

He strides toward me with purpose, his long legs eating up the distance between us. Before I can react, he wraps his fingers around my wrist, his grip firm but not painful. The heat of his touch seeps through the thin fabric of my sleeve.

"Why the hell do you have to be so stubborn?"

Instead of pulling away or arguing back, I find a mischievous smile tugging at my lips. Looking up at him through my lashes, I let the silence stretch. The tension between us is palpable, like a live wire, and every second I remain quiet, I can see the irritation growing in his eyes.

That seems to annoy him even more. With a swift motion, he pulls me in the direction of my bedroom.

"Get dressed," he orders, releasing my wrist and giving me a little push toward my closet.

Taking a deep breath to steady my racing heart, I whirl around to face him. "You can't just manhandle me into doing what you want."

"Don't do this," he murmurs, his voice gentler now. "Not for me. Not for anyone. Get dressed and you can fight me in the car on the way. You can fight me all day if you want. Just fucking fight me, baby."

I hate admitting he's right, but he is. I fight. It's my nature, but I've been wallowing, and I probably stink.

I yank my hand away. "Fine. Give me twenty minutes. You can wait in the car."

I've only gotten his scent out of the place. He can't be here again.

The slightest smile tugs his mouth upward, but he doesn't argue. Instead, he dips his chin and walks away.

I've noticed he's quite good at that.

THIRTY-FIVE

"Gather 'round, folks!" My mom, dressed in a criminally ugly Christmas sweater, shouts above the din.

Before I can blink, we're all sporting them. Elves on parade.

Mark nudges me, "She bought these right after her first email, didn't she?"

Speaking of those emails. I've been dodging daily reminders and pep talk messages for weeks. My mother's got every little detail planned out, including color-coded charts and schedules. Seriously, if she put this much effort into a military operation, we'd have world peace by now.

The town square is a sea of people, swept up in the chaos of the annual Christmas Games.

Suddenly, Sean's next to me, way too close for comfort. My clarity from the past week is replaced by anger.

One look at his face, and there's a rogue butterfly in my stomach. God, he looks good, but fuck him and his sad, gorgeous smiles.

"We've got some warmup games to begin with. Something to get us in the mood," Mom starts, her eyes sparkling. It's like watching a pressure cooker about to burst.

I'm pretty sure these games are supposed to be fun before everyone gets too competitive, but my mother is already there. She's fit to kill one of us if we mess this up.

"Don't look at me like that, Holly," she warns, reminding me how she used to scold me as a child.

"This is my face, Mom. I look like a bitch to everyone. I can't help it."

"Try. These games are my Olympics."

"Jesus Christ," Sean mutters under his breath as my mother prepares herself.

Three games in, she's at Mrs. Johnson's throat over whether *Die Hard* is a Christmas classic. (It is. Fight me.)

After some minor hiccups with carol names and movie quotes, Mom's competitiveness has ignited a feud with the Johnsons. They're throwing daggers so severe I almost feel them. Fuck it. The Johnson's kids were always little shits growing up. This is war. They glare. We glare. It's the most festive standoff Pine Falls has ever seen.

Then, we've got a ludicrous game of charades. Dad's efforts to mime *Three Wise Men* has everyone in splits. He looks more like he was trying to swat three particularly aggressive bees.

As the buzz from the prior games starts to wane, my mother's voice pierces the chatter, "It's finally time for the treasure hunt. It's the last game of the day, and we're tied with the Johnsons. This is serious." She claps her hands like a giddy schoolgirl. "We're going to split up into pairs. Me and your father. Mark, you go with Jackie. Holly and Sean, try not to kill each other."

Sean leans in. "You ready for this?"

"I was born ready," I reply, maybe too quickly.

Mom glares at us, a silent warning that speaks a thousand words. "This is still a team effort. The first team to have everyone back, wins. If you children make me lose to the Johnson's, it's grounds to disown you."

Mark arches a brow at me. It's not the first time she's threatened to disown us.

Mom hands out the clues. Sean unfolds ours, reading aloud, "Where the town clock stands tall, you'll find your next fall."

"Oh, come on," I say, "That's obviously the clock tower."

"Well then, lead the way, detective."

We begin a tense walk toward the clock tower, neither of us willing to concede the lead. Every time Sean's longer strides start to edge him ahead, I elbow my way back to his side, refusing to be left behind.

Just as we're approaching the tower, he stops abruptly, causing me to nearly run into him. He unfolds the next instruction with a smirk, savoring each word, "Partner must be blindfolded and guided only by the other's voice."

He holds out the blindfold with a cocky grin. "Ladies first?"

"In your dreams, Colson," I retort, snatching the blindfold from his hands. "You're up."

I tie the blindfold around him a tad tighter than necessary. "Remember," I say sweetly, "No cheating."

He scoffs, "Wouldn't dream of it."

Blindfolding him, I take a moment to savor the

sight: Sean, usually so in control, now reliant on me.

Perfect.

"Alright, big guy, take three steps forward and then...twirl."

His lips twitch in annoyance, but he complies, spinning awkwardly.

"Left. No, your other left!"

He grumbles, shifting direction. "I swear, if you're making me dance just for the fun of it—"

"What? It's part of the game, promise."

As we navigate towards the next clue, I'm acutely aware of the warmth radiating off his body. It's distracting, and for a moment, I lose focus.

"Step to the right," I instruct, but what I should've said was left. He crashes into a hedge, his arms flailing wildly to regain his balance.

I wince. "Sorry! My bad!"

He tilts his head in my direction, blindfolded eyes somehow still intimidating.

I regain my composure, guiding him more seriously now. "Okay, ten steps straight, then turn right."

He moves cautiously, taking slow, measured steps. It's evident he's not trusting me completely. Can't blame him.

After what feels like forever to take a couple of steps, the next instruction emerges. "For your next clue: partners must tie two of their legs together and hop to where mistletoe and wine combine."

He groans, removing the blindfold and squinting against the light. "You're kidding, right?"

I smirk, pulling out a long, red ribbon from the envelope. "Not in the slightest. Prepare to get cozy."

I tie the ribbon around his thighs and intertwine the loose ends around my own.

His hard stare prevents me from staying still for more than a few seconds.

As we take our first awkward hop, I feel his leg brush against mine. Then again. I force my gaze away, focusing instead on the ground directly in front of me. But it's so hard to keep my eyes away. Especially when I can feel his boring a hole in the side of my face.

I mean, look at him. Tall, built, commanding. His broad shoulders. His strong jaw. The way he can hold himself with such confidence.

It's not fair.

My face flushes red at the thought. What the hell is wrong with me?

His arms hang at his sides, his jaw tight.

"It's getting dark. We need to hurry."

And I need to get the hell away from you.

My head fills with the scent of his cologne. Whatever it is, it smells amazing.

The clues lead us around Pine Falls, to the bakery where they make the most mouth-watering cinnamon buns, then to the tiny bridge overlooking Frost River where couples are known to make wishes during the holidays. Thankfully, we're not always tied together. At each spot, I am unnervingly aware of Sean's proximity. The scratch of his stubble, the timbre of his voice, the warmth of his body. It's a continuous reminder of the nights we spent together.

It doesn't help that each new place we visit is bathed in memories. I wish I could say the treasure hunt was a good distraction, but it only amplifies the raw tension between us.

Yet, as much as it pains me to admit it, the ease of our dynamic means we solve each clue faster than the others. Even in our current strained state, our teamwork is pretty damn impressive.

His fingers graze mine as we decode the next hint. I force my mind to concentrate on the words. "Beneath where pine and oak trees meet, and snowmen dance to a silent beat."

Sean squints at the paper. "That's the forest clearing near the old Thompson barn. They always have those wooden snowmen decorations around this time."

"We used to play there as kids," I murmur, more to myself than to him. The memories, much like the unresolved tension, pull at my heart. The clarity of my anger begins to blur, replaced by a warmth I didn't anticipate.

More missteps later, we're outside the maze they build every year for these games.

Yes, they build a damn maze for Christmas games. This town is psychotic. But the first to reach the center, grab the final clue, and make it back, wins.

The walls of the maze swallow the world outside, silencing its exuberance and plunging us into an eerily serene sanctuary. The night's hush is only occasionally disturbed by distant laughter, punctuated by the soft whispers of other people that are in here…somewhere.

In silence, we reach the center with surprising ease, and it's like stepping into another world. Overhead, the moon shines down on a little clearing, illuminating the snowy ground. Encircling the clearing are tall, snow-covered pine trees, like age-old sentinels guarding a treasured secret. In the center stands an old-fashioned well, its stone rim encased in icicles, with a plush red velvet cushion atop it.

I wasn't lying when I said this town is a little over the top.

Sean reaches for the clue, breaking the seal, and

pulling out a parchment.

"In and out, it's all a game, find your way, or face the shame. The exit's where you least expect, a wrong turn, and you'll be wrecked."

I raise an eyebrow. "Well, that's... ominous."

"They never said it'd be easy."

But the once hospitable maze has morphed into a confounding labyrinth, its arms seemingly reshaping themselves, leaving us to wander its grip aimlessly. The cold doesn't help; with every wrong turn, our breaths puff out in increasingly annoyed clouds of frost.

"That snowman's smirking." I point at a particularly cheeky-looking snow sculpture. "I swear this turn was right."

"Right as in correct, or right as in not left?"

I shoot him a withering glare. "Sean, unless you're about to tell me how to get out of here, then keep your mouth shut."

Every so often, I catch him sneaking peeks at me, and the few times our hands brush, sparks fly. Literal sparks because of the static. Damn cold.

It's disorienting. We take several wrong turns, ending up at dead ends or looping back to where we started. At some point, it's clear we're lost, but neither of us wants to admit it.

"We're going in circles," I say, hands on my hips. "I recognize that weird-looking snowman."

"No shit."

The narrow pathways of the maze seem to close in around us, and with every wrong turn, the frustration grows.

"It's this way," I insist, pointing to the left.

He rolls his eyes, his patience clearly wearing thin. "You said that ten minutes ago, and guess what? We ended up at the same damn spot."

"Well, maybe if you'd stop trying to lead and listen for once, we wouldn't be lost!"

In his next breath, he steps closer, cutting off my retreat and trapping me against a cold hedge wall. "You don't want to be here with me, Squirt?"

His use of that nickname hits a raw nerve. "No," I snarl, trying to push past him.

He doesn't budge.

"Because you hate me, right?" His voice is low and challenging.

"Yes," I spit out, glaring up at him.

A tense silence spreads over the maze as our heavy breathing fills the air. His face tightens, rage burning in his midnight gaze.

I take a deep breath, my fingers twitching at my sides. "What's your problem?"

He leans down, crowding me. "You're my problem."

I tip my chin up "I wasn't aware."

"Good for you," he almost snarls. "Because you're all I've been aware of since you came back."

His body presses firmly against mine. It feels like an invitation, or a dare, and I can't help but consider it, despite how wrong it may be. The heat of my frustration mixing with the proximity to him is overwhelming and my head becomes muddled. I should shove him away, tell him this was a mistake, yet my feet remain glued to the ground and my eyes are locked on his as if entranced by some unseen force. His lips are so close they almost brush over mine and added to the frozen air is now his warm breath on my skin. My heart thuds wildly in my chest, and I'm unable to steady myself enough to focus on anything else except for him.

In one swift move, his lips are on mine, and all coherent thought goes out the window. His kiss is demanding and fierce just like I remember, but there's anger, frustration, and something else that makes me melt against him mixed in now too.

Walk away, Holly. You can still walk away.

Suddenly, with a surge of clarity, I wrench away, pushing him off me. The cold hedge brushes against my back as I put distance between us. My breath comes in ragged gasps, my chest heaving as tears sting my eyes.

"Stop. Just stop."

"Holly..."

"You told me there was nothing between us. You made it clear. So why? Why do this now?"

He runs a hand through his hair, clearly at a loss for words. The Sean I know always has an answer, always has a snarky remark at the ready. But now, he's silent.

"You can't keep doing this. Pulling me in and then pushing me away."

He doesn't say a word.

Nothing.

His silence is loud enough.

"What is this? I'm not someone you can call in the middle of the night when you feel a little lonely and want someone to warm your bed. So, tell me, what is this? Because if it's nothing then it has to stop. Is it nothing?"

My blood gushes behind my ears, the only sound is the pounding of my heart. I want to shake him, pound my fists against his chest.

I need him to say something.

But when he does, I want to take it back. I want to

run and hide. I want to clutch at my chest, so it doesn't hurt.

He lifts his head, those whiskey eyes suddenly detach and grow cold. "It's nothing."

My heart plummets, the weight of his words sending a shockwave of pain throughout my body. The cold, biting wind no longer feels like the worst thing against my skin; it's his words, and the raw honesty with which he delivers them.

I feel the sting of tears, hot and bitter against my cold cheeks. All the passion, the heat from a few moments ago, feels like a distant memory. A mirage.

"Right," I whisper shakily, wrapping my arms around myself. "I should have known better."

He reaches out, the desperation evident in his gesture. But I step back, the space between us growing both physically and emotionally. The maze's claustrophobic walls press in, making the divide between us seem vast.

Every fiber of my being wants to believe he's lying, that there's something more behind his words. But I can't let myself hope anymore. The hurt is too deep, the wounds too fresh.

Taking one last look at him, a figure now lost amid the twinkling lights and tall hedges, I turn away, navigating the maze by instinct. Each turn, each step, takes me further from him, even as my heart aches to go back. But sometimes, the hardest path is the only one to take.

The silence of the night is interrupted by distant laughter and Christmas carols. I'm not even aware of which way I'm going. I'm only aware of his footsteps behind me, his eyes on my back. He doesn't try to catch up. He simply remains a safe distance away.

A breath of relief gushes from my lungs as I finally emerge from the maze and rush back to the town square.

I might have found my way out of the labyrinth, but my heart remains lost, somewhere deep inside, in a twist and turn I can't navigate.

Once we're back in the square, I realize everyone is already out.

How long were we in there?

Have we lost?

Fuck it. I don't care.

"Where have you been?" Dad's voice reaches me.

I force a smile, pushing the emotions down. "Guess we just got a little lost."

Jackie wraps an arm around my shoulders. "You okay?"

"I think I'm finally at the get drunk and forget stage."

Her mouth turns down briefly before she pulls me into a comforting hug. "I'm sorry, babe."

From the corner of my eye, I see Sean rejoining the group. I don't turn to look, but his presence is palpable. Jackie seems to sense it too. She glances between Sean and me, determination in her eyes.

"Let's get wasted," she declares, taking my hand and leading me away.

THIRTY-SIX

SEAN

The night is cold, the sky ink-black above, littered with a smattering of stars. My old pickup rumbles beneath me, the radio crooning some melancholic country ballad that's doing nothing to lift the weight from my chest.

Working late into the evening usually clears my mind, especially during this pre-Christmas rush. The workshop should have been an escape. The rhythmic hum of machinery, the scent of fresh-cut lumber—it's always been my grounding point. But tonight? Nothing works.

The winding road home offers no relief. The

engine's growl can't drown out the reel of memories playing in my mind.

Holly.

She's everywhere. In the shape of the shadows, in the corner of my eye, in every damned thought that pops into my head. God, the memory of her under me, her skin heating up with every touch, her back arching in response, the soft moans escaping her lips. It's intoxicating. Maddening.

And then there's the maze. Her eyes. They've always been so expressive, but I've never seen them quite like that—vulnerable, raw, hurt. I could tell myself a thousand times that what happened was for the best. That pushing her away was the right move. But that damned look in her eyes says otherwise. It accuses, questions, and most of all, it wounds.

Since she's been back, every damn day is a test. It's like living with a ghost. There are moments I think I've moved on, that I've put the past to rest. Then, there she is—invading my thoughts, drawing me back in, challenging everything I've built in her absence.

It was simpler when she wasn't around. My days were predictable, nights restful. But now? It's like walking through a minefield. One wrong move and everything blows up.

I have to shake this off. Find a way to get back to where I was before she waltzed back into town and disrupted everything. But as I sink deeper into my thoughts, the undeniable truth hits me: I don't want to go back. Not really. Not when the alternative is this raw, this real, this…alive.

My grip on the steering wheel tightens as my headlights illuminate two women ahead, both doubled over with laughter. As they squint into the blinding light, my heart skips a beat, and my teeth grind together. "What the fuck are they doing out in the cold?"

Throwing my truck into park, I jump out, a storm of emotions brewing inside me.

Jackie, ever the comedic relief, lets out a hiccup and nudges Holly, whispering not-so-quietly, "Shit, you're in trouble." But my focus remains solely on Holly.

"What the fuck are you doing?" I demand.

She meets my gaze with those defiant eyes, tipping her chin up in challenge. "Girls' night," she retorts, her arms crossing over her chest defensively.

For a long, tense moment, it feels as though the world has narrowed down to just the two of us. It's a silent battle of wills, each of us waiting for the other to break first.

The silence is finally shattered by Jackie. "Now that you're here, can you give us a ride home?"

My hands ball into tight fists. "Get in," I order, my voice harsher than intended.

Holly leans over to Jackie, muttering something about being a traitor, but Jackie, with a dramatic eye roll, makes her way to the truck, clambering into the backseat.

Holly stands her ground, her gaze unwavering. "I can walk," she insists stubbornly.

Taking a deep breath to control the anger and concern bubbling in my chest, I step closer. "Get in the damn truck."

Despite her feigned bravado, I see her shiver. Maybe from the cold, maybe from my proximity; I can't tell. "I can get myself home but thank you."

"I won't tell you again. Get in the truck, or I swear I'll put you in myself."

"Make—" She stops herself, knowing the last time she tested me like this, I kissed the hell out of her. Her eyes widen just a fraction, but it's enough for me to notice. Just when I think I've won this standoff, she blows out an exasperated breath. I brace myself, ready to haul her in, but she stops me with a sharp retort. "Fine! I'll go."

After a silent, tense drive, we reach Jackie's place. She stumbles out of the truck, tossing a half-hearted "thanks" over her shoulder before disappearing inside her house.

Without a word, I pull the truck back onto the road, taking a left turn, as Holly shifts uncomfortably in her seat.

"This isn't the way to my house," she murmurs, a hint of anxiety creeping into her voice.

I flick the heater up a notch, trying to soothe away her shivers, though I'm still seething. "I'm taking you to my place."

Instead of the expected protest, all she does is curse under her breath, which surprises me. The journey continues in silence, the only sound being the hum of the truck and our occasional breaths.

When we finally reach the clearing where my cabin stands, I pull the truck to a stop and hop out, the cool night air instantly hitting my face. I take a second to breathe, trying to calm the storm of emotions brewing. But when I look back, I notice Holly is still seated, her eyes wide as she takes in the sight of my cabin.

It's then I realize, she's not as drunk as I thought. Her eyes are clear, only a trace of the earlier alcohol glossiness left. They reflect the warm golden light emanating from my cabin's large glass windows.

Making my way to her side, I open the door. She

continues to stare. "When I heard you built a cabin in the mountains, I imagined some tiny shack you'd hide away in to nurse your brooding."

"A tiny shack, huh?"

I reach in, wrapping a hand firmly around her waist. With a swift pull, she's out of the truck and on her feet. She stumbles slightly but I catch her, our bodies coming dangerously close.

Stepping inside, she looks around, her gaze slowly traveling across the open floor plan. The space stretches out, illuminated by the soft lighting: from the polished wooden floors to the tall beams in the high ceiling.

"You built this yourself?"

My emotions are a tangled mess. A part of me wants to pull her close, to lose myself in her once more. Another part is still furious at her recklessness earlier. It results in a non-committal grunt in response.

I guide her into the kitchen where I make her a sandwich. The scent of freshly brewed coffee wafts through the air as I set a cup down in front of her. She mutters a soft thanks before taking a careful sip.

"I'm not drunk, you know. I'm not going to vomit on your shoes or anything."

With my back to her, I close my eyes and inhale a steadying breath, my heart ready to combust in my chest.

She has no fucking clue.

"Just eat," I say, putting the plate down in front of her.

Finishing up, I pull a hoodie from one of the hooks by the entrance, tossing it her way. "Here, it'll help with the cold."

She catches it mid-air, a small smile playing on her

lips. As she slides the hoodie on, it drapes heavily around her, the fabric practically swallowing her. I didn't expect the sight of her in my clothes to affect me this much. Those days trapped in her cottage, it's what I loved most. How she would get out of bed in the morning and grab my t-shirt to cover her nakedness. It's such a simple thing, but my fingers grip the counter's edge to prevent them from reaching out to her.

Her voice breaks the silence, the playful tone back. "It's almost Christmas."

"And?"

She glances around, her eyes taking in the wood and minimal decor of the cabin. "You've got no Christmas decorations up."

I shrug. "Never saw the point. It's just me here."

"But you must have some?" she pushes.

"Yeah, they're in the storage closet," I admit, but before she can take the conversation any further, I interject, "Look, I've still got work to do. You should get some rest." I nod toward the hallway. "I'll leave a change of clothes on the bed in the guest room for you."

She simply nods, her eyes lingering on me for a moment too long. There's so much that remains unsaid between us. Words crowd at the back of my throat, a mess that I can't vocalize. She's always been this enigma, this force I never knew how to handle. With every other woman, it's been straightforward, predictable. But Holly? She's the only one who's ever made me feel this unsure, this scared.

The gravitational pull toward her terrifies me. It's like no matter where I am or what I'm doing, my senses are attuned to her presence. The way my gaze automatically finds hers across a crowded room. The way my heart stammers when she gifts me one of her dazzling smiles. The fear isn't that she's here now, but that even if she leaves, she'll still remain—an imprint on my soul.

Pushing those thoughts aside, I make my way to my home workshop, leaving her to the comfort of the cabin. But as I go, one nagging thought remains: if she smiles at me again, I'm well and truly fucked.

∞∞∞∞

Darkness envelops the cabin, save for the dim, warm lights from the Christmas tree Holly put up.

Of course she did.

As I pass by, I can't help but chuckle softly. Trust her to find a way to bring some festivity into this somber space.

There's a Post-It note on the counter.

"Sorry. Couldn't help myself.

It looks amazing though, right?

Right.

Anyway, goodnight, Sean."

I stare at her handwriting for too long. Honestly, I just need the time to convince myself not to go upstairs and drag her out of bed so I can kiss her.

Sleep. I just need some sleep, but as soon as I'm beneath the sheets, sleep eludes me. There's this restless energy, an awareness that's impossible to shake. She's right down the hall—just a few steps away. The very thought sends my pulse racing.

Turning on my side, I replay our heated exchange in the maze over and over. Every word, every gesture, every touch—it's as if it's all engraved in my memory.

I try to shove the thoughts away, attempt to bring some peace to my restless mind, but it's no use. They keep resurfacing.

And then my mind takes a cruel turn, imagining a future I have no business thinking about. Holly, here in town, her laughter filling the air, her hand wrapped around another man's arm. The thought of her, with children, with a family that isn't mine—it tightens my chest. A hot surge of jealousy and possessiveness courses through me. I shouldn't care, but the very thought of her with someone else... I clench my fists, fighting the urge to punch something.

Believe me, if I could punch myself right now, I would.

In the past, I had held on to this vague hope that things could return to the way they were before— simple, uncomplicated. But now? After feeling the heat of her lips, the softness of her skin? The memories taunt me, making it impossible to go back to any semblance of normalcy.

I'd lied to her in the maze. I told her she meant nothing, but damn it, she means everything. More than I ever anticipated, more than I'm ready to admit.

My mother was right.

I'm a fucking idiot.

Tossing the covers aside, I rise from the bed, every muscle taut with tension. The door beckons, promising relief just beyond it.

"Fuck it," I growl, deciding to throw caution to the wind.

THIRTY-SEVEN

HOLLY

The weight of being inside Sean's house presses in on me from every angle. Every object, every sound, every scent is him, and it's overwhelming. I can't seem to escape the ache that twists inside me. A sob lodges in my throat, unshed tears threatening to spill.

I roll over for what feels like the hundredth time, trying to find comfort on the plush pillows and thick duvet, but the more I try to find sleep, the more elusive it becomes. Everywhere I look, everywhere I turn, I'm drowning in him. The pain of his words in the maze digs at me like a splinter in my heart, reminding me of the void that now stands between us.

Why am I even here? Why did he bring me to his house, of all places? He could've just dropped me off at home, kept the distance between us intact. But no, he pulled me into his orbit once again, making me question everything I thought I knew.

I can't stay in this room any longer. It's stifling, and I need to breathe.

Pushing the covers away, I stand and move to the door, craving the cool air of the night. But as I pull the door open, I'm met with a sight that roots me to the spot.

Sean stands just down the hallway, his steps paused, his gaze fixed on me. The shadows cast by the dim lights carve out the sharp planes of his face, adding a raw intensity to his expression. He looks almost predatory, eyes trailing down my form, taking in the sight of me clad only in his oversized t-shirt.

I feel exposed, vulnerable. The air is thick, charged with an electric tension that makes the hairs on my arms stand on end. I can't breathe, can't move, can't think. His gaze, full of heat and questions, burns into me, demanding answers I don't know how to give.

Silence stretches between us, time seemingly frozen in this single moment. The weight of our past, the lingering pain of his words, and the undeniable attraction that's always pulsed between us collide, creating a maelstrom of emotions.

There's so much we haven't said, so much we've held back. But that look in his eyes—it's unmistakable. It's a reflection of everything I've been feeling, the confusion, the yearning, the desperate need to bridge the gap that's grown between us. That look says more than words ever could.

You can't hide anymore, Sean Colson.

"You lied," I whisper, feeling my heart ready to pound out of my chest.

He takes a step forward, the muscles in his jaw ticking. "I lied."

My hands are trembling as I grip the doorway, everything in me tensing as he comes toward me. "This is not nothing."

He swallows, his stare blistering. "It's not nothing."

What is it?

Say it, Sean. Say something.

He reaches me in the next breath, my skin achingly aware of him.

His hand cradles the side of my face, leaning down so that his forehead rests against mine, and I can feel the ragged pace of his breathing.

"You always have, and you always will be too good for me. But I'm starting to feel selfish," he begins, his voice raw. "I can't sleep. I close my eyes, and I see you, and it's driving me insane. I've tasted you. And god, it's like a drug. I'm trapped in this endless loop, craving more. Every night, I wake up from dreams where you're just out of reach, and it's torture. I've tried to fight it, tried to deny it. But after having you, I don't think I can ever get enough. You're my obsession, my torment..." He swallows again, pressing his thumb to the base of my throat. "You're my fucking reckoning."

I close my eyes, afraid if I open them then this won't be real, but when I do, he's still there. Still undressing me with just a look.

The intensity in his gaze, the huskiness in his voice, they all make me ache for him, make me want to give in to what we both know we want.

I lean into his touch, my breath quivering as his thumb brushes over my pulse point.

"I don't know what to do," I whisper, feeling like a dam is about to burst.

He pulls back slightly, his jaw clenched. "Then don't do anything. Just let me have you. Let me show you how much I need you."

Before I know it, he's pressing me back against the wall, his hands sliding down my sides to grab my hips. I gasp as his lips crash into mine, hungry and urgent. There's no holding back now, no pretending that we can resist what's been building between us for so long.

He lifts me up effortlessly, my legs wrapping around his waist as he carries me back to the bed. I'm lost in the sensation of his touch, the taste of his lips, the feel of his hard body against mine. It's like we're both drowning, and the only way to survive is to cling to each other.

He lays me down on the bed, his hands roaming my body, igniting a fire that's been smoldering for too long. I tug at his shirt, desperate to feel his skin against mine. He pulls away long enough to take it off, revealing the hard planes of his chest and the taut muscles of his abs.

"God, I need you," he groans, his lips finding mine once again.

His hands slide under the hem of my shirt, pulling it up and over my head. I feel exposed, but empowered, like I'm shedding a layer of myself that's been holding me back. He takes in the sight of me, his eyes dark, before trailing kisses down my neck and over my collarbone. I arch into him, wanting nothing more than to be consumed by this moment, to forget everything that's happened before and just be here, with him.

He moves down my body, his lips tracing patterns over my skin as he goes. I gasp as he reaches the waistband of my panties, his fingers trailing over the fabric.

"God, you're so beautiful," he murmurs, his breath hot against my hip.

He flicks his tongue over the sensitive skin just above the band, and I moan, my body already wound tight with need. I want him, need him, and it's like he knows exactly how to touch me, how to make me feel alive.

He slides my panties down my legs.

I'm exposed in the best way possible. I'm completely vulnerable to him, and he knows it.

"Mine," he whispers close to my ear, before sinking into me with a deep, guttural moan.

His?

I am. I'm his. He branded me and made sure I wouldn't belong to another.

We move together, my body adjusting to the stretch while lost in a haze of pleasure, our bodies striving for release. It's like nothing else exists in the world but the two of us, the electricity between us sparking and crackling with every touch.

When we finally come together, it's with a raw intensity that leaves us both gasping for breath. Sean collapses on top of me, his breath hot against my neck.

"Still hate me?" he asks, his voice heated.

My lips twitch. "So much."

He presses his lips to mine before whispering against my skin. "I hate you more."

THIRTY-EIGHT

The first sensation that breaks through the haze of sleep is warmth. It's not just the warmth of blankets or the dappled morning sun filtering through the curtains. It's the heat of a body, the rhythmic thud of a heartbeat against my back, the rise and fall of a chest syncing with my own breathing.

I blink my eyes open and am immediately aware of Sean's arms wrapped securely around me, holding me close. Memories of last night flood back—the passion, the words, the vulnerability laid bare. A tingling mix of contentment and anxiety washes over me. As much as I yearn to sink back into the embrace, the weight of my pending deadline gnaws at me.

Quietly, carefully, I extricate myself from the cocoon of his arms, stealing glances at his sleeping face. The tension that often marks his features is absent now, replaced by the serene expression of deep sleep. But I can't stay. Not now. I need to finish that book.

After dressing and managing to slip out unnoticed, I'm back at my cottage, lost in the flurry of final edits, tweaks, and last-minute touches. The story comes alive under my fingertips, flowing effortlessly onto the page. Just when I'm about to exhale in relief, having sent off the final draft, a thunderous knock disrupts my peace.

Sean stands on the other side, looking like a storm about to break. A storm made of anger, concern, and a hint of betrayal. "You left," he declares, voice gruff, devoid of any question.

The guilt, combined with the newfound shyness after last night, pulls my gaze downwards. "I had a deadline. I didn't think you'd want me hanging around after...after last night."

His brows knit together as he steps forward, crowding me back into the confines of the room. "I always want you around."

"But...that was before we...you know," I stammer, trying to find the right words but failing.

His hand comes up, fingers grazing my chin, tilting my face up. "Did you listen to a damn word I said last night?"

Our eyes lock, and in that split second, a torrent of emotions pass between us, unspoken yet unmistakably clear.

"I meant what I said," he says, his hand still holding my chin. "I want you, all of you, and I don't care about anything else."

"Sean..."

"I've been in love with you since you were nineteen. Nine years you put me through hell just by looking at you and knowing I couldn't have you. But I can have you now, and you better think again if you expect me to let you go."

All that comes out of my mouth is air.

He loves me?

Is this a joke?

"Don't mess with me. That's not funny."

But the way he's looking at me makes me think this is anything but a joke.

My eyes widen. "You're only telling me this now?"

He shrugs like it's nothing. "You were busy."

My heart races in my chest as his words sink in. A tear streaks my cheek but he's quick to brush it away with his thumb.

I want him too, more than anything.

But...there's always a but.

"We'll drive each other insane," I say, my back pressing into the wall where he cages me in.

"I fucking hope so."

"You're my brother's best friend."

"So I'll have a black eye for a couple of weeks. You'll find it sexy." He winks, that cocky smirk plastered on his face.

I don't know why I'm fighting this. Maybe I'm not. Maybe I'm testing him, seeing how hard he's going to fight.

"This could ruin everything," I say, feeling his breath across my face, the awareness of his hand on my waist sinking lower...and lower.

His eyes lock with mine. There's a pleading there, a pain, but there's so much fire. "Too late, baby. You've already ruined me."

"We're jumping off a cliff."

He smiles like he's getting amusement from this. From this pathetic struggle I'm putting up. "But we're jumping together."

"Stop having an answer for everything. What if I get cold feet?" I whisper.

"Then I'll chase you until you're out of breath and

remind you of nights like last night, and why we jumped together."

"Sean—"

"What are you scared of?"

"You," I answer honestly.

His broad shoulders shake with a light laugh as he tucks my hair behind my ear.

"Something funny?"

"Yeah, because you are, without a doubt, the most terrifying woman I have ever met."

The moment feels suspended, drawn out between heartbeats and breaths, waiting for a decision, a definitive path forward. The silence in the room, filled only with our shallow breaths, is like fragile glass—one wrong move and it could shatter.

I can feel the tremble in my hands, the heat of his body so close to mine, the intensity in those dark eyes that don't just see me, they see through me. It's overwhelming, it's frightening, and yet it's the most alive I've felt in...well, ever.

"Why me?" The question slips out, genuine curiosity mingled with the remnants of self-doubt. "You could have anyone. Why wait for me?"

He leans in closer, so close that I can count the dark lashes framing his eyes, feel his breath mingling with mine. "Because it's always been you, you infuriating, incredible woman. It was you when you were off limits, and it's you now. The waiting never bothered me. It was the not having that did."

My heart clenches.

"Sean, I—" The rest of the sentence gets stuck in my throat, but he understands. Of course, he understands.

"Don't," he whispers, his forehead resting against

mine. "For once, stop fighting me. You can go back to fighting me later. I want you to keep fighting me every day after this. But right now, I want you to tell me to kiss you. Stay here with me and let me kiss this stubborn, beautiful woman."

And so, I stay. I stay as his lips finally capture mine in a kiss that feels like a resolution and a new beginning all at once. I stay as his arms wrap around me, not just holding me in place, but making it clear they're where I belong. I stay because, despite the fear and the uncertainty of the future, there's nowhere else I'd rather be.

THIRTY-NINE

The festive lights from Holly's parents' house cast a warm glow on the snowy walkway. The sound of chatter and clinking glasses spills out as her father swings the door open. "Sean! Brenda! Merry Christmas. Come on in."

I nod at him, trying to keep my nerves at bay. It's not the holiday celebration that has me on edge—it's the secret Holly and I have been harboring. And now, the very room I'm about to walk into is filled with the very people we've been avoiding telling.

I put the gifts down just in time for little Mia to lunge into my arms, breaking my stream of thought.

Her giggles and the weight of her small frame ground me for a moment. But as I step into the living room, filled with tinsel-strewn decor, gifts, and the delicious aroma of roast wafting from the kitchen, my gaze is magnetically pulled to one person.

Holly.

Our eyes lock. There's a hint of mischief in hers, but the blush creeping up her cheeks is pure embarrassment. Ignoring the sensation of Mia's small hands squishing my face together, my lips twitch into an amused smile as I take in Holly's outfit.

"What the hell are you wearing?"

Perched atop her head is a damn wedding veil.

My mother, ever the romantic, lets out a delighted sigh. "Oh, Holly, you look stunning. You're going to be a beautiful bride."

Chuckling, I tease, "Planning a wedding already, Squirt?"

The deepening shade of red on her face is adorable. She rolls her eyes, clearly searching for an escape. "No, my mother thought it would be hilarious to make me wear her old wedding veil. She practically ambushed me. You're lucky I'm not in the dress too."

Before she can elaborate, Karen intercepts with a bright grin. "I just thought she could use a little motivation. What's wrong with envisioning the future?"

Then, like a snowball effect, one by one, various family members jump in with unsolicited advice about Holly's non-existent wedding. My mother talks about the best season to get married, Rachel predicts the lucky guy's profession, Karen discusses the ideal honeymoon destination. Each comment pushes my buttons, my possessiveness growing with every word.

I feel a heat, a rage, starting to build in me at the thought of them pairing Holly with anyone other than me. It's irrational, but it's there, growing with each passing second.

I press a kiss to the top of Mia's head and put her down. My steps are measured but swift as I close the distance between Holly and me. I see the realization dawning in her eyes, the nervous anticipation of what I'm about to do.

Without any hesitation, I cup her face, pulling her into a deep kiss. Around us, the room goes pin-drop silent, the previous cacophony replaced by stunned stillness.

I pull away just to hear her whisper, "What the fuck?"

Wrapping my arms around her waist, I pull her close and address the open-mouthed crowd gawking at me. "At least now you can envision the groom too."

It takes exactly ten seconds until Mark's face is in mine. "Let go of my sister and take two steps to the left."

"Mark, stop it," Holly pleads, but I knew this was coming.

Dipping my chin, I step away from Holly. "It's okay, baby."

I'm hardly able to finish the sentence when Mark's fist connects with my jaw.

The room erupts as I clutch my throbbing cheek and stand upright, working my jaw back and forth. To be fair, he could have hit me harder.

Slapping me on the back, he pulls me into a hug. "Had to be done, brother."

I hug him back. "I know."

"Don't fuck with her," he warns.

"You have my word."

Holly fuses over my swollen face as the room falls into another tense silence.

"It's about fucking time," my mother mutters, sinking into the chair. That tongue of hers is a permanent thing as of late. "It took you both long enough."

Laughter ripples through the room as my mother's comment breaks the tension.

Holly's father chuckles. "Merry Christmas everyone."

Holly shoots me an apologetic look, her hand gently cradling the sore spot on my face. "I'm so sorry. I didn't think he'd actually do it."

"I think I deserved that one," I admit, smirking despite the pain. "Happy Birthday by the way."

Another blush. She's fucking breath-taking.

"Thank you."

Karen, grinning from ear to ear, approaches us with a tray of drinks. "Well, since we have that sorted, how about a toast to the new couple?"

Mia, who's been watching the entire scene wide-eyed, finally pipes up, "Does this mean Uncle Sean marry Aunt Lolly?"

Holly's blush returns in full force as she tucks her face into my shoulder, and I laugh, pulling her close.

The room cheers as Karen raises her glass, "To Sean and Holly, may your love be as strong as that punch."

As the night wears on, Holly and I steal glances at each other, our hands finding each other's under the table. The veil may have been a joke, but there's no mistaking the certainty I felt in my chest at the sight of her, the unspoken promise between us.

I'm going to marry that woman one day. One day

soon.

We may not have planned to reveal our relationship tonight, but in a way, it's fitting. Surrounded by the people we love, the ones who will always have our backs, we're creating our own little world, one where we can be ourselves, no secrets or fear.

The future may be uncertain, but as long as I have her by my side, I know we can face anything.

∞∞∞∞

As I sit on the couch, nursing my drink and nursing my sore jaw, Holly sidles up to me, sitting on the arm of the chair.

"Your mom seems to be doing good."

I glance over at my mother who is smiling down at Mia as she shows her the new toys she got for Christmas.

"Yeah. She finally agreed to some home help, and the doctors have found the right medication. I know there'll be darker days, but I'm grateful for today."

"I'm here to help too." She runs her hands through my hair, content. "Thought I'd give you another present," she murmurs, handing me a neatly wrapped package.

I glance at it, then back to her. "We've already exchanged gifts."

"I know," she says with a playful shrug. "But I also know you give your mom one of my books every year for Christmas."

I smirk, taking the package from her. "Noticed that, did you?"

"I was a little late on my deadline, but somehow managed to get my publishers to print me an early copy."

As I peel away the wrapping, her blush deepens. It's sexy as hell. Removing the book from its confines, I catch the cover—her latest novel.

"You might like the dedication," she adds, biting her lip and trying to suppress a smile.

Curiosity piqued, I arch a brow and swiftly flip to the dedication page. My eyes scan the words, and a moment later, I throw my head back and laugh.

She's beaming down at me, her eyes filled with that familiar mischief. In the next breath, I pull her close, capturing her lips in a searing kiss that communicates everything words fail to.

When we finally part for air, I lean my forehead against hers, grinning like a fool.

Her fingers play with the collar of my shirt. "Thought you'd appreciate it."

"I do," I murmur, pulling her in for another kiss. "More than you know."

"Oh, there's one more thing."

"Holly, I don't need more gifts—"

"I love you."

I smile so wide my face hurts.

Now that's a gift.

She grazes her lips against mine. "Merry Christmas."

"Merry Christmas, baby," I tell her, pulling her onto my lap before I reread the dedication:

To my local carpenter,
Thank you for the inspiration.

EPILOGUE

Nine years later

HOLLY

The winter air bites at my cheeks, turning them rosy with more than just the chill as everyone around us counts down. "Three... Two... One... Happy New Year!" The crowd in Pine Falls' town square erupts. Up above, the fireworks burst, splashes of color against the starry night, mirrored in Sean's eyes as he turns to me, his grin an infectious curve in the darkness.

I barely have time to catch my breath before his lips find mine, a warm, familiar promise that's always echoed in every kiss. It's a conversation of laughter, of tears, of arguments so heated they could start fires, and reconciliations that could put them out. It's our own language, refined through the years.

He breaks away, his breath a whisper against my mouth. "Happy New Year, Squirt."

"Happy New Year," I whisper back, heart full to bursting as Sean bends down to our little man, Ethan, who's cheering on the fireworks display. He's all Sean, especially that mischievous spark in his eyes. "Happy New Year," Sean murmurs, kissing Ethan's forehead. "Daddy loves you to the moon, kiddo."

"I love you even bigger!" Ethan yells, his tiny arms grappling for Sean's neck, his small frame buzzing with unrestrained joy.

"And what about my princess?" Sean grins, shifting to bring down our daughter, Lily, from her throne on his shoulders. She giggles as Sean kisses her flushed cheek. "Daddy loves you, sweet girl. More than there are stars in the sky."

"Love you!" Lily coos, her little arms hugging him tight, her laughter melding with the night's festivities.

I can't help the smile that splits my face, watching them. My heart feels like it might just explode. This man, this incredible, infuriating man I married, has grown into a father who still manages to take my breath away. He's all the Sean I fell for—stubborn, infuriating, quick to challenge and quicker to joke—but with our kids, he's also everything gentle, patient, and kind. It's him, but amplified, and after all these years, it still gets me.

The fireworks fizzle out, the last of the sparks surrendering to the night, as we huddle close, lost in our own little world.

"Alright, team," Sean's voice cuts through the post-celebration hush, his hands rubbing together. "Who's ready to see if Santa came by the cabin with some New

Year's presents?"

I roll my eyes. He spoils them rotten. He went from a man who didn't decorate his house for Christmas, to a father that tells his children that Santa comes twice a year, but only to them because they're extra special. Every year since Ethan was born five years ago, Santa has crept back into our house on New Year's Eve to leave a little gift.

"Me, me!" Ethan and Lily's voices jumble together, their fatigue forgotten.

Our walk back to the car is a chorus of their excited theories, Sean and I throwing in our own wild guesses, eyes meeting over the top of their heads. Their energy is a living thing, and I find myself caught up in it, wondering just what might be waiting back at the cabin. I never know either. This is all Sean, and he takes pride in it.

We're all buckled in and barely a minute into the drive before it hits—the day's adventures catching up all at once. Their chatter slows, then stops, heads lolling to rest against each other in the backseat.

"They're out," I observe, twisting in my seat to catch Sean's eye, his face intermittently lit by the passing streetlights.

"What do you think the chances are they'll actually stay asleep when we get there?"

I laugh softly, shaking my head. "Oh, they're down for the count. Way past bedtime, and all that sugar and excitement? They'll sleep until morning, no doubt."

"So, that means we can...?"

I raise a brow, a smirk playing at my lips. "That means, Mr. Colson, we'll have to check if Santa left something for the two of us."

"I'm sure he did," he quips back, his eyebrows

doing this ridiculous dance. "I've heard through the grapevine we were exceptionally good this year."

My laughter fills the car, echoing against the windows as we fall into a contented silence, the kind only years of comfortable love can craft. It's in these quiet moments, amidst the beautiful chaos of our life, that I find myself reflecting on the world we've built together.

It hasn't been easy. Marriage, the real kind, is never a smooth ride. We've weathered storms, clashed in a way that would make thunder cower, but we always, always come back to each other. Our love is the eye in the storm, the calm in the chaos. We're more than just husband and wife; we're teammates, best friends, and sometimes the fiercest of rivals. But through it all, we're us. And I wouldn't trade that for the world.

The cabin comes into view, our cozy world tucked away from reality, and as predicted, the kids are still out. Sean scoops up Ethan and I take Lily, and we settle them into bed.

The door clicks softly as it closes, and then it's just Sean's arms around me, his voice a low rumble. "And then there were two."

"Two very tired adults who probably should call it a night," I joke, my body, however, humming with a very different kind of energy.

"Tired? Speak for yourself, baby." His breath tickles my ear. "I'm just getting started."

"Oh, is that so?"

"That's so. I'll have you know—"

But his words are lost as I pull him down for a kiss, slow and deep, a spark that ignites the familiar fire. When we part, there's a new heat in his gaze, his breathing a tad more ragged.

"What was that for?" he breathes, though he's already leaning down for another.

"For being you," I whisper, lost in everything that is him.

"Well, in that case…" He doesn't finish, leading me instead to our room, hands locked like they were always meant to be in each other's grasp.

The new year might have begun, but time seems to stand still as we cross into the sanctuary of our bedroom. There are no years here, no hours, just the timeless expanse of us.

Nine years ago, we decided to jump off a cliff. We did it, but we did it together.

The End.

We love hearing your thoughts.
If you enjoyed It Should Have Been You, please
consider leaving a review on Amazon or Goodreads.

WANT TO READ MORE BY
LAURA ASHLEY GALLAGHER?

CHECK OUT THE REST OF HER
BOOKS AT
LAURAASHLEYGALLAGHER.COM

GET IN TOUCH

You can reach me on my website. I would love to see you there.
www.lauraashleygallagher.com

You will also find me on Facebook, Instagram, and TikTok.

Printed in Great Britain
by Amazon

36134438R00163